SHAME
ON
YOU

Amy Heydenrych is a writer and book blogger based in South Africa. She has been shortlisted twice for the acclaimed Miles Morland African Writing Scholarship. Her short stories and poems have published in multiple anthologies including *Brittle Paper*, *The Kalahari Review* and the *Short Sharp* Stories anthologies. When she is not writing her own fiction, she ghost-writes books and columns for global tech and financial companies. She is currently working on her second novel.

SHAME ON YOU

Amy Heydenrych

twenty7

First published in Great Britain in 2017

This paperback edition published in 2018 by

TWENTY7 BOOKS
80–81 Wimpole St, London W1G 9RE

This is a work of fiction. Names, places, events and
incidents are either the products of the author's
imagination or used fictitiously. Any resemblance to
actual persons, living or dead, or actual
events is purely coincidental.

A CIP catalogue record for this book is
available from the British Library.

Paperback ISBN: 978–1–78577–094–4
Ebook ISBN: 978–1–78577–095–1

also available as an ebook

3 5 7 9 10 8 6 4

Typeset by IDSUK (Data Connection) Ltd
Printed and bound in Great Britain by Clays Ltd, Elcograf S.p.A.

Twenty7 Books is an imprint of Bonnier Books UK
www.bonnierbooks.co.uk

For my son Zach, who grew alongside this book and entered the world with it

Prologue

McDonald's is an unholy mess of drunks at this time of night. A bunch of lads scoff fries as they whoop over a video clip on one of their phones. Some porcelain dolls touch up their lipstick while quickly getting rid of their Big Mac packaging, hoping nobody noticed how much they ate. Then one interrupts the application of her red lipstick to reach for her iPhone. She holds up the camera and films the young woman running towards the counter. Although partially obscured by other customers, something about her hair, her stance, the way she moves, suggests that something is about to happen.

As the girl shifts into focus, Red Lipstick bleats in gleeful recognition. This is no ordinary woman, but *the* face of healthy, organic, gluten-free eating. The girl who cured herself from cancer and posts pictures of salads and smoothies every day. The girl who just put Oprah on a new diet. A girl who definitely does not belong in McDonald's. Is she here on a secret burger binge? Is she covering her face to avoid recognition? Either way, it must be recorded, saved and used as currency somewhere.

The girl falls to her knees a few steps in, prostrating right in front of the queue. Customers turn as one, eyes narrowed, annoyed at the craziness that has somehow blown inside. A security guard thunders towards her, his ketchup-stained tie flapping over his shoulder.

'Excuse me, miss! Excuse me! You can't—'

The girl rears up like a snake. A dark, throttled scream curls the fat off the walls. She removes her hands from her face. Her palms are red. Dark, war-like gashes on her cheeks. Blood pouring now, soaking her neck, her shirt. As one shaking phone calls an ambulance, the others rise, silent, unblinking, capturing the writhing human form before them. This moment, so uncomfortable, so striking, had to be recorded.

Chapter 1

Holly

'You'll kill yourself if you keep doing that.'

Holly creaks her head upwards, shifting her gaze from her iPhone to the striking stranger grinning down at her. She can feel the urgency of the likes and comments collecting on her latest Instagram post prickling up her arms, but she resists the urge to look down. The shock of sandy hair against wide green eyes demands her attention.

He gestures to the stethoscope dangling from his top pocket.

'Trust me, I'm a doctor.'

The trace of an accent curls around his words. A real Londoner would never just walk up to someone they didn't know.

'Do you always give out random medical advice to strangers in Starbucks?'

He laughs, pulls out the chair next to her, removes his overcoat (Burberry, she notices, clearly new) and takes a seat. 'No, only the beautiful ones nursing an obvious neck spasm.'

Game on. He's definitely flirting. Besides, he's right. She hasn't been able to turn her head either left or right for weeks. They clutch their coffees in silence, and he draws in a deep breath. She braces herself for the inevitable awkward moment when he shoehorns into the conversation how he knows her from Instagram. The air always shifts when this happens. A pregnant pause as the other person gathers their courage. If he's discreet, he'll tell her he loves her photos. Or, disappointingly, he may reveal that his girlfriend is a huge fan of her recipes and could she please sign a copy of her latest recipe book *Holly's Home-Cooked Health*?

Fans would be surprised to know the despair that beats through her as they coo over her long, blonde hair. They'd be bewildered if they could feel the panic grinding her teeth as she poses for a selfie. All they see online is the confident Holly, the likeable Holly, the perfect Holly.

The unthinkable has led her here. A shock diagnosis of cancer. Hours of excruciating chemotherapy. Then a decision to turn her back on it all and try to heal herself through a raw, vegan diet. Her love for cooking and healthy recipes blossomed. Throughout her cancer, remission, and further cancer scares, the likes, shares and comments of her followers pulled her through – each notification gave her a surge of adrenaline and purpose. Now, she's been clear of cancer for two years. She knows who to be for these people when she's arranging fruit for a picture or writing a sunny caption, but who is she when she comes across them off the screen? She wants to shake her fans by the shoulders and plead with them, 'Tell me: what is it you see in me?'

The doctor turns to her, licking the foam of his cappuccino off his spoon. There is a disarming childishness about him.

'You haven't told me your name yet,' he says.

'You never asked . . . but it's Holly.'

He holds out a giant hand, 'It's a pleasure to meet you, Holly. You can call me Jack.'

'Well hello, Jack.'

'Now, how about we get you out in the fresh air and away from the glare of that phone?'

Holly's gone home with strangers before. Usually from pubs, but not in the past year though, not since her first book came out and her glowing face smiles down on the masses at London's tube stops, but before, when she was new to the city and drunk on its potential. All encounters blur into one. A sloppy greeting, a drink, some superficial chitchat and a stumbling journey home soon after. Yet for all her one-night stands, the prospect of leaving a coffee shop with a stranger seems exciting, dangerous even. He's sharply dressed, glistening with promise, so she picks up her bag and follows him out of the door. Imagine how happy her fans would be if she started dating a *doctor*.

Jack walks quickly, but looks across at her often. Maybe to check she's keeping up, or that she's still here, or that she's real. Can he tell she doesn't do this often, that she is never the girl that is chosen for good, never the vixen that edges from the shadows into a girlfriend? For all her beauty, her most romantic affairs have been imagined. The 'connections' she felt with male friends never acted on, the 'spark' of a one-night stand never igniting her phone with a call the next day. But something about Jack, the intent with which he looks at her, makes Holly hope that this is different.

He makes up a game called 'Never Turn Left'. They walk aimlessly, turning right whenever they reach a dead end. She loves an explorer, someone who knows how to get lost in the city. Familiar landmarks – Marks & Spencer, Angel tube station, Sainsbury's – give way to a private London language. Restored Victorian flats with floor-to-ceiling bookshelves visible through bay windows. Quiet streets occasionally interrupted by girls in tea dresses and worn brogues whizzing past on bicycles, their belongings in a straw basket at the front.

Their conversation flows in a rhythm as natural as their steps. He asks her questions incessantly. His enthusiastic curiosity bubbles up quicker than he can speak. It makes him instantly likeable. He doesn't just ask questions; he asks them as if the world's orbit depends on her answer. For every one of her replies, there is a long, considered silence. He runs his fingers through his mop of hair, so it grows higher and wilder. They cover favourite books, movies and songs, carefully mapping each other's tastes, marking the places where they intersect. Searching for the source of the hot static humming between them.

'So, what do you do, Holly?'

'I'm a food blogger.' She can feel her face growing warm.

'Full-time?'

'Yes . . .'

'That can't make you enough money to survive, surely?' That's what my father always says, Holly could tell him. He is practically willing her to fail – it's there in every terse phone call. Yet to admit that now would open up a soft part of her she's not ready to show yet. Instead, she takes a deep breath and recites her patient, scripted explanation.

'Well, not always. But if a lot of people start becoming interested in what you do, you start to get advertisers, sponsorships, book deals . . .'

He stops dramatically in the middle of the pavement, busy commuters sighing as they push past him. 'Wait a second. Am I walking through the streets of London with an author?'

'Oh gosh, it's not as big a deal as you'd imagine! But yes, you are.' She laughs.

'What do you make?'

'Mostly healthy stuff – raw food, juices, meals made from superfoods. It might not seem as fun as burgers or fries but I think my followers connected to my story, you know? My life was very different from what it is now; I used to be really sick, but I turned it all around by changing the way I eat.' He doesn't say anything, so she's compelled to justify it a little more. 'I just wanted to share my joy with the world. The popularity of the whole thing still feels quite surreal.'

He touches her shoulder; desire pounds in her chest. 'What was wrong with you, when you were sick?'

Holly's hands start shaking. She can't tell him, not now. He'll ask too many questions.

'Let's not talk about it. It's kind of a second or third date conversation.'

'I don't understand – you think it's too intimate to share with me something that you were comfortable sharing on the Internet?' He's smiling, but his voice is barbed. There's an undercurrent that seems at odds with his gentle demeanour. Still, she'll take it. It's better than explaining.

'Enough about me, anyway,' she purrs. 'What type of doctor are you?' It feels hot between them again, the air stretched tight.

'Guess . . .'

She examines the contours of his face, his brimming smile. He's a charmer, the good-looking type, who probably sees repeat visits from divorcees with nothing wrong with them but loneliness.

'General practitioner!'

'No, more specialised.'

'Oncologist.'

A shadow passes over his smiling face. He looks down.

'Too morbid. Try again.'

'Gynaecologist?'

'Wrong again.' He sighs. 'I heal people, like you do. Not through food, though. I'm more traditional than that. I help people through cutting them open. I'm a surgeon.' His hands move back and forth in manic, slicing movements. It's not that funny but she laughs anyway.

He takes another breath, as if he wants to say more. Instead, he takes her hand and they continue walking. A summer dusk fades into a cool night as they find themselves in the lantern-lit streets of China Town. *Just enjoy it, Holly. Oh please, just try to enjoy it*, she thinks. But her mind is whirring with the risks of the meal ahead, the pressure of holding his interest. He likes her, she really thinks he likes her, but her gluten-free, sugar-free, vegan requests may make her look like a freak. He wouldn't be the first man who found her diet too high maintenance.

A small door in a dark side street reveals a dim sum bar she's never seen before. The cool, grey interior soothes the strangeness of their previous conversation. She snaps a photo of the pink neon sign against the wall, that says THE GOOD LUCK CLUB, her instinct to capture the moment as quick as a reflex. She'd filter the colours later to make them brighter before posting it to her feed, her perfect composition matched by a rush of dopamine. They sip jasmine tea and she beams at him, overcome with gratitude for her new life and the precious things that keep entering it. This is something special here. She can feel it.

Holly picks on a salad and pushes the spinach-and-cream-cheese dim sum into her lap, then onto the floor. Isn't this what everyone does on a first date anyway, act as agreeable as possible? Faking normality has its rewards.

Her face is sore from smiling by the time the dinner ends. They stand facing each other in the narrow alley, the chaos of Oxford Street roaring on the other side. Her hands ache to touch him as he moves closer to her, running his fingers over her arms. He smells like bergamot and sandalwood. It seems expensive and grown-up, hinting at an adult life she hasn't quite built yet.

'I want to tell you something,' he whispers, arms snaking around her waist. She edges closer and tilts her chin upward, finding his face for a kiss. She knows what's coming next – she's lived this moment at the end of many nights, in many quiet streets.

'Tell me anything you want.'

'You don't know how much I ached to find you,' he whispers like a romantic hero. 'I've been waiting for this night for so long.' Her stomach flips. This feels dangerously good. A glint of silver catches her eye. She doesn't under-stand what it is yet.

His arms tighten around her, holding her. She can't breathe; she can't think. This must be a game, surely he's playing a game? But his clenched jaw says no. The way he viciously contains her struggling says this sudden hatred is real. It spits out of his pores, acrid and urgent. 'Holly Evans, you're a fucking fraud.'

People always say just poke your attacker in the eyes, just kick him in the balls, because these are static targets carelessly overlooked. But he is everywhere and nowhere, efficiently pushing her down, slamming her golden head over and over again into the filthy muck on the pavement. It's the pain that makes her freeze eventually. The horror as he holds his scalpel above her face in triumph, and calmly presses it into each cheek while holding her jaw in a strong grip. She tries to scream as it breaks the skin, yet by the time he tears through the muscle her voice is a hoarse whimper, the otherworldly sound of an animal. Blood rushes down her temples and chokes in her throat. The cool night air hits the gashes in her face. As he disappears into the darkness, she raises her hands against her wet face. One thought blinds her, she never once told him her last name. Not once.

Chapter 2

Holly

Sleep is a black pit Holly can't crawl out of. She grabs at consciousness, then collapses back to where she came from. Finally, she becomes aware of the stiff sheets wrapped around her, of the pillows propping her up and the soft gauze caressing her face. Her face. A reminder of the horror of the night before. Her mind strains and grasps at fragments that don't make sense: his bright smile, the heat of his hand in hers, the shocking hatred burning behind his eyes. Holly's breath catches in her throat – this was no accident.

She scans the room, searching for something that will help her understand. There are signs of visitors. Bunches of flowers crowd the room in makeshift vases. An empty coffee cup teeters on the side table. Cards are stacked on every surface like a shrine. The air around her aches with care. Tears push at the corners of her eyes – the sheer, uncomplicated love is overwhelming. A fear pulses beneath the calm, ugly and urgent. If he could find her in a coffee shop in Islington, how much easier would it be to find her now, trapped within the confines of a hospital bed? All the love in the world can't save her now.

She takes a deep breath in and out, trying to still her heart. She gives in for a moment to the pale blankets and the soft edges of the morphine that swells in her blood. Pushes away the fear for a few more minutes. The panic. Nobody would guess how complicated this is. Nobody needs to know. Get well soon, get out of here. Carry on as if this never happened. Everything will be just as it was in no time. If only she could remember what he said to her! She tries once more to touch the night before in her mind, but the memory of how she got here is out of focus, a blur making its way out of the room, down the passage, past the sad hospital coffee shop and into the streets of London.

Despite her throbbing face, a familiar delicious sensation overcomes her, just like every other morning. Her phone, untouched for hours, has accumulated likes, shares and messages she hasn't read yet. Although her throat is crying for a glass of water, this is far more urgent. She summons the strength to strain past the tubes and paws through the drawers next to the bed, until a cool rectangle slips into her hand. While the tubes, flowers and cards look like a dream, what people are saying online will make her pain feel real, even justified. In the white silence of this room, she needs to hear a chorus of voices cry out, 'Something terrible has happened to you, and we are all so sorry.'

Of course, Holly's chorus of voices is larger and more practised than most. They joined her one by one as she struggled through the devastating lows of her illness, and travelled with her into this brave new life. Like a circle of friends, they are outraged that she has been cursed with yet another struggle. But she is not their friend. She is a brand that people believe and invest in. A symbol. It surprised her, the first time someone called her that – 'a brand'. She'd blushed and humbly batted the compliment away. Now it's become a natural wonder, a force with a destiny of its own. However, in this desperate moment, it doesn't matter what they think she is. There is nothing she needs more than this all-encompassing feeling of love.

She goes to Facebook first. Thousands of hysterical fans have been posting on her page. A trend has started where people share pictures of when they met her at book signings. Image after image of her with her arms around red-faced, emotional, smiling young women. She, the luckiest girl in the room. Holly starts to wonder if she's already dead and her spirit is hovering over her body, flicking through her social media profiles with ghostly fingers. There are angry demands to the 'managers of her Facebook page' to deliver a statement as to what happened and how she's doing. Nobody would guess that, besides her publicist, she has no staff at all. Every post made on that page is a result of her own hard work.

Instagram is even more overwhelming. After she works her way through the cluster of likes on her latest post (an atmospheric, warm-toned portrait of her almond-milk flat white taken at Starbucks), she gets to the tags. More than eight thousand people have tagged her in photographs in the past few hours. She scrolls through the bright rainbow of food photographs, being sure to like each one, until they all start to look the same. She almost misses the first blurry photograph of herself collapsed on her knees, hands over her face. Then they keep coming, a flood of pictures from all angles that swallows her whole. There's no need for her to remember even a single moment of that night. Everything, from her blood-soaked clothing to the paramedics lifting her from the floor, has been casually recorded. While the captions and comments to each photo are compassionate, Holly can't help but feel the force of everyone tugging at her trauma, trying to grab a piece of it to claim as their own.

Still, it is soothing to go through all the get-well wishes and imagine a world of strangers gathering to support her. Surely, if so many people are outraged, she doesn't need to feel so uneasy? Surely there would be signs that she did something to deserve it, signs other than the sticky mass of guilt clinging to her chest?

Years ago, when she was in and out of hospital and hunched over her computer researching alternative therapies, she felt desperate and isolated. But with every milestone reached and picture shared, she found new followers and friends, all connected by the basic human desire to survive. These same fans, and more, will carry her again. Panic rises. Her thoughts turn to the horror that lies beneath her bandages. Ugliness. Shame. Invisibility. She has to be stronger than the pain that lies ahead of her because it's the only power she has. If there is one thing Holly knows, it's how to heal.

No matter how many hundreds of likes or comments a person has on social media, eventually they all run dry.

The room has darkened by the time she gets to the last one. It's not enough. She's always waiting for something just out of her reach that she can't quite make out. Sometimes she thinks she keeps checking her phone in anticipation of receiving something important enough for her to want to put it down for good.

The aching shadow of her concussion begins to close in on her. She really should get some rest. But wait, there is one more message. A private message. She sees it in a flash of orange out of the corner of her eye. A video from a private account. It plays automatically, before her shaking fingers can stop it. It keeps looping long after she has dropped the phone to the ground with a gasp. Over and over again, a scalpel slicing a signed photograph of Holly's face into ribbons. A caption that taunts, 'This is only the beginning.'

Chapter 3
Holly then

'Tell us what it feels like to have cancer in your twenties?'

Holly can't form any words. All she can think about are the bright lights in her face, the sweat collecting on her shaven head. Her endlessly moving hands. It's the first time she's done this. Where the hell does she put her hands?

The interviewer stares at her, a smile frozen on her face. She has perfect eyebrows, thick and lush. Holly's fingers reach for her own. There is nothing but skin. The last round of chemotherapy took her hair away.

The silence stretches. She wanted to be here, and now she has to say something. Holly takes a deep, ragged breath.

'Like any woman in her early twenties, I didn't have my life completely figured out. Although I had done well at school and uni, I took a boring retail job to make some money and, before I knew it, a few months had turned into a year. I thought feeling constantly stressed, fatigued and lonely was my normal. I just felt horrible all of the time but I thought it was a phase I would get past when I grew up. So I missed my symptoms and by the time I saw a doctor I'd probably been sick for a while.'

The interviewer nods, eyes on Holly and not on the clock. She's doing it just right. The thrill shakes her tired bones. Her voice changes, stronger now, deeper. Maybe her words will have the power to reach out and educate someone before they get sick.

'Of course, that was before I had to come to terms with the possibility that I may never have the chance to grow up. When the doctor first said "cancer", I was numb. Only a few days later did it sink in and I just cried about the big things I wouldn't get to do: discover who I really was, have a career, get married, have a baby, travel. Then there were the little things, like the daily stories from my friends, tasting different foods, dancing, yoga, walking down the street with a really amazing song playing through my headphones. I mean, shit, what about all the songs and the playlists of songs that I would never discover?'

The life she spoke of sounded so sweet, imbued with the rosy glow of tragedy. She'd always wished for a life like that and imagined it was right around the corner. But Holly never danced or did yoga. She didn't really listen to music. Most of all, there were no friends with daily stories or messages fighting for attention on her phone. Before her cancer diagnosis, nobody gave her a second glance. She slouched through the world collecting clothes she hated and eating food that made her feel worse. Fat. Tired. Unlovable. Another washed-up consumer trying to numb herself to survive the drudgery.

How could she tell the interviewer that getting cancer in her twenties was the best thing that happened to her? That she finally realised she had something to fight for? That it was toxic, but not as toxic as the home it helped her pull away from? She turns to the camera and digs the words out from deep within her heart, flashing a smile that overwhelms her small, gaunt face.

'My profile has grown quickly and suddenly, and I am so honoured and overjoyed that so many people want to walk alongside me on this healing journey. But if I have this platform, I want to do something good with it. I want to inspire you and have a real impact on your life.' She points a finger, graceful as a dancer. 'Don't wait. You are enough. You are beautiful and talented and smart right *now*. If you are not feeling completely in love with your life and in awe with your luck, you have the power to change things. Nourish your body and your mind. Get healthy, get fit and get your head strong, because there is no challenge this world throws at us that we cannot fight till the death: not even cancer.'

Chapter 4
Tyler

Tyler steps into his Chelsea apartment, bloodied brogues swinging in one hand. He wipes them with a deft flick of a dish towel and places them on the counter so his cleaner can't get out of polishing them.

He makes his espresso on the stove with a cheap little gadget he found in Istanbul. The whole thing spills fucking everywhere as he lifts it off the heat. Bloody shaking hands.

He shouldn't have come home. The buzz is still crawling on his skin, seeping into every pristine surface it touches. It's not welcome here. What he's done, what he did. It was just this once. Like a one-night stand or trying out coke. A small, necessary diversion from an otherwise perfect path. A rite of passage. She deserved it, and now it's done. His eyes flick towards the dish towel, now stained brown. How many times has he come home from the hospital, with some unfortunate bodily fluid marking his clothing? It's all been innocent enough, collateral damage of a job he loves. But this mess just won't do.

He laces up his Stan Smiths – so clean, so classic – and heads out again, dish towel bulging in his pocket.

The buzz stings through his thighs, down to his toes. He paces past Harrods. Kings Road is quiet and slicked with rain. The dish towel is thrown – going, going, gone – into an empty bin outside a pastel-hued ladies boutique. The solitude should make him feel invincible, but it only makes the buzz grow louder. His steps quicken until he finds a bar in Fulham and orders a double Jack and Coke a few minutes before they call last orders. He strikes a conversation with a pretty, yoga-lean young thing who laughs at whatever he's saying and clutches his arm with a desperate grip. It's the last chance to find someone to go home with for the night. Panic shrills around him in a tinny falsetto. But it's not as loud as the buzz. Yoga girl is dancing now, brushing against his thighs. He imagines the inside of her bleak south London house share, the mouldy walls decorated with shawls from India and the scent of incense masking the damp laundry airing on a crowded clothes horse. The sex would be high-pitched and experimental enough to drown out the buzz for a few minutes, but her neediness would kick in quicker than his hangover. The investment is not worth the return. Besides, he hasn't been able to get hard in six months. He disappears while she is mid-twirl.

An off-licence provides an easier short-term solution in the form of a quart of cider and a loose cigarette. He takes it deep into Hyde Park and settles in front of the lake. What would she make of him tonight, drinking cheap booze out of a plastic bag? Oh, what is he on about? She would have loved it. She loved him best when he loosened up, when he acted as outrageously as she did. Even though she's long gone, he still feels as if he's performing for her, as if she's standing somewhere in the distance, just out of sight and smiling.

There was always a bit of a 'fuck you' spirit coiled within her bones. She could be spotted from a mile away, wild red hair raging against the collar of her vintage Harris Tweed Chanel suit, reading Machiavelli on the tube. No matter how wealthy she was, or how successful she became, she had the ability to shock him when he least expected it, to remain the principled, audacious woman she was when they'd first met. You don't meet girls like that every day, ones that truly don't give a shit.

Thinking of her pushes the buzz to a shrieking pitch. It aches in his temples. She would be proud of what he did tonight. He's sure of it. He wouldn't need to explain to her that it was justice for everything Holly had done to them, a small step towards rectifying the order of things. She'd have understood that sometimes things needed to be destroyed for the greater good. The heavy ink sky has diluted to a transparent grey. It's that sickening hour when the lost and the lonely from the night before collide with the achievers of the morning.

The pavement is sticky and littered with the debris of a night that has had the joy wrung out of it. He sidesteps a broken beer bottle as he takes out his mobile phone.

He's not sure what he expected, but Holly's Instagram is unchanged. Despite him feeling the scalpel pressing down on the soft meat of her cheek a few hours before, her photographs aggressively portray a life well lived. There she is, smiling radiantly while holding a green juice. In another shot, she arches herself into a yoga pose on an unnamed beach – girls like her are always in tropical locations for no apparent reason. A 'no make-up selfie' shows her pale and glistening before the camera with wide, searching eyes. The last shot – an elegantly lit flat white americano – he knows well. He watched her take it from his corner at Starbucks as she huffed, rearranged and strained to get the right angle. He'd smiled then, scoffing from the corner at the triviality of her last meaningless moment as the scalpel grew hot in his hand.

Tyler's not very good at social media – he prides himself on keeping a healthy distance these days – but he knows enough to click on the little icon to the right. Here are the photos of Holly, the ones other people take of her, the ones she doesn't have the power to edit and frame. The screaming interior of McDonald's instantly fills his screen. In its centre, Holly kneels on the ground, clutching her face, soaked in blood like a warrior emerging from battle. Despite the fuzzy footage and awkward angles, there is something iconic about it. It feels like a moment in history. A warm feeling swells in his gut. He delivered Holly's reckoning and stripped the mask off her face to reveal the quivering fraud below.

But the comments on the photos tell a different story. They wail in a cloying crescendo:

@SusieS
How could this happen to such an angel?

@SarahTaylor
Oh Holly, you represent everything that is good in my life! I feel like this attack happened to me!

@VegansofLondon
We love you babe, you've healed once before and you'll heal again! Be strong, we are all supporting you!!

The words of support seem endless. Intimate messages crowd every picture, from women who act as if they personally know the sunny blonde on their screen. It's suffocating. By the time he reaches his apartment and slumps on his bed, the buzz overcomes him like a sickness. He didn't teach Holly a lesson at all. Instead, he has created a martyr.

He goes into the dark, musty room next to the kitchen. In contrast with the rest of the house, it is undecorated. A smell of old incense clings to its scant contents. He digs into one of the boxes to find the folder of scraps that adorned the fridge when they used to share it. An old shopping list with DISHWASHING LIQUID underlined twice. The take-out menu for the curry place down the road. A silly picture of them posing in a photo booth at a wedding, she in a top hat and him in a tiara. Finally, the thing he was looking for – a magazine cut-out of Holly in tiny denim shorts and a floral bikini top, smiling into the camera. Frankie kept it up there as inspiration. He can still hear her laughing, saying 'Holly will remind me *not* to eat the entire box of chocolates,' like that extra softness around her hips mattered. Bright, radiant Holly, an invisible, pious goddess. Teach us, wise guru, how to abstain. Teach us how to be good.

He takes the picture with trembling hands. Holds the still-bloodied scalpel in the air. Presses down the record button. He means to slice the image only in half, but the buzz takes over, screeching in his ears, shaking his hands back and forth, over and over again, insatiable. 'It's not over yet,' he whispers as he presses send. It's not a fully-formed plan, but a dark feeling without a shape. It's only the beginning.

Chapter 5

Holly

'Hey there, sweetie, it's time for another test. I'm so sorry, my love.'

A thin nurse with a warm, Mancunian accent fishes for Holly's arm under the hot sheets.

'Oh, it's OK,' Holly says brightly. 'I'm used to it. How many am I in for today?'

'Just the one. Doctor wants to make sure you didn't pick up tetanus. That's all.'

'Well, that's a walk in the park then, isn't it!' She tries to smile but her cheeks feel weighed down and numb from the dressing. There is also that creeping fear that any sudden movement could break her. Gently does it. Still, no matter how scared she is, she likes to be that positive, cooperative patient everybody remembers. 'Oh, the funny blonde girl in Ward A, of course I'll take her some water!' 'You're looking for Holly? Oh yes, she's everybody's favourite on this floor. We'll be sad to see the back of her.' Countless hospital visits have taught her that you want the nurses on your side, and word gets around. They deserve a little brightness in their relentless slog.

The nurse bustles around her, checking her blood pressure and the incision where the drip had been placed.

'Oh, by the way, your boyfriend stopped by while you were sleeping. Such a kind, gorgeous guy. You had us all green with envy!'

'Boyfriend?' Holly cries, the innocuous word scratching in her throat.

'Yes, he stayed for ages, just watching over you. We offered to wake you but the poor thing said you needed your rest. He brought you some things from home too.'

She gestures towards a worn-out weekend bag on the ground with the faded logo of her university. She uses that bag for everything – from visits to the gym to moving cities, but seeing it here fills Holly with terror. It takes everything she has not to pull out her drip and run. How did he get into her home? How does he even know where she lives? She can't bear to unzip the bag and look inside. Should she tell the nurse she has been single for as long as she can remember? That something is desperately wrong?

Maybe it would set into action a series of events that would keep her safe. Holly's eyes flick between the bag on the ground and the medical file in front of her. She can't tell anyone anything yet, not until she understands it herself. It's too risky.

'What's your name?' she changes the subject, speaking slowly and carefully so as not to split her stitches. The nurse's face breaks into a wide, snaggle-toothed smile. 'It's Aurelia.'

'Fancy. French?' Her voice sounds painfully garbled, like she is hearing herself speaking through the fuzz of a radio.

'Yes, legend has it I was conceived in Paris. I know, I know. My parents are so original.'

Holly tries a laugh, which sounds more like grating metal.

'At least it was romantic. My parents have hardly ever left the country. I was probably conceived in a toilet while the pub was having a lock-in.' Holly's mother and father have coexisted miserably for as long as she can remember – so much so that she wonders whether their union was owed to some unfortunate series of events that cemented their despairing inertia into something resembling a family.

'Pretty little thing like you couldn't have had a beginning like that.'

There's an uncomfortable silence. Holly could tell the nurse that she wasn't always considered pretty. It used to take work and chance and luck for people to look at her twice. Their silence, however, speaks of something else. She *was* a pretty young thing, and now isn't quite so pretty anymore.

Aurelia turns her attention to the medical file at the end of the bed. Each flick of the page is like a paper cut to her throbbing face. 'Stop looking!' Holly wants to scream. Her intense gaze burns into the nurse's skin. It's not healing being here, trapped in this white room, the workings of her body analysed in a file, naked for all to see. Her body sluggish with drugs, vulnerable to attack. Her mouth is dry, panting, frantic. Her lips are cracked. The blood on her tongue pulls her mind to her mangled face. The force of her guilt is as persistent as a migraine; she would do anything for a private moment to collapse beneath it.

'Is everything OK pet? You're breathing like you've run a marathon!'

Holly looks away. A tear sinks into her bandages. Aurelia, mercifully, pushes the file shut.

'I think I should give you some space, yeah? It's been a long day.'

Her private room is so silent, Holly can hear the pounding of her breath. The metallic taste of blood still lingers on her tongue. There are no chattering families or dramatic, heaving patients. She could be lying in a hotel. Crisp sheets. Hard bed. A loneliness that bites through every surface.

She spoons mashed butternut into her mouth, a special vegan request. The rich taste of butter makes her heave. The hospital kitchen must have forgotten that dairy is not vegan. She forces the rest of it down, determined not to turn her nose up at their kindness. She'll run off the fat in a few days and feel in control once again. These awful emotions will bend beneath the force of her will. That is the beauty of a healthy lifestyle – no matter how uncertain the world's politics appear or how tormented your own life is, you can always return to a clean kitchen with some fresh produce and create a better life, a better world.

She tries to watch *Friends* reruns on the fuzzy television above her, but wearing the headphones make her feel exposed. Her heart won't slow down. The skin on her arms tingles and, every now and then, a bolt of pain shocks her face. She has started to remember his eyes, wild and hungry, as he grabbed her around the chest. Worse still are the flashes of moments leading up to the alley – her light, musical laugh, her hand tentatively grazing his, her disgusting ease with this person she had just met. She made it so easy for him to hurt her. But there is something else haunting her this evening, something more. The silence around her has a weight to it, like a held breath. It moves with a hidden presence. She is convinced he is watching her.

Being here alone is too much. She can't take it. Holly pulls her gown tight and eases herself off the bed, grinding her teeth against the pain of it. It's not only her face that's damaged. He threw her to the ground with such a force that her back is black with bruises.

She takes small, gentle steps, edging forward from the sanctuary of her room into the beating heart of the ward. Neither the nurses nor the patients glance at her bandaged face. They look ahead determinedly, the patients probably grateful they're only in for something superficial. Holly imagines them in the comfort of their living rooms, deep in a nest of blankets and love, saying to their families, 'Honey, you wouldn't believe who I saw today.'

Breathing physically hurts, but her legs push her deeper into the hospital, walking through the corridors like a ghost. All those tiny, tense Pilates moves must have counted for something. She settles on a soft, purple sofa outside the maternity ward. It smells of milk, women and vanilla. Visitors are not allowed inside, but she can sit and stare at the babies lying in rows, their wails giving a voice to the tightness in her throat. Their faces poke out of their snug swaddled blankets. Each one has a sheen to it, that new baby sheen. Nothing has touched their cheeks yet, so soft and round. Her fingers rub together, imagining the feeling of the skin. Their perfection is like a punch in the throat. The sour-milk taste of vomit burns her mouth. She was beautiful once. Everybody loved to look at her. Everybody was interested in what she had to say. Not anymore.

As desperately as she wanted to leave her room, she now desperately wants to return to its safety. She needs to lie down, close her eyes, get some more pills. The walls blur through her watering eyes. The floor sways beneath her bare feet.

Her room is a cool, dark contrast to the relentless light. The silence that unnerved her has shifted into soothing stillness. No more sudden moves.

The covers of her bed have been pulled up tightly, tucked in with regimental precision. Someone must have thought she had been discharged. Yet the magazines next to her bed remain in disorder and the flowers have been untouched. Holly squints into the darkness. Was that the shape of a figure, or just the curtains blowing in the breeze?

It's too much work to get under the covers, so she climbs on top and curls into a ball. Too hot to be trapped under blankets anyway. The bandages make her cheeks feel as if they are on fire. She shifts to get comfortable, and the bed crackles beneath her. Her breath catches. She shifts again. Something lies beneath the covers.

Heart pounding, she bunches the sheets in her fists and tugs them to the ground. Flicks her phone-torch on and shakily aims it towards the mattress. Rows and rows of faces stare up at her with small black eyes, features melted into each other. Each one so scarred their skin looks more like a mask. A low howling sound escapes her lips as she crouches on the floor, head between her knees, away from the eyes. The eyes that know.

Nobody must see this. It's a statement, a conclusion. This was no fluke. The attacker meant to hurt her and her alone. For this, she feels complicit. Nobody attacks unless they are provoked. She gathers the pictures quickly and pushes them into her handbag. They're good quality photographs. Printed out properly in a way she doesn't see much these days. It's a detail that haunts her. There is no note, no explanation, but an unsettling amount of forethought. He is here. He is always watching. And now she knows, he won't stop until she is torn to pieces.

Chapter 6
Tyler then

Tyler was five years old when they moved from London into the glass house in Weybridge. Drawings and detailed plans of its angular edges and lush gardens had been strewn about in strange places for years – his mother had a knack for creative filing. But to his small mind, the leap from touching those rough sketches to running his fingers over the newly varnished railings confirmed his greatest belief: his mother was a magical being, able to breathe life into anything.

At night, the stars glistened through the glass walls so vividly, it was as if the house didn't have walls at all. They were a family of wild things – mum, dad, boy – free as blackbirds and fast as foxes. His mum's magic only grew, as they hid from each other in the rose gardens and chased each other up and down the endless stairs of the house she had dreamed into life. He'd wanted to be like her, and hung on her every word as she explained why the ceiling sloped just so and the windows opened to the west. He tried to draw fantasy houses in the hope that she would make them real as well, but he always threw them away. Not because he was ashamed, but because he just couldn't think up a house as beautiful as the one they already had.

His dad still worked in the city most of the time, leaving them to endless, unstructured days of 'don't tell your father' bliss. Once they made a pillow fort and pressed their noses against the glass wall all night, watching for barn owls and shooting stars. They paged through his bird book together, choosing a favourite one on each page. He woke up squinting at the sun the next morning, cosy under the covers, safe in the crook of his mother's arm.

She still performed her magic, but not far away in the city like dad. She sat upstairs surrounded by books and sketches. Hours went by as she calmly plotted and planned on the big silver screen in front of her, flattening people's homes and rearranging them until they were perfect. 'Don't look so bored, it's just like the Lego you play with!' she used to laugh, but he always liked her sketches more.

When his dad was not around, Tyler would do all the important stuff. He would bring his mother biscuits while she worked. He'd walk with her hand in hand as they jiggled every door and window at night to make sure everything was locked. They were a team, and together they kept the glass house safe and full of magic.

The spell wasn't broken all at once. It happened slowly over time. First, it took the form of his mother's thin hand held up as he tried to show her the book on insects he'd got out the library.

'No, Tyler sweetheart. Not now, please.'

The catch in her voice turned the glass room cold. She didn't want to play as much anymore. She was always tired, always sleeping, always sitting dazed in front of the television, battling to catch her breath after walking up the stairs. She was a faded, thin-smiling version of his real mum, and in his dark, raging moments he wanted her gone.

He thought it was his fault. Why else would his mother and father hold tense, tearful conversations in whispers so shrill it could make his ears bleed? He lay awake at night listing all the bad things he had done: not sharing, not eating all his vegetables, lying and saying he had eaten his vegetables when really he'd hidden them and thrown them out when she wasn't looking. None of that seemed bad enough. Through some dark sorcery, the glass house folded in on itself. Wide-open spaces turned into closed doors. The garden was full of screaming faceless spirits. His mother's explosion of sketches was neatly arranged into piles by a housekeeper who didn't know how things were meant to work in the glass house, a housekeeper who took his jobs away, like bringing Mum tea.

He sat outside her bedroom while adults paced in and out. Behind the shut door, he heard her screams. Long before they told him she was sick, long before they explained the word 'cancer', he knew. He wanted to kick and bite them and shout in their faces like a savage. He knew, he knew. He had smelt the sickness on her skin first. When it came to her, he was always first.

Not that she let him close to her anymore. He longed to hold her hair in his hands and roll it into little ropes that his army figurines could climb. He cried at night because he needed to feel her hand resting on his forehead to fall asleep. It wasn't her fault. They were keeping her locked in her own glass house like a fairy-tale princess, and it was his duty to save her. He drew up plans and armed himself with weapons (a plastic cricket bat and a towel cape) and tried to sneak inside. He slammed into a wall of grown-up legs and screamed in his father's grip as he was carried away to the other side of the glass house.

Tyler and his father sat side by side like strangers, as he gruffly explained, 'Your mother loves you very much, my boy, but you can't go into her room anymore. You've got to be a good boy and not sneak in. The cancer has made her very sick and she doesn't want you to see her like this, OK? Do you understand?'

He didn't understand. The books that she and he had read together said that when someone is very sick, they get into an ambulance. They didn't stay locked in their glass house, lying there getting sicker while strangers walked in and out carrying strange equipment and packets smelling of herbs. They went to hospital to get better. So why wasn't she? His tea, while it took a long time to make, always tasted more delicious than any other tea. Why wouldn't she let him bring it to her? All these questions made his head pound, so he just cried into his clenched fists.

Tyler's father sighed and pulled his fists back into his lap.

'Look at me, Ty. This is enough, you hear me? We need to be strong now, and you need to get out of Mum's way.

All of this . . . this performing. It's not helping. You're not helping.'

You're not helping.

Tyler didn't see when they carried her body out. But he knew. Rocking back and forth sitting on his bed, he knew. Because the glass house had lost its breath. Its spirit had crumpled until it was nothing but a dream, a sketch of a dream life that belonged to somebody else.

Chapter 7

Holly

The footsteps bang against her ears. They jolt Holly awake from a fitful sweat-stained dream of sharp things breaking the surface of her skin. Pressure. Surrender. Blood. The feeling of ill will lingers in her consciousness, soon taking the sickly shape of guilt. This is worse than anyone could understand.

'Holly, open your eyes, my darling,' the nurse coos. 'You have more visitors.'

Three men stand at the end of her bed. The meds make her eyes water; they still stick together with sleep. From where she lies, their ruddy faces and shadowed eyes blur together like ghouls. Even in their awkwardly formal suits, there is an on-edge awareness that reveals them as police. As they carry through some extra chairs and seat themselves next to her bed, she feels a pang in her chest. They're a threat to her. They're here to hunt.

One gestures to the nurse. 'Can you give us some time alone please, ma'am?'

'Yes, yes of course. Holly, just buzz me if you need anything.' She tries to lock eyes with the nurse. *Please, please don't leave me with them.*

He turns to Holly. 'Hey there, pet. My name's Pete. My boys here are Darren and Dean. We're here to ask you a couple of questions about the crime that took place two nights ago. We're going to turn on this recorder, see? And write a few notes too so we can get a formal statement from you. The nurse here says it hurts for you to talk too much, so let's make this quick and painless, yeah? You ready?'

'Yes,' she whispers.

'Let's start at the beginning. Where did you meet the attacker?'

'I was at Starbucks drinking coffee and he came up to me.' The moment glimmers in her mind, that everyday stillness before everything changed. Was it something in her posture, the pout of her lips that made her seem available?

'What did he look like?'

'He was tall, about a head taller than me. Uh, sandy hair. Green eyes. Square jaw.'

'And you spoke to him.' The part she feels most ashamed about – how willing, how innocent she had been. Other girls would have known better.

'Yes, he was, uh, very charming.' She tries to find the right words, desperate to please. She's attuned to their reactions like a trapped animal, searching for a half-smile, an encouraging nod, anything to make her feel safe.

'OK, so just confirming that you spoke to an unknown male whom you had never met before.'

The three men exchange a loaded look between them. Oh God, this is her fault. She brought this on herself, didn't she? What the hell was she thinking? The other boys dance through her mind. Her history is written across London, in the sordid anecdotes of men whose surnames she cannot remember. It wouldn't take much digging for it to surface. It wouldn't even be the worst of her secrets. The cop writes for five agonising minutes in his notepad. He can't be writing word for word what she is saying. She hardly said that much. He must be adding insights, judgements of his own.

'What happened next?'

It feels so stupid now, so embarrassing. She pulls the covers a bit higher over her chest. She's got no bra on under her gown and it makes her feel vulnerable.

'We went for a walk around the city, and then had some supper. It was just like any first date really.'

'Except it was a date with someone you had never met before,' he qualifies.

Her cheeks ache, and her mouth is dry. The pain is too great for her to tolerate his sarcasm.

'That's usually how first dates are: a meeting of two strangers.'

'Now, now,' he laughs, 'No need to get pissy. I'm just getting my details straight.'

'And where did you have dinner then?'

'At a place called THE GOOD LUCK CLUB, in Soho. I remember walking from there to the place we said goodbye.' The dark alley, at that moment still heady with anticipation.

All three men stare at her pointedly. 'Now, tell us a bit about the, uh, incident.'

She shifts in her bed. This is the part that disturbs her the most. 'My problem is that I don't remember too much after a certain point. I remember leaning in to kiss him while standing near the restaurant where we had dinner, and then suddenly my memory goes.'

'You don't remember the attack at all?'

God, how she has tried, but it is like pushing against a cement wall. Immovable. She could mention his eyes, but it wouldn't be of any use. She cannot describe their colour or shape, only their coldness. They narrowed the same way her father's used to when she had done something wrong.

'No.'

'What about when you ran to get help?'

'Nothing.'

The men exchange glances again. She has a feeling she just failed an important test.

'Were you drunk?'

'No! I mean no, um, I don't drink at all. It's a health thing.'

'When you were found, you were screaming that your attacker knew you. Do you remember this?'

She closes her eyes. All she can remember after the blankness of the attack is the stark interior of the ambulance, and a kind, curly-haired woman holding her hand.

She was repeating something over and over, squeezing the woman's hand tighter. The words assumed a ghastly, distorted shape as they left her slashed face. *He said my full name. He called me a fraud. He knew exactly who I was the whole time. He called me by my name.*

'Yes, I do. Whoever it was definitely knew me. He did it on purpose.' Saying it out loud makes her hands tremble. He intended to harm her, and he'll return to do it again.

'Why do you think that would be?' The judgement drips off his tongue, thick as syrup.

Holly Evans, you're a fucking fraud. Bile rises in her throat. Her aching mouth tries to form the words to tell them about the video, but something in her closes up. How can she trust them? They could be collecting clues to pass the blame on to her, taking her fragments of memory and building it into something she does not recognise. For now, she needs to protect herself and keep this memory a secret.

Their leader slams the case file shut. He has heard enough. He holds up a plastic ziplock bag with her bright yoga leggings and stripy white top. 'Your doctor gave us your clothes for evidence – is there anything else you have that could be of assistance?' Is it her imagination or is he looking at her see-through leggings with distaste? And are his two sidekicks smirking knowingly behind him? They don't have to say a word; she knows what they are thinking. Nothing good ever happens to girls who wear clothes like this.

It's in the silence and the unsaid where her fears swarm like flies. She asked for it. Through her clothes, her Instagram pictures and her brazen flirtation with him at the coffee shop, she made him pick her.

The cop pats her on the arm as they get up to leave, 'We'll call you if anything comes up.'

Wait! She almost whispers. *There is more evidence.*

Wait. To make them turn around so she can push the video clips and the pictures – oh those horrible pictures – into their hands.

Wait. Please. It's a real case, he's a real person. The video clips and the pictures – flickering on the phone, crackling in her bed. The possibility that he was in her apartment, rifling through her things. This wasn't a random attack. It was deliberate, pointed, and the threat is far from over.

Holly Evans, you're a fucking fraud.

She cannot tell. They would have questions. They would look at her more closely, too close for comfort. Panic tightens her throat. It's far too risky. It would surely destroy her for good.

The men walk away, punching each other's arms and laughing at a shared joke. A bus roars in the distance. These moments are so screamingly average. Yet the horror beats impatiently behind her eyes.

Zanna arrives a few hours later in a cloud of Chanel No.5 and dressed in jet black. The peanut butter smoothie and almond latte she carries in her hands are too late to soothe Holly. She is panting and fidgeting like a caged rat. Nothing can hold her attention – not Netflix, not the stack of magazines her mother brought her, not even the activity on her Instagram feed. There is no remedy to quell the sick feeling that something terrible is about to happen. It's feeling closer now.

Although she aches to be alone and out of sight, she wants to call the nurses back every time they leave her. It only took a few minutes for him to prepare that horrific bed of pictures, what will he do with more time? What cruelty is he capable of if she is lying there trapped under the covers and waiting for him?

She focuses on the good things. Zanna is the only visitor with the ability to make her feel better. Her slick, silver-dyed hair, angular black wardrobe and Louboutinned strut turn every occasion into something impossibly stylish. While she survives primarily on sweets, cake and soft drinks, her body is as lean as a lioness. She also happens to be the hottest publicist in London, representing everyone from politicians to boy bands. Every magazine cover Holly's had, every TV appearance and radio show she's appeared on, has been aggressively negotiated by Zanna to give Holly the best exposure possible. She has a bit of a crush on Zanna, the way women often do. She even tried to emulate her edgy look once or twice, but on her it came across as garish and awkward.

Zanna flings her giant metallic tote bag on the bed.

'Hello, *mon petit chou*. I'm so sorry it's taken me three days to get here! I flew back from Cannes as soon as I could.' Of course, Holly recalls blurrily, Zanna was on a publicity spree at the Cannes Film Festival. Just the week before she was fretting about concealing her movie star client's latest on-set fling.

'Zanna! I can't tell you what a relief it is to see you.'

'Are you surviving in this hellhole? Oh God, forget I asked. Clearly you're not – you're as jittery as an LA socialite coming down from cheap speed.' She winks at her. 'And I've seen that shit on more occasions than I'd like to remember.'

'Well, I guess that's one way of putting it. The police were here. They made me feel like I was asking for it.' Saying it out aloud relieves some of the pressure. Darling Zanna, the only person Holly can admit her secret fears to so plainly. Well, some of them at least.

'Oh, sweetie, don't mind them. You know the truth and that's all that matters.'

She studies Holly through narrowed eyes. Unlike everyone else, she doesn't look at her with sadness, pity or discomfort. She stares at her dead-on, assessing the situation for what it is.

'Real talk now. Are you staring into the abyss?'

That's their code for when a situation feels so overwhelming there is no way out of it. Being a public figure comes with unexpected and unusual anxieties after all. Thankfully, through some steely resolve of her own, Zanna is a specialist in bringing her clients out of the abyss, or cajoling them away from the edge.

'I feel sore and tired. I can't really get my head around what happened. I don't usually mind the hospital, but after this morning I woke up desperate to go home.'

She thinks about her soft, cotton sheets. The jars of seeds and flours in her kitchen. The feeling of sinking into her couch with her cat curled upon her chest. Nobody prepares you for how to deal with the little inane things in situations like this. Tragedy is like that – a big, life-changing moment followed by a never-ending sequence of logistics that dull the aftershock.

As if reading her mind, Zanna says, 'I sent my assistant to get your keys out of your bag and feed your cat the night you were attacked. Just before I came here I went over myself to put some non-dairy milk in the fridge to prepare for your return. Oh, and I stocked you up with an enormous amount of fruit. Seriously, the amount of fruit you health bloggers eat is *obscene*.'

Relief rushes through her.

'I owe you one, Zanna.'

'You can say that again – your apartment was such a mess, it could have been ransacked!' she laughs. 'Seriously, what the hell were you making before you left the house that day?'

Panic clenches in Holly's chest. She loves her apartment and takes pride in keeping it tidy. There's something grounding for her in knowing that everything has its right place. In fact, she had spent the morning before the attack rearranging her spice cupboard to include the latest masalas she had found at her favourite little spice shop in Euston. Now, he's been there. His strange fingers grazing her belongings. His cold gaze taking in the soft, vulnerable ordinariness of her daily life. She knows nothing of him but the brief flashes of his face that evening, yet he has left his mark on everything she calls her own, even her face.

Holly has to remain calm. She's stronger than this, than him and she has wonderful people by her side, like Zanna.

'I can't believe I almost lost you, Holly!' A grey trail of mascara slides down Zanna's cheek. 'Jesus, look at me. I'm a mess. No matter, in a few hours we will be safely ensconced in blankets on your sofa watching TV as if none of this happened.' Holly desperately tries to imagine an afternoon free of worry but it's just not possible. The terror of her new life will confront her every time she walks past a mirror.

'Wait, am I going home soon?'

'Yes! You get to go today.' Zanna takes in a deep breath and furrows her eyebrows. 'Which is why I'm here to brief you.'

She rustles inside the tote bag, 'Here's a beautiful blush See by Chloe dress. A scarf to cover your face, oh, and some flats. I've got some dry shampoo for your hair and some perfume for a general increase in self-esteem.'

The hyper-feminine dress is hardly something she would pick out for herself. Despite her job in Topshop, clothes are still a foreign language to Holly, loaded with unintelligible meaning. She was never one of those girls who could throw on an ironic vintage jumper and Doc Martens and look cute. Even when she figured out how to look sexy, it was never in a subtle way. A short skirt, a plunging sequined top. Smooth shaven legs. Dressing for men was always easy; it was the women that she had no idea how to please. When her following got into the tens of thousands, she relied on brands to dress her in their latest neon athleisure. Finally, something fitted. She embraced her role as the fresh-faced, active girl next door, always on her way to yoga class, latte in hand. She thought she looked so wholesome, so inno-cent. Now, shame holds her in its cold grip as she recalls the way the policemen looked at her clothes tangled in the evidence bag. Inappropriate. Provocative. She needs to be a heroine now, and a heroine is more acceptable in a demure dress than a pair of yoga leggings.

The dress is only part of the problem. It's the perfor-mance that worries her, standing outside with the wind beating her bandages and all the people, *the journalists*, standing waiting to hear what she has to say. It would take just one question to poison them all.

'Is this really necessary?'

Zanna looks appalled. 'Holly, I don't think you understand the impact your attack has had. There are news crews from all around the country camping outside, waiting. And that's not even including your hundreds of followers either, and the thousands going hysterical online.'

'I don't understand . . .'

'You're female, beautiful and famous on the Internet. Your fans have lived through everything with you, so it feels to them like they have been attacked too. For the media and commentators, it is worrying proof of how dangerous it is to be a woman online. People are calling for regulation and some sort of justice. And right now, you're the poster girl for all of it.'

'But what's the dress for?'

'Well, my crisis communications strategy is to help you look poised and strong. You are not a victim. You are not defined by your tragedy. I want you going out there dressed like a winner, with a slick new signature style and a life philosophy still intact. The monster who did this to you wanted to take that away from you, so you're going to hold your head up high and carry on. And between you and me, Chloe gifted me with the dress on the way here – once you wear the thing, it's guaranteed to sell out online within minutes.'

As structured as Zanna's approach is, it actually seems natural. On Instagram, every moment is part of Holly's brand. No matter how horrific, it contributes to a bigger picture, earning the empathy of her fans. For now, this gives the tragedy a feeling of purpose. Maybe someone will see her struggle and feel less alone.

'And the scarf?' Holly asks, although she's not sure she wants to hear the answer. She's petrified that Zanna is ashamed of her new, mangled face, and wants to hide the horror from prying eyes.

Instead, she takes Holly's hand and looks into her eyes. 'While you've shared so many intimate details about your life online, you need to draw some boundaries. Some moments in life are too sore, too private to be flattened on a screen to satisfy the human appetite for gore. Let's be clear – every one of your fans, no matter how loving, wants to see your cut-up face. They probably don't even understand why themselves.'

'But I still have my dressing on!'

'Doesn't matter – they still get to gawk at the extent of the damage.' She shakes her head. 'I hope they get this guy, whoever did this is as malicious as they come.'

Holly's legs feel like lead. Is she insane to leave the comfort of the hospital for her flat, now sullied with his presence? He knows where she lives and wants her to know that he can come back any time he wants to. Maybe it's not too late to pull Zanna aside and tell her everything. But there's a signed discharge form, a packed bag, and people outside waiting.

'Should I say something?'

'Read through this statement I have prepared for you. I will help get the mic beneath your scarf and you will read it outside the hospital. One hour later, you'll post it to all your social platforms with a picture I have selected from your archives. Once that is over with, you will have some space to rest.'

Every moment after that feels hyperreal. Her mother, cloying and unprepared, clutching her arm. Her father, conspicuously absent. *You deserved this.* The delicate lace dress, alien against her skin. The signing out of hospital. The doctor, concerned that her saliva will infect the wound, fitting a drain. Her hand, clutching a plastic bag filled with clear liquid mixed with her blood.

As she stands before the crowd, she takes in every tear-stained face, wondering what brought them here on a weekday. How did they get off work? Why did her private pain matter so much to them?

Quietly, beneath the rustle of the crowd, a darker thought. What will happen when they all stop loving her? Will she still be remembered then? Beyond all the joy, support, smiles and encouraging eyes, she feels the shudder of a tower swaying in the wind, the earth shifting beneath her feet, threatening to pull everything to the ground.

She feels Zanna's arm around her shoulder and the mic slipping underneath her scarf. Another power takes over. It's time to speak.

'Good morning, everyone. Thank you all for being here. I am overwhelmed by the outpouring of love and support in the wake of my attack. Not one message has gone unread, and each one gives me hope for the innate kindness of the human race. What happened the other night was a toxic, freak incident. I don't know why someone would wish to attack me. In fact, I'm not sure why anyone would want to hurt someone the way this attacker hurt me. As many people have said, it is a sign of our increasing vulnerability on the Internet. That being said, I started my Instagram and my blog in order to consciously share my vulnerability with others in the hope that it would empower them to live better, eat better, and embrace their true selves. There have been so many stories of healing as a result, and a loving health conscious online community has been built because of my journey. I will not let one sick person take that away from me, or reduce the impact I have had on others. I will be taking some time to heal in private, but I will be back in the near future, carrying only a message of love. Have a good evening.'

The crowd roars. Holly tries to still her shaking hands. The words she just spat out were empty, the words of a hypocrite. She doesn't feel powerful at all. She feels small, fearful, reduced to the most pathetic version of herself. To an outsider, her eyes may look resolute, but in reality they are searching, heart in her throat, for a flash of golden hair and a brand new Burberry coat.

Zanna's fingers graze lightly her bruised shoulders as she ushers her into a waiting car. 'You did great. Everything is going to be OK now. You'll see.' The image of her sliced photograph burns behind her eyes, those unnamed scarred women crackling beneath her weight. He's found her, and now he flickers in the corner of her eye. The glint of a scalpel. She will learn what it means to hurt. Then, there is the secret that aches within her bones, the fear that coils around her ribs so tightly they may shatter. If they looked hard enough, they would see. It's hidden in her Instagram feed. Now it is clear that somebody out there knows.

Chapter 8
Holly then

Six o'clock. Right on schedule, the keys jiggle in the lock. Dad's home. Holly runs to the door behind her mum to greet him. It's partly out of excitement to share everything that happened that day, but also partly to check the temperature of his mood. A stooped posture and sour grimace means a night of shouting and broken glass. An easy laugh and swinging briefcase, a sign that tonight will be one of the better nights. She has to read the signs and adjust herself accordingly. If it's a bad day, anything – a careless comment, some mess in the living room, the way she has arranged the knives and forks – will cause him to explode.

Her breath quickens as she leans in to hug him. He holds on to her tightly in his smell of cologne and cigarettes. It's OK. Today is a good day. Thank goodness because she has so much to tell him. Youth group is on at church tonight for the first time since the school holidays, and this afternoon she went with her mum to Office to buy some trainers for the occasion. It had taken her weeks to decide which ones, but after carefully observing her peers, she finally had her heart set on one pair and one pair only: pitch-black Fila high tops. One of the most popular guys at youth group, Oliver, has the boy's version. She imagines them walking together, holding hands. Changing from thirteen and never been kissed to steady girlfriend of the hottest guy in town in an instant.

They weren't sure about the colour at first. Holly had never owned any black clothing before. Her dad could be quite the religious nut sometimes, and he thought the colour was satanic. Maybe she should only put them on once she gets to youth group. But her mum had said it was fine, and he had only made those comments once or twice before and those were on particularly bad days. And anyway, he knew she needed some new shoes.

She runs up to her bedroom and pulls on a pair of jeans and a plain white T-shirt, lacing up the new trainers as the finishing touch. Holly is not one of the pretty girls, or even one of the cool girls, but maybe tonight is the night things change. The embroidered logo on her feet winking up at her is her ticket. She grabs her denim jacket off the bed and smiles as her dad's laugh bellows from the kitchen.

'OK, Dad, I'm ready to go now!'

She shifts from foot to foot.

'Just a minute, my girl,' he says, finishing the last of his coffee. His eyes dart to her feet and narrow into thin slits. '*What* are those?'

Her mum steps in. 'She needed some new trainers, Ralph. All the kids are wearing ones like these.'

'Not my kid,' he says, growing redder, more danger-ous. The air contracts around them both. She shouldn't have taken the chance. She should have looked in his eyes properly when he came home. It's always there in his eyes if you look hard enough.

She's not in her body after that. She's outside, floating above them as he calls her evil, a follower, a slave to her friends. Black shoes won't make her prettier. Black shoes won't make them like her. Doesn't she see how nobody cares about her? Stupid, superficial, chubby girl. She doesn't react as his voice gets louder and he shakes her, trying to scream a reaction out of her. Eight red marks where he has gripped her. No, she floats just above the chaos like a balloon tethered to his eyes. The wildness in them shows Holly just how far he's lost control, and encourages her to hold on to it herself.

These fights used to follow a well-worn pattern. He would go too far with a punch or a push; she would start to sob and he'd wrap his arms around her. *I'm sorry, my baby, I'm so sorry.* He'd make it all better and they'd forget. Well, she's not a little girl anymore. She doesn't break like she used to. Even as he speeds through the streets of Exeter, spitting insults, slamming his hands on the steering wheel. Even as he swerves and her body slams into the door. Even when her stoic silence pushes him over the edge and he makes her take the new trainers off and throw them into the bushes. *You deserve it. You deserve it.*

She stumbles into youth group ten minutes late, face stinging from bruises yet to form. While her footsteps echo through the empty church hall, nobody turns to look at her. They're all huddled in a circle around blonde, perfect, popular Emma, who is crying neat tears into her fluffy pink jumper that falls seamlessly over her prematurely developed breasts. Oliver is right there, rubbing her shoulder, mesmerised. God, she was so stupid to think it would only take a pair of shoes to be one of them, a stupid pair of shoes now getting soaked somewhere in the rain outside. How crazy she was to hope that they would run to her as she came in from the rain, that they would hold her while she sobbed.

'Hey, Holly, come join us in prayer for Emma. She found out today that she is very sick,' the youth leader says. There's no space for Holly's pain today. Nobody can see the bruises yet, or worse, the cuts across her heart from the things her dad called her. So she wipes the mud from her bare feet, kneels down and lays her hand on the sick girl, the special girl, and prays to God to make her well.

Chapter 9
Tyler

The simple act of walking to St Mary's hospital is too much for Tyler to bear. Idiocy taunts him around every corner. Right now, he's stuck behind a middle-aged man idling on his phone.

Tyler is angry about a lot of things: the traffic, the bleak weather, people who wait till the last possible second to take out their Oyster card at the tube station turnstiles, tourists dawdling on Regent Street, the way his hair didn't cooperate with its styling wax today. Like every day, it has no discernible source. How many times has he wondered what it would be like to kick the person standing in front of him on the escalator? How satisfying would it feel to roll his car ever so slightly forward and onto the pedestrian crossing at the wrong time?

When he cut Holly, he felt a sweet release for a few seconds, as if his own anxiety was seeping out with her blood. It wasn't like when he performed surgery, where he was surrounded by other people and focused on a specific outcome. The moment was more sacred. A private indulgence. It felt like a solution.

It started to wear off the instant he walked away, but the memory remained. He clung onto it as he fell asleep at night. He acted it out during moments of frustration in his day. He could feel it vividly, viscerally, the sensation of the scalpel pressing against his palm, the 'will he / won't he' rush as the evening came to an end, the tensing up of her frantic body in his grasp. She'd felt as fragile as a caged, fluttering bird.

He had been gearing up to that moment ever since he convinced her landlord to give him a key to her apartment months before. All he had to do was act like her worried boyfriend and make up a critical emergency. Charming as he is, the landlord gave him a key for the morning, long enough for him to make a copy. There was a thrill in being close to her whenever he wanted, and occupying her place of safety without her knowledge.

A part of him had thought that the moment he attacked her would be enough, but he feels the sheen of the memory wearing off every time he revisits it in his mind. The little details and sensations begin to feel distant. It wasn't a solution after all, but a start.

The tightness in his chest opens slightly as he walks through the grand red-bricked entrance to St Mary's. In the short time he's been here, he's become known among the other doctors, maybe even loved. It's not the hardest thing to achieve. Anyone will love you if you ask them questions about themselves. They will love you more if you pay attention and stay interested. Rachel, the night nurse on duty in the psychiatric ward, competes in Irish-dancing tournaments at the weekends. Rob, the gynaecologist, came out as gay last year and is proposing to his boyfriend when they go on summer holiday to the Maldives. James, one of the new trauma surgeons, dreams about going to South Africa to experience working in their trauma wards, but until then he binge-watches *Grey's Anatomy* on his nights off. This information means nothing to him, but appearing curious makes his world a smoother one to live in.

'Doc! You're in the paper today!'

A sudden surge of panic. Has he been too confident? Was he too careless? But of course not. It's something else. Namely, the reconstructive facial surgery he had performed on ten women in Bangladesh. Some journalists from the *Guardian* travelled to the home where they were recovering and wrote a glowing report on his selfless work. He felt a thrilling jolt at the sight of their smooth faces. The skin grafts had taken beautifully. The slack muscles had become infused with new life. Most importantly, the women bubbled with a confidence born of the relief that they will fit into society once more. Shame, isolation, loneliness. These things are more poisonous than a scar could ever be.

The headline reads PLASTIC SURGERY WITH HEART. They don't understand. He doesn't perform plastic surgery with his heart. He performs it with his mind only. He purposefully doesn't get too involved in the backstory, in the person behind the broken mask. What does interest him is the intellectual riddle of moulding and shaping their singed skin. He is interested in the magic of bringing their frozen faces back to life. There are no challenges of this nature in

London. Everything here is too sterile, too average. There is a limit to how many breast implants he can shove into women each day. Cutting for no real reason feels like a crime, a gross misuse of his skills. He can only really see his full potential in an unequipped clinic, with a lost cause lying broken and malleable in his hands. He took pictures of every woman to document their progress, pictures that he put to use two nights ago. He takes one look at the article before folding it and putting it into his pocket. Breathes a deep sigh. The media's obsession with creating heroes without any evidence is exhausting. Still, he'd rather be recognised as a saviour than as an attacker.

'Hey, Tyler, have you seen this story?' The nurse hands him the front page of the *Telegraph*. Holly stares back at him with a face of jagged cuts swimming in blood. This must have been taken just after it happened. The blood had hardly got a chance to clot. Oh, how it had turned his stomach to make such careless, messy incisions! His worst work by far. The article stumbles over itself in its praise of Holly. He can only read the first paragraph.

Self-made online entrepreneur Holly Evans has become the face of the nation's outrage towards online harassment. The young blogger, blessed not only with good looks but also business savvy, has a wellness empire valued at over £1 million. This includes one published recipe book, media appearances, sponsorships and an upcoming range of organic skincare.

While there is no clear motive for the attack, Holly claims the attacker knew who she was. This is the most drastic instance of harassment of a female online figure to date in the UK. Evans's attack has seen an outpouring of support from her fans and sponsors . . .

The tone of it makes him sick. Do online entrepreneurs like Holly really need to have an ounce of 'business savvy'? Or do they simply happen to be in the right place at the right moment in history, with a face that is fresh enough to match their idea? He graduated from university a few years before Facebook hit. He was at his best-looking and at his most dynamic in a time before Instagram. What could he have achieved if he'd lived out his life in front of the camera? Instead, he's had to work for his success the hard way.

The nurse fidgets in front of him, eager for his opinion. He remembers now that she's one of those types that gets fixated on a news story and devours it from every angle. The prettier the injured party, the better. She wants something exclusive, something she hasn't found yet in the articles she's read. 'What do you think of the damage, Dr Wells? Do you think she'll ever look herself again?'

He smiles at her and flattens the paper on the desk in front of him.

'Unfortunately, no. While this looks like the work of an hysterical opportunistic attacker, they have actually done an excellent job, cutting in such a way that will promote the most scarring possible. It may be a fluke, but they have gone for the softest tissue, and made small, jagged incisions that will not only be a nightmare to fix, but are open to infection. Give her a week or two under the wrong doctor and there will be some serious problems.'

'Would you treat her? You've dealt with much worse!' Her eyes are hungry. The excitement at some drama in her dreary day is too much to contain.

He stiffens at the thought. The risk is too great. But imagine, oh imagine the sweetness of her soft, helpless body lying in front of him again. A rambling script begins to form in his head of everything he would say to her, maybe even *do* to her. She needs to understand what she did wrong. You can't just do what she did without some form of repercussion. You don't just take someone else's life and then slink away to enjoy your good fortune. It's just not right.

Throughout the day, his heart keeps lurching back to infinite afternoons in Hyde Park. Frankie's red hair tangled in the grass, a book resting on her chest. The inevitable moment when she grew bored, burrowed under his newspaper and slept on his chest. 'What are you reading now, Tyler? Huh? Huh? Tell me the news I should care about.' Nothing was as important as her softness against his skin, so he would give up his futile attempts at processing current affairs to roll with her in the sun-soaked grass. She'd always make him go and buy ice cream, even when it was overcast and they could feel the prickle of rain against their bare arms. Not just any kind, she liked flavours swirled with rich caramel and chocolate, with bites of brownie or biscuit. She would drag him down to South Kensington to get her favourite red velvet cupcakes for later. She ate sugar then, with child-like abandon. She inhaled eggs, cream, butter and steak. The good things, the juicy things. It was clear in the fullness of her breasts and the arch of her hips, when she was swaying down the street, running to the tube, gesturing to him to follow her, to catch up, that there were endless things left to explore.

His rage quieted in her presence. She teased him about it of course. She found his superficial annoyances and the discomfort with which he lived everyday life absolutely hilarious. 'Darling, they're just people trying to go about their day. What do you want them to do? Not everyone can be as perfect a specimen as you!' Wild kisses then, all over his face. Eyes, nose, cheeks, mouth. Love sinking into his skin and calming the places that hurt. Turning his screams into sighs. He should have never accepted them. He should have pushed her away before he got hooked. He should have known that she would leave him eventually.

Chapter 10

Holly

Holly jumps at a frantic banging on her door. Panic has ground up any sense of perspective. Her nerves disintegrate at the slightest disturbance. Her imagination loops, taking her down the darkest paths, over and over again. There are many ways to break a woman. She is cornered and cowering, with nowhere to run. He is going to cut her again and make her beg for mercy.

He knew her well enough to pounce on her in the Starbucks she always visited after yoga, so what else does he know? How long had he been prowling in the shadows, taking note of her innocent routine? The stain of his watchful gaze makes her whole life feel dirty.

Tofu, her beloved cat, stirs in the warmth of Holly's arms. Sweet thing – she hasn't left her side since she returned. Holly strokes her silver fur and watches her blue eyes open and close in bliss. It's hard to believe that the purring creature snuggled next to her was too petrified to even eat in front of her six months ago. She pats the side of Holly's face gently, regarding her fraying bandages with interest. If anything happened to Tofu, Holly would never forgive herself.

The banging continues. Holly pulls herself up, careful not to strain the aching muscles in her neck and face. As she goes to open the door, she can feel the physical force of her mother huffing in the next room and finally heaving herself up to respond to the racket outside. Ever since her drawn face appeared next to Holly's bed, she has made it clear that every moment of her care comes with immense personal sacrifice. Holly would push her out of the door if she could, and push away the agonising reminder of home, but nobody likes an ungrateful patient.

Don't answer. She wants to scream but her voice doesn't come. *Don't let him in.* His eyes pierce through her fitful dreams, hungry for so much more. Eyes like his could calmly take a life.

'Who's there?' her voice echoes across the apartment. She imagines his sick smile, the one she can't wipe from her memory. It's so clear, that he could be standing right in front of her with his scalpel pressing into her throat. Nothing's stopping him. The police don't have any leads. Her only comfort is the number they scrawled on an oil-stained scrap of paper to be used in the event of an emergency.

She's also meant to call it if she remembers any more information. What could she possibly say? That she is convinced he will quietly return to finish what he started? That she wouldn't blame him? Her future unspools ahead of her: a shadow of a man lurching towards her in the night, months spent in hospital until the world forgets about her, a pitiful return home to heal her scars and pay off her debt.

Her scabs are rough against her fingertips. The stitches prickle and itch. This skin that she once knew so well is alien to her touch. She can't look in the mirror, not yet. Her reflection will confirm the worst – this really happened, and now she is the tentative inhabitant of this strange new life. While her cancer memories have soft, undefined edges, this feels hard and brutal.

She shrugs on her dressing gown, hands shaking. It's not him. Not today. It's simply another drop-off of juices, smoothies and soups from a raw food restaurant in Portobello. Since she got home, she gets a fresh 'love pack' from them every day. This is only a small slice of the abundance crowding her flat. Her small kitchen is heaving with healthy brownies and cakes. Her bed is strewn with the wrappings of hundreds of earth-friendly creams and oils that were gifted to help her with the scarring. She's never felt such an overwhelming outpouring of love.

While she regards the product drops with healthy suspicion (one Instagram on her account equates to thousands of pounds in advertising), the letters from her followers have stuck. One girl got harassed on Twitter for calling out a guy for promoting rape culture in a disgusting picture. In response, he sent her a direct message of her photograph with his semen all over it. A beautiful woman in Barcelona sent Holly an email saying she was forced to remove her yoga account from Instagram after the constant comments about her DD breasts almost drove her to have a breast reduction. Then there was the sixteen-year-old black beauty blogger who had to go on antidepressants after a slew of racist comments over her natural hair. This is the curious, contradictory heart of social media. Women are encouraged to be visible, to mark their presence with their beauty and their talents, yet if their expression doesn't fit in with another person's definition of normal, it is seen as an invitation to be harassed.

In a way, she is better off than these women. At least the damage of her harassment is mapped across her face. He abused her in a language that is recognisable as wrong.

Uncomfortable visions keep pushing to the surface. Maybe it's the feeling of brokenness that sets off old memories, or the compulsion to tell only part of the truth, the part people are ready to hear. Or maybe it's the relentless flashing of her attacker's face in her mind, quivering with the type of anger she last saw in her father's face.

He gave her a black eye once. England had lost at the cricket and he switched the TV off, finding a distraction in taunting her about eating a plate of chips. She was getting too big for her age and no lad would fancy her. She said something rude – *yes, Dad, I'm a fucking pig*. When he hit her, his signet ring caught on her brow bone. The story she stuck to was about sleepwalking and falling. The real shame, quivering and raw, remained hidden.

She already understood then that some hurts received sympathy, and other hurts received judgement. If she shared the truth with her classmates about her swollen eye, would they understand or would they wonder what she did to deserve it? As she holds her breath in anticipation of what Jack will do next, she can't help but wonder the same thing now.

Chapter 11

Tyler

The fact that Tyler met Frankie at all was a mystical act of fate. Like in any big city, two people could happily share the same space without ever crossing paths. The place they met was one neither usually went to and, after meeting, neither visited again.

That day, Tyler was rushing to meet a friend visiting from out of town. Despite his protestations, his friend was insistent on meeting in a dank, charmless pub near Warwick Avenue tube station. He had his reasons, something to do with a treasured memory, tradition and a barman who poured heavy-handed gin and tonics. Tyler was never much of a drinker – the lack of control unnerved him. Frankie always told this part of the story differently, ruffling his hair and saying he was imagining things, but no memory in his mind is clearer.

Frankie always says – said – that they saw each other for the first time outside the tube station, but that's just not true. He saw her on the escalator. Something about her bright hair, and the way she was swaying to the song on her earphones, told him that this was a girl who knew how to live. It's hard to believe that was just three years ago, when he was working double shifts at the hospital, trying to prove himself as a young doctor after decades of studying. His life revolved around grim hospital hours and a staple diet of Tesco ready-made pasta. His spare time was spent pounding punishing running routes along London's streets – anything to numb his constant rage.

How time can build things up. How time can break it down. Spotting Frankie in her long, red Indian-style dress that day was a startling vision. Fire was spun in her every gesture and in her orbit glowed the promise of new life. Lord knows that by that stage of his life he desperately needed to live. She could have been just a sweet dream that passed through his consciousness, only to be forgotten. Yet as he walked out of the station she was sitting on a bench waiting for a bus, chewing on a cheese straw and engrossed in her book. The surprising ordinariness of it almost made him laugh out loud. He could have just walked on, but the cover of her book was like a calling. His dream girl wasn't reading just anything, she was reading *Perfume* by Patrick Süskind, the defining novel of his university days. Her choice of literature was like a siren song, affirming everything he wanted to believe about her. So he walked up to her.

'Great book, that.'

'Excuse me?' She had the guarded mask women wear around strange men. Her hands reached in her bag, perhaps for a sharp key to defend herself with if necessary.

He tried again, careful not to stand too close. 'Sorry, I just couldn't help but notice the book you're reading. It's one of my favourites.' It sounded so stupid out loud, but judging from her half-smile, she was softening.

'Really? It seems a bit slow-going right now.'

'That's what I thought. I almost put it down a number of times, but I'm so glad I stuck with it. The ending, wow, I don't know how to explain it. It's like nothing you've ever read or will read again.'

'That's quite a review.' Her eyes opened up like flowers, her fists uncurled.

'I mean every word.'

Her tongue flicked over her lips. He held her eyes.

'Will it change my life?'

'Oh, I'm not so sure about that. But listen' – a strange impulse took hold of him – 'why don't you take my number, and if you love the ending as much as I do then you can let me take you for a drink?'

'I must warn you: I take my alcohol seriously and in large quantities.'

'Is that a yes?'

'It's a "let me see how the book goes".'

That was their beginning, at a bus stop on Warwick Avenue, and then a bar in Hoxton. Tyler, a striving young doctor and Frankie, a young investment banker blazing her way up the corporate ladder. They were so unmoulded then, all rough edges and untarnished gold. What a perfect pair they made, walking hand in hand through Camden Market, dancing in the rain at festivals, staying up all night at punk concerts held in deconsecrated churches, walking out of obscure Finnish vampire-movie screenings, running along the South Bank, dancing, drinking, smoking, learning. What a fresh, unbreakable, London love. What a disaster.

Chapter 12

Holly

Holly shuffles to make herself coffee, eyes darting for anything irregular in the room. The past few days have been unnaturally quiet in her home, but he has made his presence known in other ways. Emails keep coming through saying someone is trying to hack into her YouTube, Instagram and Facebook accounts. It's too frequent and persistent to be anyone but him. He doesn't just want to end her physical life, but her digital life as well. Holly has to wonder which he finds more offensive.

Despite her pounding heart, the beauty of her apartment still takes her breath away. The absence of her mother – now thankfully back home in Exeter – also allows the place to fill with a sense of peace. Morning light exhales on a bunch of fresh peonies. Her walls are decorated with magazine covers and articles about her blog. Her recipe books rest on the bookshelf next to Jamie Oliver's and Nigella Lawson's. It looks like the space of someone who knew what they were doing all along, someone worth the fame they have achieved.

Most people who make their money from being loved on the Internet sidestep the question of what made everything change for them. Everyone wants access to that magic, that secret alchemy that turns an average human into a star. Most will say there was no big turning point, that they simply posted pictures every day and their fan base grew and grew. They want to believe that their destiny is down to more than sharing the right content at the right moment in history with a willing audience. It's just luck, nothing more.

Holly knows the exact picture responsible for everything. She has memorised its light, shade and composition by heart. It shouldn't have been a success. The colours were brash. The angle seemed a bit off. It wasn't that different from other haphazard pictures in her feed. At that stage, she had 250 followers, mostly acquaintances or spam accounts.

The photograph was taken a month after she had been to the doctor. She'd got scared, and embraced a healthy new lifestyle. Amid all the hysteria of being ill, of being broken, she had found a reliable comfort in cooking. The antidote to sickness lay in the kitchen, in the crushing of spices, the dripping flesh of fresh fruit and the sharp tang of herbs. Like a nun in her restraint, yet like a witch in her gleeful communing with the earth.

The first recipe she was ever proud of was a green smoothie, which she posted on Instagram. Her lumpy, pasty face loomed above a glass with contents the colour of swamp water. The caption read: 'It's time to commit myself to good health. Food is medicine. It prevents; it heals; it cures. This smoothie looks vile, I know, but the combo of bananas, spinach, almond butter and spirulina powder does something special.' She added some hashtags to show off her handiwork and inspire others. She typed #smoothie #healing #radiation #cancer #survivor and posted. The recipe was that good.

She got a few likes, as well as a few comments from friends wishing her well. Nothing out of the ordinary. Back then, Instagram felt a bit new and awkward and wasn't something she checked every few minutes. A bit later she'd racked up a few more likes and a comment from someone she didn't know: 'Just tried this after a shitty day at chemo. Was also the only thing I could keep down. Sharing your pic with all my mates now. Thanks doll! #fuckcancer.' Holly checked her profile – it seemed to be one of those girls from the latest hit reality TV show, who'd gone public with her breast cancer struggle the previous year. That first surge of validation was sweeter than anything she has ever experienced since then.

By the time she had turned on her phone the next morning, she had more than 5,000 likes and 1,500 new followers. Among them were other reality TV stars, women's magazines and cancer support groups. It turned out the *Daily Mail* had published a story with the headline, 'Reality star swears by girl next door's all-natural smoothie during cancer treatment.' In the body of the story was an embarrassing selfie that showed she needed to get her roots done.

She had released one of a multitude of moments into the great, wide world and now people wanted more of one particular frame in her life. Just that. So she traded her phone for a better one and got a blender. She started reading more books on natural healing and how food affects the body. She could evangelise on the benefits of ginger and design the ultimate meal to cleanse the body of toxins. She did more squats and sit-ups and posted a few bikini pictures. She lightened her hair and went for treatments to make it shine. She got a YouTube channel, where she shared candid vlogs about what she ate in a day. She was surprised to find how much she enjoyed being in front of the camera and sharing her passion. Her natural sense of humour and caring nature – usually hidden by her shyness – started to shine through. Her followers grew, and soon she became a woman worthy of her hype. But if she was honest, it all started because of that one random moment, when somebody coated in the temporary glitter of fame chose to reach out, and some of that glitter rubbed off on her. Yes, it could have been anyone. But it was her, and she was going to hold on to it until her knuckles turn white.

Holly is wrenched into the present as her door flings open. She's screaming and screaming, hands over her face. The moment has finally arrived – he is here to finish what he started.

'Oh fuck! Sorry! It's just me – you gave me a key, remember?' A familiar voice. Zanna, it's just Zanna.

She walks tentatively towards Holly, as if she's different now, an injured animal that has grown unpredictable.

She's slightly flushed from one of her fad exercise classes. Judging by her black ballet shoes and satin wrap skirt, she's now discovered Ballet Barre. Her hand rustles through one of the media drops and pulls out a raw cacao brownie, crinkling her nose at the sharp shock of unrefined sugar.

'Should I ask how you are doing today?'

'Oh, I'm OK.' The light is too bright. The heat on her face feels angry. She cannot shake the feeling that he is nearby watching her, mocking her. Still, she is desperate to make things right and match her friend's sunny disposition.

'That greeting you just gave me tells another story. You sure everything is OK?'

Her secret, just for a moment, unfolds on the tip of her tongue. It coats her mouth like acid, and she would do anything to spit it out. Zanna would have a plan, as she always does. How many times has she cried on her shoulder after a meeting with a cynical journalist or a comment from a bitter troll? She's the only person Holly can really talk to in that raw, unmasked way that she imagines real friends do. She may even get her to laugh about it! But then as quickly as it came, the secret folds back on itself again. She says, 'Well it's not very comforting that the police have found nothing at all. Every potential suspect picture they have shown me looks like a thug. This guy was elegant in a way that nobody could fake.'

'It gives me the absolute creeps. He sounds like one of those rich boys that avoid rape charges at Oxbridge because their daddy is a donor.'

A chill spreads down Holly's spine. Zanna pulls her silver tote onto her lap and rifles through it.

'God. Zan! What do you keep in there? You're like a monochrome Mary Poppins!'

'When you're in PR you have to be prepared for any eventuality. Anyway, this time it's something you'll be pretty happy about.'

She dumps a pile of newspapers onto the coffee table with a loud thud, spreading them out with lean fingers. Holly's name is on every single cover. Some have even printed a shot of her in a bikini, taken on a press trip to Hawaii at a time when she still had a six-pack.

Zanna laughs, 'I submitted your sexiest pic to the press. I hope you don't mind. I always find it so unnerving that nobody has a choice in what picture represents them when tragedy strikes. I mean, not only have you been attacked or murdered, but now you have to cope with the whole world judging you from one random photograph a journalist managed to save from your Facebook page which is usually one of you wearing a pink sparkly cowboy hat and looking like an arsehole. It's anti-feminist I know, but hey, being sexy makes the world want to save you.'

'No, no, it's great. I like it! Although it does make me wonder if I'll ever be that beautiful again.'

Saying it out aloud brings with it an urgent despair. A realisation. On Instagram, she is just a face and body, filtered until pure. Even the behind-the-scenes, 'real' snippets of her life in her Instagram stories are curated to show her best side. There are hundreds, thousands of women just like her. Some are thinner, more exotic, more put together, sexier, dirtier, funnier. There is always somebody newer who has the chance to be the next 'It Girl'.

A genuine sadness flashes across Zanna's face. How many times has she stood witness to a young beauty burning to the ground? She clutches Holly's hand.

'You're beautiful now, babe, you're just a bit buggered up. It is what it is.'

It is what it is.

Zanna is on a mission now, arranging each paper side by side.

'OK, now I bet you're wondering why the press are going crazy over you again. There's been a new development.'

Her mind flits to the doctor's shiny shoes walking into the police station. What does he have on her? It could easily be everything.

'What's happened?'

'When the police released a statement saying that they have no definitive leads, your fans went completely mental, crying that it's a failure of justice and yet another way that women are not protected in the UK.'

She crosses her legs in a neat little lotus position. She can't hold back her brimming smile.

'They won't stand for it, so they've taken the matter into their own hands. Pass me your MacBook, babe?' She types furiously. 'Come look here. Everyone who was in the vicinity of that Starbucks in Islington that day has been sharing their photos, check-ins and Instagrams on this site. The result is a digital map of all the people moving through the area. They're hoping that someone will have seen your attacker or, even better, that he crops up in the background of someone's selfie. It's a ground-breaking use of social media for good.'

'I'm . . . I'm speechless. It's remarkable.'

'They have received far more data than they could have dreamed of. Starbucks have also submitted their security camera footage from the evening. The police are caving in under the pressure, saying that they are almost certain that whoever did this was a professional, as he kept his face hidden from the security cameras the entire time.'

'Nice of them to let me know,' Holly says bitterly. Something, anything would be a welcome validation at this point. All she wants is for them to definitively say they believe she was not to blame, that there was nothing she could have done to prevent her attack.

Pictured next to the article is a selfie of a jubilant group of girls. They're posing in front of a messily painted banner that says, 'We love you, Holly!' Grinning for the camera, teeth glinting white. Eyes aflame. Thin arms clutching each other, bone against bone.

She doesn't voice the other thought that pounds in her mind. If people can see so much of one moment, what has been inadvertently captured of other moments? Her hands shake as she remembers the way she moved up for him to sit next to her, and then leaned into the space between them, holding his eyes, laughing at his jokes. To an outsider, they could have been a new couple meeting after work. Any picture of her that evening would reek of her interest in him. Whoever captured those hours on camera would know how much she wanted it, and how she had walked willingly into the trap he set for her.

Zanna continues, 'Yeah, and the best part is that it's growing bigger by the day. You have a whole squad of amateur detectives digging through your life, with much better tools than the cops. Someone's bound to uncover something soon, I can feel it. Oh . . . my phone's ringing.'

Zanna squeezes Holly's arm as she glides into the next room. While she should feel some sort of relief that so many people are on her side, there's something unnerving about a swarm of strangers being so invested in her case. It feels less like kindness and more like an imminent threat.

Chapter 13

Holly

Pots and cutlery clatter behind the pounding bass of this year's summer hits. Any passer-by would smile at the sight of a flash of blonde hair swinging and arms waving in time with the beat. Look how much fun that girl is having while she cooks. Look how *happy* she is.

Holly shakes her hips and gathers her ingredients for tonight's dinner. Can anyone see her? She keeps up the performance just in case. There's nobody on the street outside, but that doesn't mean he isn't watching.

She twirls and sings into her makeshift microphone – a wooden salad server with her name engraved on it. Besides, isn't it about time she lightened up? Had a little dance to take her mind off her troubles?

If he wants to watch her through her window, then he should be shocked by what he sees. He should see that she is not fazed at all. Of course, like everything in her cursed life, reality is different close-up.

The wooden spoon shakes in her hand. The sunny music fails to drown out the looming sense of despair. It cannot calm the panic that has set in. Since she woke up this morning, Holly has noticed something both sweet and acrid in the kitchen. It claws at her nostrils and makes her dry heave in the basin. The mystery makes her feel frantic. The daily deliveries must have started to smell.

This is no cloying earthy ripeness, however. It is a sharp, maddening scent she cannot place. Where the hell is it coming from? She tries holding her nose to each of the boxes. It reeks in the sodden packaging of some cashew nuts. It rises from the soil of potted herbs. Her breath grows ragged. The smell has branded the inside of her nostrils. Faster and wilder, she pulls each of the deliveries towards her, sniffs it again, and pushes it to the floor. The smell coats her tongue, constricts her throat – why can't she place where it's coming from? She tries to tell herself it's a cat that's jumped in, or maybe she knocked over her bottle of apple cider vinegar but she knows she's fooling herself. It's human urine. Pungent, invasive, unmistakable. Her worst fear made real. He's been in here again, she's sure of it, marking her house with the scent of his anger like a dog.

Every bad thing is pushing its way into her consciousness, no matter how hard she tries to press it down. She stood in front of the mirror for the first time this morning. Naturally, her eyes gravitated to the new ripples of cellulite above her knees and her jutting belly. You turn your back for one second and your body betrays you by starting filling all the spaces. Only after this cold assessment did her eyes travel up to her face. Deep, purple scars, surrounded by hot angry skin, cut across her face. She tried to smile and the left-hand side of her mouth remained slack. Broken,

broken, broken. She is dehumanised. She is a prey quivering until the predator picks up her scent. She needed to release the restlessness jumping in her legs; she needed to hold in her scream, which is why she started dancing.

Now sitting on the floor, surrounded by stinking boxes, she chokes with the unfairness of it all. She's only had four years to show the world the person she really is. There was the fame, of course, but also opportunities that she really loved, like speaking at cancer events or reading to the sick in Hospices. The charities that approached her were always so grateful for her time, but Holly knew that she was the one who benefitted the most. All her life she just wanted to make a difference, to be *good*.

Now she can feel a lack of purpose creeping back and settling into the blank greyness of her skin. She built her life on being nourished, inside and out. She created a career out of being well. Will people still be interested in her story now that she has been robbed of the parts that made her? Body, legs, face? Even curiosity has its limits, and one day soon the world will grow used to her scars and turn their eyes to something brighter. She'll have no other choice but to sink back into the despair from which she came.

Why did he hate her so much? All she ever did was strive to be better, cleaner, washed out and pristine from the inside out. That's what succeeds on the Internet these days – the good girls, the clean girls, the fit girls. This is the new holiness, this is the new way to mark yourself as chosen and stay safe. She was a shining example to them all and took her role seriously. This coveted corner had to be constantly defended. You can always be a bit more perfect. With every picture she braced herself for underhanded jeers that she wasn't being quite healthy enough.

@Trixie21
Babe, should you be eating all that fruit? You're looking a bit rounder lately.

@FitgirlsIG
What training are you doing love? Good on you for promoting a chunkier, healthier look?

@Plantbasedandproud
Is honey vegan? Not saying you're wrong or cruel to the animals for having it. Just asking out of interest, you know?

This girl-on-girl violence she was prepared for. But a gorgeous man coming at her face with a scalpel?

Holly's tried to hold tightly on to her mind, forbidding it to endlessly loop over every detail of that night. But sometimes the effort is too much and the grip loosens. The actual cutting is still unclear. Sometimes she thinks she spots the flash of a memory but is it real, or just something she spotted in the endless stream of photos from the night? Mostly her brain sticks to all the things she did wrong. Why was she so quick to talk to him? Why did she follow him out of the door and spend the whole evening with him? Why was she so damn confident that she could just close her eyes and turn to kiss a stranger in a dark street without anything going wrong? It was reckless, foolish. There were so many moments when she could have turned around and said, 'No, it's time to call this a night,' but she never did.

Worse still is the waiting. She keeps telling herself she is waiting for something definitive, something she could pin on him, then maybe she'd change her mind. But then why did she stupidly throw away those horrifying photographs? Or hysterically push all the urine-soaked boxes in the trash? The police could have got some DNA, maybe even find out whether he had done this before. His harassment of her is so brazen, so assured, as if he knows she won't have the guts to report him. This can only mean one thing: he knows that she is hiding sins of her own.

So she continues, frozen in fear, scanning her inbox every day for something new, picking through the new comments on her Instagram and Facebook to find something, anything that stinks of his spite. When she leaves the house, all footsteps behind her sound like his. In a gust of wind, she feels the warmth of his breath. But it's never him. He crouches in the shadows silently, gleefully, waiting to unfold some new horror. He is everywhere but nowhere, impossible to pin down. And she is powerless to stop him.

Chapter 14
Tyler

What was it like to love Frankie? Tyler tries to remember but it has the fuzzy texture of a dream. As much as he tries, love doesn't live in the big moments. Rather, it is a shapeless force that occupies every inane moment, just out of his field of vision.

She loved marcasite jewellery, the genuine antique kind. She collected so many pieces, some small and elegant, some loud and dramatic. Together they'd make up ridiculous stories of each piece's origin. According to their folklore, she was the keeper of treasures last seen on duchesses, fortune-tellers, performance artists and concubines. She had the charm and danger of all those women dangling against her skin, with the freedom to choose, or discard, whoever she wanted to be that day.

He could go on forever listing the things she liked and didn't like. He was the one who knew her best. He had made a study of her, down to every freckle on her soft skin. He willingly lost hours of his mornings to the intoxicating pull of her, the magic she conjured. This was no ordinary love affair, but one that rearranged the very atoms of his body into something better. Though she felt the same, Frankie was always charmingly perplexed at the level of his devotion, always coyly batting him away, always just out of his reach. This only made him love her more.

Her jewellery seemed so inconsequential at the time, mere possessions contributing to a sensual whole. Now she lives on in them, a most welcome haunting. Tyler still likes to walk through Portobello market and pick out pieces she would have loved, imagining how they would rest against her elegant collarbone. Today, the rain taps against his clean-shaven face and his fingers flex against the cold. A few traders brave the dismal weather, including his favourite, a withered man with perfectly round spectacles and the most authentic antique jewellery collection.

'Good morning, sir.' He coughs. 'Are you back for more of the marcasite?'

'You're a perceptive man.'

He reaches beneath the trestle table and pulls out a wooden box.

'I have some new stock then, not even unpacked yet. Did your fiancée love the rose you got her last time?'

Tyler grinds his teeth. Smiles. 'Oh yes, she wears it all the time.'

He holds up an intricate necklace of marcasite lilies, all bending into and away from each other in endless symmetry. He can imagine it lying against her freckled skin, leading down to her chest and her beating heart.

'It's incredible. I'll take it.'

Tyler loves this part of the ritual, where the old man creaks around and finds a soft velvet box and paper bag to wrap it in. Today he puts it all in another layer of plastic, to protect it against the rain.

'Is that all for today? What about another antique bronze spoon for your mum?'

He gestures to a row of patterned bronze teaspoons, just like the ones Tyler's mum used to hang from the wall in the magic house. He has too many already, filling up his cutlery drawer.

'Oh, go on then. Better get something for the old duck,' he laughs good-naturedly. Just an ordinary guy with too many women to please.

He paces down the street, oblivious to the people stepping out of his way. The new treasures clang in their bags as he places them on the floor of the café opposite Holly's apartment where he settles down, unfolding his copy of *The Economist*.

'Nice to see you again. Can I get you anything?' the waitress asks, smiling as she pats down her sleek, pixie-cropped hair. Her eyebrows are distractingly perfect. Tyler has her pinned as one of those try-hard women who came to London to make something better of themselves, but got sidetracked along the way. Everybody thinks that they will be the one buying the lattes, warming their hands on a takeaway cup, and not the one serving them.

'My usual please – cortado, with one of those shortbread slices. Do you have them today?' Tyler asks this casually, as if he is merely interested. The truth is he needs the sugar more and more these days. A little sweetness takes the edge right off.

'Of course! There's a fresh batch about to come out the oven in a few minutes. Anything else?'

'No, but leave the menu here. I'm going to be here a while.'

This place, with its hand-illustrated cups and perfect photogenic lighting, is a pretentious shithole. The servers have to be professional models with a bachelor's degree to even have the chance of a job. His waitress – Eyebrows – gets flirtier with every visit, as if he's coming for her, as if he is going to reach down into the pit of her mediocre life and save her. The forced genteelness makes him want to douse the place with acid, but it happens to have a perfect view of Holly's front door.

It's almost time for her to leave the house. After a few days of observation, it turns out that Holly is quite the creature of habit. He taps on Instagram to pass the time. Visits her profile first. She's not as high-pitched as usual, but she's still out there, healing herself for the whole world to see. Today she's posted a tidy little shot of a self-help book, with some healing essential oils. 'This is the only thing I trust to help me heal my scars!' Oh, baby girl, those ragged red gashes aren't going to calm down any time soon.

There she goes, walking out of her door in yoga pants and a sweatshirt. His fingers tighten around his espresso cup and he bites his lip as he spots her familiar hunched posture. She only leaves the house once a day to hurry to the Bikram yoga studio down the road. There is always a floral scarf wrapped around her face like a balaclava, complemented by oversized sunglasses. From afar, she could just be another starlet in the city, skipping to a secret location in disguise so she's not photographed before hair and make-up people smooth her over. But he knows. He knows. She paces quickly, hands in tight balls next to her body, looking hunted.

It's his fifth day here and every time he sees her, the muscles in his thighs strain to get up. His hands involuntarily clench into fists. He should follow her. But every time, he doesn't. He just lets her leave. He gets the bill, feeling a bit sheepish. What's stopping him? He can't even say, except that it doesn't feel quite right to see her face to face. Not yet. His next move should have the same poetry as his first. So he watches Holly as she disappears down the street, feeling the imaginary warmth of Frankie next to him, watching him and egging him on. *Go on, darling, show that bitch what happens when she hurts your girl.* Running her fingers through her red hair, which is long gone now. Fuck forgiveness. It's time to deliver justice.

Chapter 15

Holly then

The deepest pain is not the one you would expect. It pulses beneath the skin incessantly. It is a nail being pressed into a nerve. People have gone crazy over less.

For Holly, that pain is made of tiny beads of anticipation. Every night she goes home and scans the horizon for signs of a threat. Her dad has triggers – mess, gluttony, noise, jokes he cannot understand, sex scenes on television. If something is not godly enough for him, the devil comes out.

And how the devil is going to come out today! Holly thinks, as she walks home from school, her mid-year A-level results shaking in her hand. She did OK in English and French, better than she expected actually, but her Maths and Science marks are atrocious. She'll have to make some big changes if she wants to pass by the end of the year. He's going to zone in on that, no question. He's going to explode and she can barely breathe with the fear of it.

She pushes her bedroom door open and feels under her bed for her asthma pump. 'Spontaneous seasonal asthma,' the doctor calls it. Holly knows better. It is her throat seizing up with panic, reacting to the world closing in on her. A few puffs opens her airways, but her mind turns in circles. This day will only play out in one way. They will go to his leather-scented office and she will quiver beneath his gaze, like an employee. The envelope will crack open, and he will read its contents.

Two hours until her mum and dad get home. One unused razor in the bathroom cabinet. Holly stamps on it until the plastic edges break off and she can pull a thin silver blade out. She turns her music up, hikes up her school pinafore and takes a jagged breath. In a lightning motion, a deep red line appears on her pale thigh. Finally, the pain turns into substance, scarlet and glistening. It drips down her leg, away away. For a second there is only the bright sting of agony, nothing more. The music on the radio swells around her, she reaches for a tissue next to the bed and cleans herself.

Six o' clock but his car doesn't appear in the driveway on schedule. Holly helps her mother prepare dinner as they wait. Every minute burns like acid and makes the end of this evening disappear even further from sight.

They run out at seven o'clock to greet him. He enfolds them both in an embrace, enveloping them in the scent of beer and meat.

'You ate already?' her mother asks quietly, careful not to use a tone.

'I can always eat more!' he laughs. It's a whooping, uncontrolled laugh, like a wild animal. It's utterly disproportionate to the joke. Holly digs her fingernails into the wound on her thigh. Tonight, she is a rabbit in the den of a wolf.

Her eyes narrow on his signet ring as he slices through a piece of dried chicken schnitzel. Will it be too dry for his liking? Will he notice how Holly is pushing her food around her plate? Starvation is as much a sin as gluttony in his eyes.

He took some of the boys from work out for a drink, that's why he was late coming home. They had a cracking sales day, with everyone meeting their targets and more. 'Lucky girl.' He gestured to Holly with a giant hand. 'Looks like I'll have the money to keep you in that posh school of yours.'

She jolts in her seat at the imaginary blow. Not that he notices, his mind is manically jumping from one topic to the next.

'Speaking of which, aren't your A-level results coming out soon?'

Her mother looks panicked.

Holly freezes. Her heart can't take being ridiculed again. Her body, if shaken and pushed around, may break. She runs a finger over the scab beneath her skirt, her pain made concrete. Another path begins to take shape.

'Oh, yes! Mrs Ede spoke to each of us about them today one by one. She is so happy with my results. I'm averaging B's in everything!'

'Everything? Even Maths and Science?' Her father almost looks deflated.

'Yes!'

'Can I see?'

It felt so easy. It just rolled off her tongue, 'Oh sorry, Dad. We didn't get a printed copy. It's just mid-year results after all.'

It's just a little white lie. She'll fix it over the next few months by studying hard and going to extra lessons. He'll be none the wiser. She'll go to school and watch the girls stare at her long scar while they change for swimming, and hope they imagine the very worst. They will look at her twice in the school corridor now, and whisper tall stories. Hopefully they will be curious enough to ask, kind enough to reach out and touch her. Perhaps in the comfort of their concern, she will let herself cry. Her father nods appreciatively under the power of her lie, and her mother smiles in relief. They continue chewing in silence, while a whole new world opens up for her.

Chapter 16
Holly

Holly sits cross-legged on her bed, watching YouTube clips and picking through a kale salad. As she has mentioned many times in her recipe tutorials, the folate in kale makes it a great mood enhancer, so it is the ideal food to eat when you're depressed. Today, it only tastes bitter. Maybe there are some things that food cannot fix.

Still, this is the most normal she has felt since the attack. She doesn't have to be the sum of her injuries. She can still be an average girl, passing the time by watching video clips of other people's interesting lives. She looks up at the time on her computer screen: 7 p.m. already! Time for a shower, some television and an early night.

No matter how content she is in her own company, there is always a moment when the silence turns sinister. Every creak of her wooden floorboards turns into a footstep. The sudden flutter of a pigeon perching on her windowsill makes her jump. This is even more pronounced since the incident.

She needs the comforting sound of bathwater and the blaring of the television in the background. She changes the channel to her favourite baking reality show, runs a bath flush with pink bath salts, shuts the bathroom door and closes her eyes.

Holly must have dozed off, because when she opens her eyes the water has turned cold and the house is silent. Did the television somehow turn off on its own?

A sharp, clattering sound, like a pot falling to the ground echoes through the apartment.

'Hello? Zanna?' says Holly, immediately feeling foolish. It must have been the wind, it could only have been the wind, but tomorrow she will take better safety precautions and change the damn locks.

Although the television is off and the clattering has ceased, the apartment is not quite silent. Holly can hear the sound of running water. She steps out the bath, dries herself off and braces herself for a leaking pipe or, worse, a flooded kitchen. She hasn't been herself and keeps leaving the oven on, and taps running. As she rifles through her cupboard for a set of clean pyjamas, she notices her laptop has moved from her bed to her dressing room table. A voice inside her screams:

That's not where you left it. That is definitely not where you fucking left it.

She inches closer and unlocks the screen.

YouTube is still open, but it is playing a different video. The title of the clip is HOT GIRL DANCING IN SHOWER and has over five thousand likes. Holly clamps her hand over her mouth to stifle a scream as she watches the tanned, lean woman dance in the shower. The glass door clearly shows the lick of her blonde hair that leads to her firm buttocks . In one frame, she turns to wash her hair, revealing the curve of her breasts and a taut stomach. Holly feels sick, she knows this body. She spent hours nourishing it with healthy foods and working out at the gym after all. She knows this shower. She was the one who thought the see-through glass doors were sexy and edgy when she first moved into the apartment.

'I know you're here somewhere!' she shouts, voice shrill and out of control. Softer now, 'Don't think I don't know.'

Hands shaking, she scrolls up to see when the video was uploaded. June this year. A whole month before he attacked her.

Chapter 17
Tyler

It's going to be one of those horrific days at the hospital. Tyler can feel it in the buzzing static of the air. The panic setting in before the patients are even pushed through the door.

Everything feels a bit too raw today. The old man with dementia smoking outside, telling him that his daughter will visit today, he's sure of it. The sobbing Muslim family filing into the prayer room to surrender their mother's health to Allah. The smell of infection that his keenly trained nose picks up immediately, despite the disinfectant liberally applied to every surface of the hospital.

He tries to numb the sense of foreboding the day ahead holds with some filter coffee and a moment spent scrolling through Holly's latest posts. There are no signs of cracking, even after the stunt he pulled last night. Her captions are just the right amount of vulnerable. The style of her photographs never falters. It is like a robot has kept automatically producing content while the real Holly, the Holly he holds in his grip, begins to lose control. It's only a matter of time before she does, he just knows it, and he has all the time in the world.

His phone lights up. He is needed. As he runs to the surgical ward, he sees the patient ahead of him. The writhing body is too little. The pool of blood soaking into the sheets too great. High-pitched crying of random words, 'dog', 'mummy', 'light', 'shoe', 'bye bye'. Poor little girl, she is repeating every word in her vocabulary to impress them, to stop them from hurting her. By the time he's scrubbed up and inside the theatre, she's passed out.

She is just two years old, and still wearing the muddy red wellies she was playing in. Her dark brown pigtails are damp with drizzle. Her T-shirt has a picture of Peppa Pig. There are deep fang marks clustered around one eye, and more still over her nose. Dog bites.

His hands shake as he assesses the damage.

'What the *fuck* happened to this kid?'

One of the nurses says softly, 'She was playing in the park with her mum and this Rottweiler ran towards them out of the blue and attacked. The mum tried to fight it off – she's downstairs in the ER getting her hand stitched up. The mum said it looked possessed, on a mission.'

The blood on the sheet continues to pool around her neck. He knows what he's about to discover before his hand even touches it. Two deep bites, one on her back and the other on her neck. He swallows the panic in his throat. He doesn't have much time. Stop the bleeding. Close the wounds. Perfect the stitching. Disinfect, disinfect, disinfect. The world around him is a blur. His only focus is to get through each step, to make her well.

It's happened before, often even. He's performed a miracle at the last possible second and left everyone high-fiving bloodied gloves across the table. He's run down the stairs and into the waiting area, found the waiting family and said, 'I have good news.' But not today.

The little girl, with all her grown-up words and favourite things, remains limp in his hands. Her heartbeat, that must have flashed so brightly in her mother's pregnancy scan, is now a flat line on a screen. All because some dog got loose and mistook her for prey. All because her mum thought it would be lovely to take her to the park to feed the ducks. He kicks a table behind him. Steel instruments clatter to the ground. The nurses stay out of his way. There is no discussion. The assistant surgeon makes the dejected trip downstairs to her mother.

Tyler finds a dark storeroom and slams himself inside. The tears, hot and angry, are a surprise to him. He wipes them away with clenched fists. A sob sticks in his throat. He screams it away into his sleeve. Saliva bubbles down his chin. They used to be just patients. But he can't take the injustice anymore. It's just not fair. The best people, the innocent ones, are always the first to go.

It hurts to breathe, to think. The buzz is back, shriek-ing in his ears. He pulls out his phone. His typing sounds like a swarm of flies slamming against a closed window. Words and images come out that he has never used before. Disgusting words. Appalling images. But with every letter the pain constricting his heart releases until he can dry his eyes, slide his phone in his pocket and walk out the door.

Chapter 18

Holly

There's got to be something Holly can feel other than this. Her eyes water and the edges of her mind feel blurry. Memories, dreams and fearful fantasies become one. It's hard to keep a solid grip on anything when he could always be just around the corner.

She tries to focus on her blessings until she can no longer feel his eyes on her. She attempts to manage the gaping expanse of her day through the timing of her various medications, meals and tasks. She tries to not be so self-centred, and do something nice for Zanna. After spending hours agonising over the perfect thank-you gift, she has a Jo Malone candle and a bunch of exquisite black roses delivered to her studio apartment across town. For a second, that felt good, although nothing could really show just how grateful she felt for her loyalty. These days, just the sight of her fast, determined walk through the door is enough to bring her to tears.

She sits in front of her mirror and recites her daily affirmations through hot tears:

I am worthy.
I am beautiful.
I am strong.

She doesn't feel any of this, but she's read enough spiritual literature to know that positivity attracts positivity. What you put out into the world comes back to you. She recites the words again, voice shaking, battling to feel anything other than revulsion at the scars on her face and the situation she is in. If only there were words that could act as a salve for the guilty, for those who feel they deserved everything they got.

She's put herself on her signature detox system to cleanse her body of negative energy. This involves a ruthless regime of lemon water, regular vegetable juices and a colourful handful of sulphuric supplements. Her hours are spent in nun-like dedication to making sure that every minute is a sacred act of devotion to herself. She should use her experience to help and heal others. This is supposed to be her greatest revenge.

If only Holly could stop screaming. She does it without warning, unprovoked. Her violent, strangled cries turn everyone's eyes on her. It happened in Sainsbury's the first time. As she was reaching for a packet of spinach on the top shelf, a teenage boy appeared out of nowhere, leaning forward for some apples. Next thing, she had dropped her groceries and was screaming in his face. Everyone was shocked, but understanding in that tight-lipped, awkward British way. Every time, it leaves Holly breathless and with her heart pounding for hours afterwards. What is this unpredictable beast that coils within her throat?

She can't help but feel him edging closer. Nowhere is safe. There are little signs wherever she turns. The rubbish bin outside her door appears to have been rifled through. She sees the footprints of a man's shoe in the dust on the stairs. Sometimes she thinks she sees him, walking across the street in that cursed Burberry coat, but the second she looks closer he is gone. He lives in the silence, and in the space that swells around her as she falls asleep.

She received a message from an unknown number late last night. The words blurred into one another and she threw down her phone. Sick, sick, sick is the only way to describe it. Long and rambling, the message described exactly how he wanted to torture her and make her plead for mercy. She ran to the bathroom to retch. It was him, because only he would think of doing that. And every time he taunts her, she is even more certain that he knows the one thing she has tried so hard to keep hidden. If she were to go to the police now, if they were to trace his number and bring him in for questioning, her secret would be the first thing he would mention. She deleted the message, took a deep breath and tried to remain calm.

The signs point to an impending danger that has begun to keep her awake at night. He has access to her apartment. He knows her habits. Or is her mind playing tricks on her? Did she really see those pictures and smell urine in her home? Did she really see that YouTube clip playing last night? Or is she becoming unhinged? She's started to fear for Tofu, who has finally found a sanctuary in Holly's quiet home. Would he hurt the thing she loves the most just to get to her?

Still, how could she admit to anyone what she truly fears? It seems hysterical to say it out loud, the self-centred ranting of a social media celebrity used to the world revolving around her. She saw how the police looked at her, smirking at her tight, provocative yoga leggings – if she voiced the depth of his hatred, they would wonder what else she has done to ask for it.

Until he emerges out of the shadows, she performs for him. She tries to invoke him, like an evil spirit too absent to be fought, but present enough to make her sick. The brazenness of her plan makes her feel out of control and dangerous. She pictures his pretty face reddening as she posts another picture of some artfully arranged fruit. She records long YouTube videos about how she is dealing with her scarring, hoping that one of the four hundred and seventy thousand views is his.

Look at my personal, untouchable army. Look how much I am loved.

This popularity was hard won. Before she was famous, something about Holly set her apart – it was like the other kids could smell it, as if it was a contagious disease. At school, she was the girl who walked home alone, a few steps behind the other girls, the better girls. They were on their way to another boring, candy-scented afternoon of trading secrets and fears over frappés. All she had waiting for her back home was a reality TV marathon, a fridge full of snacks and the constant sense of foreboding. That kind of loneliness has its own substance; it builds up into something.

She made a friend eventually at work, Andrea. While prickly at first, Andrea came into her own when Holly was sick, and became somebody she could call and cry to when the hopelessness of her situation overwhelmed her. However, her compassion only lasted a second. She remembers Andrea's sneers clearly, the disgust that clouded her face when she found out the truth.

I heard what you did.

How could you?

Her scorn left a mark she couldn't erase. What she had done felt essential at the time, but it warped into something shameful through her friend's eyes. The guilt followed her to London, where she couldn't quite settle into herself and find the new friends she had dreamed of. There was no tight-knit, smug circle of healthy women who all stretched each other after Pilates and giggled over their Bumble prospects while drinking non-dairy chai lattes. As much as she didn't feel she deserved friendship, she wanted it, so deeply and urgently. The love she received online made her think that maybe, just maybe, real friendship was around the corner. But the health bloggers saw her as a threat, and their interactions never moved beyond a few empty greetings at a launch or a posed lunch for a brand they were promoting. How surprised her adoring community of thousands would be to learn that she always ate alone.

Her closest friend came in the form of Zanna, who, at their first ever meeting, poured sugar into her oversized hot chocolate until it was difficult to stir. 'I don't know what your whole lifestyle is about, but I know it's fickle as fuck and you need me,' she said.

She'd captured Zanna's attention at a star-studded cancer charity event, when Holly was struggling to string a sentence together about her dress that night to a TV interviewer. It was cruelty-free Stella McCartney, obviously. Zanna made it all feel real – the followers, the fame. This hobby of hers became something that could sustain her and make her money. The road to success wasn't as smooth as she would have liked, but this was someone else's responsibility now, someone who understood the game. Over meetings and exercise dates and eventually long nights watching TV box sets together, Zanna became her truest friend.

Zanna always challenged her to sell what made her different, to stand out from the ever-growing pack of beautiful, healthy girls. Zanna always surprised her with unlikely interests and clubs. Who knew she collected first edition comic books and autographed fantasy novels? That she had a tattoo of Tank Girl sneering on her shoulder?

Zanna is fascinating, really fascinating. She carries a whole world inside her, marked with unlikely landscapes and turbulent weather. Holly knows only how to occupy extremes: sick or healthy, bad or good. She doesn't know how to fill the space in between. Her soul is a shapeless thing, assuming the form of whatever will make people like her the most. Only Zanna with her boundless faith in herself has enough faith left over to believe that Holly's soul is made of something more. How could she tell Zanna everything and disappoint her? How could she possibly reveal that her pictures are all she ever was, that there is nothing real behind them?

Chapter 19

Tyler

Here lies the root of the problem. Today's world is characterised by pervasive access to anything and everything. Luxury, fame, beauty – all these rich pleasures that used to be only accessed by the worthy – are now free for anyone with a credit card and an Internet connection. Anybody can walk into a Louis Vuitton store and purchase a handbag. Anyone can apply a filter to their face and erase decades of poor diet and grooming. We choose our avatars and wear them like masks. They allow us to be whoever we want to be. Yet too often we fool ourselves into thinking that our mask is who we really are.

When he sees Holly again, this is exactly what he will say. He fell short on this last time – savagely cutting her face as if he could reach behind the skin and muscle, and tear off her mask for good. He should have pinned her down for longer and explained exactly what she did wrong. That would have calmed the hurting; that would have released the hating. Yes, he will hold her firmly next time and tell her everything. Who knows how a fake, wax excuse for a person will react to the fire of the truth. She will melt to nothingness in his hands.

He never understood Frankie's attraction to Holly, why she of all people would want to be like this bland carica-ture of health. Frankie was real, in a way you could sink your fingers into and caress with all your senses. She was down to earth, her casual demeanour undercutting her top-drawer education and healthy trust fund. She lived life *in* the moment, not for the capturing of it.

The two of them were equally matched in their pedigree. He had never felt so comfortable, so calm with another person. From their very first date, everything fell into place as if the very universe had intended it. They shifted from wild, smoky dates in bars, to cosy nights eating pizza around the corner from her flat in a matter of weeks.

He knew she was the one from the start. This sense of purpose crystallised into a path that nothing could set off course. Although it was still early days, every date, every night spent together held this electric potential. When the time was right, he would commission a reworked mar-casite ring with a giant ruby stone in its centre (she had an ethical thing against diamonds). He would blindfold her and lead her through the city until they reached the bench on Warwick Avenue where they first met. There, under the gaze of amused bus commuters and a rocking meth addict, he would ask her to marry him. Together, they would build his new family: husband, wife and, one day, a child, maybe a little boy with Frankie's auburn hair, pulling a wooden toy behind him through the park. A magic house in Brox-bourne with a big tree at the bottom of the garden. It was meant to end to the brokenness; it was meant to make everything whole. He could have never predicted that Holly would bludgeon through his life and destroy it all.

It was that power that got to him the most. It was the thing that kept his mind hooked on to Holly. How could one person, *a stranger*, have the power to randomly destroy another person's life? He thinks of the freshly printed documents he slipped into a folder on his desk this morning. At any moment, he can reveal their contents, and truly end this thing. Now *that* is true power.

Chapter 20
Holly

She follows the same path every day. It unfolds unremarkably, despite her imaginings of a hand around her throat, an elbow in her ribs, a punch to her stomach. Holly jumps at the sound of every footstep. He has plans for her. She can feel them thickening like glue in the street outside.

When she first arrived in London with a bank account full of money from a protein shake sponsorship and a flat sponsored by a convenience store, the city seemed endless. There was no street, no person, she had seen before. She would ride the tube, blissfully anonymous, and smile conspiratorially at the young, thin girls who looked at her twice, the growing army of women beginning to recognise her from her blog. It was so comfortable then, so innocent. Even if she didn't know who she was yet, she knew who she wanted to be.

Now, London had been reduced to 100 steps from her stale-sweat apartment to the Bikram Yoga Studio and back. It was Zanna's idea of course. She thought yoga might soothe her nerves. Then there are the unmentioned benefits – the tightening of her thighs, the flattening of her stomach. Without her face, she needs to rely on other muscles to earn her living.

If he had cut any other part of her body, she could have pushed the pain away and tried to forget, but he took her face, her fucking face. It confronts her in the mirror, a clown-like mockery of her original features. It draws the attention of passers-by, who want to both stare at her and pretend she doesn't exist. It aches in her smile, the pain jolting her out of any tentative happiness. Her beautiful face drew people into her beautiful soul. It allowed them to see the gentle, giving heart that swelled beneath her awkwardness. Now she feels hideous, a monster – what do people think lies within? God, she would love to do what Zanna suggests and believe all the positive 'can do' quotes she keeps sending her, but the truth is that she's angry. She hates her attacker and she hates her fans. Most of all, though, she hates herself.

Instead of turning left towards the front of the Bikram Yoga Studio, she carries on straight to a smaller room at the back. This black, padded studio stinks of bitter sweat and wound-up men. Something wild clenched inside her feels at home here. She can feel it pressing beneath her skin, changing her into someone stronger, someone different.

'Hiya, Holly, right on time!' Jono, the bald, diminutive instructor stands before her, looking more like a monk than the cage fighter his flyers outside promise. Esoteric symbols and Latin phrases compete for space on his tanned, shaven limbs.

He starts her off with a warm-up run. Her shaky legs pound the treadmill and her heart threatens to give up. She can feel the extra weight from the past few weeks pulling her down. A little voice in her head whispers *fat, fat, fat,* before she can stop it.

'Great, very good, you're a natural! Now let's get onto the mat to have a quick chat.' He sits serenely, cross-legged and stares earnestly into her face. 'Let me start by sharing a bit about me.' He flicks through a few pictures on his phone. An even smaller version of him snarls through a blue gum-guard.

'I used to be a mixed martial arts cage fighter. I did well, got my trophies and got into my fair share of brawls outside of the ring too. One night, well, some shit went down.' The way he says it so casually hints that whatever went down was darker than anything Holly could ever imagine.

He continues, 'I saw God, in one of her many incarnations. In that moment, I chose to leave cage-fighting and use my skills for good.'

Jono regards her smiling, unflinching. 'What about you, Holly? What brings you here? Nobody comes through this door without having faced some darkness first.' As if he hadn't seen it on the news, as if it's not literally staring him in the face.

She includes no detail, only the things she feels. Despair. Rage. Hatred. Fear. Mostly the acrid, pervasive fear. Holly assures him she doesn't want to box to lose weight or tone or any of the things women come to him for. Like some of them, she may be doing this for a man, but she hopes the outcome will be different.

He winds black straps around her palms, pulls chunky red gloves over her hands. Turns up some pumping house music. Bounces across the room towards her, ready to spar. With every movement, she feels herself shedding the old, afraid Holly and moving into her own power. She is tougher than her past, and she is stronger than him.

'Don't hold back,' she shouts, spurred on by the beat. 'Teach me how to fight.'

Chapter 21

Tyler then

After he shared the news of Frankie's death, the hospital gives Tyler some time off work. There were whispers among the nurses about how frayed he had become. He was losing his grip, they said, and the Chief of Surgery was afraid it would begin to impact his delicate work. It all came from a place of care, but that didn't stop him from feeling like a fool. Tyler had been on the other side of this conversation when an operation had taken an unexpected turn for the worse, gently coaching a grieving family through the screamingly banal logistics of death. He'd awkwardly ended his speech with the saccharine line, 'Now remember to take some time to look after yourself.'

He of all people should understand the exhaustion and relief that come after months of watching your loved one succumb slowly to a long-term illness. His colleagues force him out of the hospital, even when he begs them to let him work just a few more weeks. His patients need him. He needs the work to feel whole.

No such luck. They stand firm and soon he finds himself pacing his family's unused apartment in Monaco, scowling at the yachts going by. He walks the Cercle d'Or and buys a three-piece suit on a whim, but the perfection of the fabric sickens him so much he can't even take it out the bag. Such beauty exists, but Frankie does not. Relax? Who are these people kidding? Under the acute throbbing ache of guilt, it is impossible to sit still.

A holiday was an absurd idea, repulsive even. He leaves so early the sheets barely have a chance to hold the scent of his cologne-soaked sweat. Only one rinsed espresso cup in the sink hints at his fleeting presence.

Home is no better. Before the rot of cancer took hold, their lives had begun to blissfully intertwine. He had left a change of clothes and a toothbrush at her place, and she'd begun to leave her distinct mark on his apartment. It used to give him such a thrill, knowing that she was folding into his space so effortlessly. It was a dress rehearsal for their inevitable shared future. But now the signs of her presence taunt him. Tyler sees her everywhere – in the unwashed throw pillow that smells of her perfume, taken on a whim from her apartment; in the scrunched tube of Aesop orange-rind body balm she favoured; in the smug picture of Holly she had placed on the fridge. Holly, chosen goddess blessed with all the luck. How did she manage to heal her cancer and Frankie did not?

He goes through every picture on her page, from her first dismal-looking smoothie to her smug sermons on monthly cleansing colonic irrigations and alkaline nutrition plans. She's beautiful, he can see that, but not as beautiful as his Frankie. She is open and authentic and all those other things that get celebrated on social media, but something about her gets under his skin. Holly is unnervingly poised. Even in the posts from during her chemotherapy, she seemed strangely engaged and open to chatting with hundreds of readers. When Frankie first received her diagnosis, she found the sudden influx of interest into her health stressful and upsetting. She wouldn't even speak to him about it. From what he has witnessed in cancer patients at the hospital, this reaction is commonplace – in the moment you receive the most attention, you don't want it.

But Holly certainly did. Not only did she want it, she actively encouraged it, posting pictures of the most intimate treatments. As he reads through every emotive caption, he understands what is unsettling him: she is manipulative.

The realisation comes like a deluge, as he looks at the photographs over and over again. Not one photograph during her 'unsuccessful chemotherapy' contains a nurse, or her family for that matter. She is always alone, the picture closely cropped to only contain a glimpse of the equipment. Her hair is too clean-shaven – cancer patients have their hair fall out unevenly, in clumps. Also, the 'cut' from inserting the drip is too jagged. No self-respecting nurse would bludgeon a patient like that.

He runs to the bathroom and vomits, his body registering the truth before his mind can even process it. There is no proof yet, but he doesn't need it. Every cell in his body rages: the bitch was faking it all along.

Chapter 22
Holly

'The thing you have to know about Holly is that she has one of those powerful minds, you see. She will do *anything* she sets her mind to.' Holly's mother twitches earnestly in front of the camera and utters every word like a threat. Heaven knows why they approached her for an interview. Heaven knows why Holly's mum chose not to reveal this information during their phone conversation last night, but the resulting, never-ending interview makes her panic. The right question is all it will take. A lowering of spectacles. An expression of interest. Her mum will lap it up and say something she shouldn't. For once, Holly wishes for the looming presence of her father in the background to cut the whole thing short.

Her mum adjusts her hair and turns to face the camera. The skin on her cheeks crinkles as she twists her mouth bitterly. It's the same expression she had years before in Exeter, when she stormed into Holly's childhood bedroom uninvited, eyes widening as she saw everything laid out on the floor. Her mouth curled in disgust as she told her that the hospital had called to discuss a 'sensitive issue'. There had been some complaints. They were worried, apparently. That sickening moment of realising how everyone was talking about her was the worst she had ever felt. The facts spoke for themselves. There was no room for her mother to comfort her and no doubt her father would crucify her. A pile of clean laundry was dumped on the floor. Next to it, an old suitcase. A sum of money appeared in her account. While the Holly on Instagram continued to be celebrated by her doting fans, her own family had made it clear that she was no longer welcome. It was time to move on.

Now her mum carries on and on, incorrigible. 'I'll give you an example. When Holly was a little baby, I knew that when she made up her mind about something, that was it. Hah! You should have seen when I gave her soya milk for the first time – she gagged and threw her bottle across the room! And let me tell you something – she didn't toilet train. No. One day she just walked up to me, held up her filthy nappy and said "no more nappies"! That was the end of it. After that, she used a proper toilet and didn't even wet her bed during the night.'

'Perfect,' Holly groans. 'Now everybody knows about my childhood toilet habits!'

Why are they giving her so much airtime? Surely there is another disaster to cut to? Holly bites down on her lip, hard.

'Well, I'm just thinking about how your soya milk sponsors are going to feel about your childhood aversion to their product.' Zanna laughs next to her. 'Seriously, though, it's about time you told your story in your own words. I know it's petrifying getting back in the game and you definitely needed some space, but people are going to impose their own angles and theories on your ordeal if you don't speak up.'

What kind of angles? What kind of theories?

'But what do I say?'

'Just tell them the truth about what happened, and how you're moving on. You're the victim here, babe. All you have to do is show them how tough you are and that you're going to keep fighting.'

There is the truth, and then *her* truth, swimming with shadows. Nobody would understand if she laid it bare, not even Zanna. She'd look like a monster. She'd never be forgiven. The richness of her life would be drained of all colour and she'd be left to rot. She would have to go home, palms open, begging for money. The world would forget. Maybe this is what she deserves, a fair punishment for what she has done. Somebody braver may free themselves of the truth, no matter how daunting the consequences may be. Somebody else may feel less attached to the perfect girl she has created on screen, and sacrifice her for her own safety and for the greater good. But not her, not yet.

Three days later, they are huddled together in the back of a black taxi on the way to the BBC studios. Holly's heart is pounding – she's not sure if it's from excitement, fear or a mixture of both.

Zanna babbles on. 'You know what really surprised me about this particular interview is that a hard news channel is interested in hosting an in-depth interview with you. Olivia Williams usually interviews politicians and activists, not bloggers. It shows that what you're doing is really important, Holly.'

Or does it hint at something more sinister? Any good journalist could look deeper into her story and follow a few unlikely trails. God, she felt so untouchable back then! Yet the foundation of her life is as flimsy as paper. Holly's dry lips change shape as she practises her defence.

The car slides to a standstill and they are hustled through the back entrance of the building. The bright lights make her feel like she is entering the afterlife. A team of angels descends to take care of her, preening over her hair and face until she is transformed into someone once again palatable to the public eye. She used to wish the hours of hair and make-up away, eager to get on screen and charm her fans. Now she wishes she could be suspended in this time forever, like a butterfly preserved in amber. It's over all too soon, and suddenly she has been propped in a seat like a horrific doll. The lights descend. They are live.

'This is World News Today with me, Olivia Williams. The practice of online trolling has been a problem for Internet users for some time. Women in particular have been subjected to ongoing insults and abuse with little to no support from the platforms on which this trolling occurs. Just a few weeks ago, we witnessed a worrying shift as globally renowned health writer Holly Evans was physically maimed by someone who appears to have discovered her through her online brand. Although she is still recovering, Holly is giving us an exclusive interview, for which we are incredibly grateful. Holly, can you give us a bit of background about you?'

'Hi, Olivia, thank you for taking the time to report on this serious issue. I'm a full-time health blogger, and I am about to release my second cookbook. My recipes all focus on addressing physical problems in a holistic way. I believe the body is meant to be in balance and eating the right foods helps us achieve this and ward off chronic and degenerative illnesses, including cancer.'

She smiles encouragingly. 'What were you doing before you went full-time?'

'I was a store manager for Topshop in Exeter. After about six months of running my Instagram account and blog, I had enough advertisers and sponsorships to quit my job and move to London.'

'So you had no prior experience or training in the health industry?' Trouble. Sweat gathers at her forehead. Heart racing.

'No, but my recipes and Instagram posts are all based on extensive research. I never post anything that I have not tried myself or wasn't part of my own healing journey. In fact, I plan on studying nutrition now my second book has been published.'

A gloomy slideshow of Holly's cancer journey flicks on the screen behind her. There are more selfies than she remembers taking, some sickly, some hairless, all with her trademark stoic smile. According to her website, she only went through one round of chemotherapy before turning to natural remedies. Nobody ever questions why that brief period was so obsessively recorded. Seeing her past packaged and polished for the world to see sends a jolt of sadness through her. The woman in those pictures looks so desperate she hardly recognises her.

'Ah, how do you feel about releasing your second book in light of what has happened?'

Her second book, that promising follow-up. Her first compendium of her wisdom had been such a success after all. Her old face, beaming on the cover over a basket of fresh kale. It seems like a lifetime ago that she approved the final proofs and held her breath when she heard they had gone to print. Her advance is long gone, spent on trainers and spa days and heaven knows what else. Holly's royalties are her only shot at a future income. She swallows hard, and says, 'I'm more motivated than ever about educating others about the benefits of a raw, vegan, lifestyle.' She turns to face the camera directly, wondering with a sick twist in her stomach whether he is watching, 'I will not be beaten by the unfounded rage of another person.'

'It's been widely reported among informal sources that the attacker targeted you because of your online empire, is this correct?'

If only they knew.

'Yes, I believe it is.'

'What makes you believe this was his motive?'

'He whispered something in my ear just before he . . . uh sorry . . . you know just before he . . .' Holly coughs and covers her face. Something feels wrong, like she's sliding down a steep slope and can't find a grip to pull herself back up. Her scars ache, as if they are about to crack open and burst. How many people are watching her, judging her, right now? All over the world, people are seeing her for the ugly, maimed creature she has become. Maybe, this is who she was all along, skin raw and breaking. Maybe her father was right.

'It's fine, Holly. Take your time. Now, your attacker . . .'

'Jack.'

'Were there any signs of someone trolling you before this happened? Did you suffer any other form of online harassment?'

She probably doesn't mean it, but there is an intimation there similar to that of the police. Had Holly noticed anything before her attack? Could she have prevented it? Would anyone observing the facts conclude that Holly was ignorant or reckless and that this was somehow her fault? Still, it is a question that demands a response. She takes a deep breath.

'I didn't receive any online harassment that I could identify as coming from him. Obviously, as a woman publishing content online, you receive the usual comments. You know, people calling me fat or telling me that they wanted to . . . well, they expressed themselves using some disgusting sexual innuendo that I'd rather not repeat. But not him.

The moment I met him in Starbucks was the first time I had ever seen him in my life. I have no idea why he would want to hurt me. I think that's what troubles me the most – why me? Why did he choose to hurt me?'

'And the police have uncovered nothing so far?'

'No, none of their suspects remotely matched him.'

The police officers jeering faces burn in her memory, their eyes darting across her medical file. The shame feels like a physical pain in her side. Did they see something? Are they preparing a case against her? Is everyone faking a smile while they prepare to entrap her?

'What do you think this says about the challenges of being a woman online?'

'Any woman who shares an idea, image or video online is automatically one of the hunted. You are walking into a field of wolves, foxes, and snakes in the grass. There are men, but also women who turn on you. The worst thing about it is that as soon as you post, you are seen as voluntarily entering the hunting ground. People question why you walk into the field of wolves, but they never question why there are wolves in the first place.'

'Well put, Holly. Luckily, it's not all bad news. I think the thing that unsettles most of us is the fact that your attacker is still out there. Do you ever worry that he will hurt you again?'

The sound of him grunting as he pushed her to the ground. His eyes, laughingly holding hers as he cut her face. The video clip, slicing her photograph. The pictures of the broken women. The stench. The text message that made her retch.

The footsteps, the sense that he is there, that he has always been there, and one day he will snuff her out for good. If she listed his actions one by one, they'd see his determination, they'd know that the first attack was no mistake. Every act of violence was meant for her. They'd call her paranoid, mad, but she can't shake the feeling that every act of violence is a token that she somehow earned. It won't stop. Maybe it never will. It's the anticipation that drives you crazy, the hand held in the air preparing to strike.

Her hands feel detached from her body. They crawl like serpents up her face and tug at the microphone and the earpiece.

'Um . . . sorry, Olivia . . . I'm feeling a bit sick . . .'

(*Broadcast ends*)

'GET THIS OFF ME!'

Holly's screaming and screaming, and she can't stop. She can feel the silence all around her, hands touching her. A faceless crowd is trying to contain her agony. In the heart of it, she hears a steady familiar voice.

'Sweetheart, what's going on? Let me help you.'

Holly holds her hands up to her face. It feels like it's swollen to twice its size and it's being sliced all over again.

Having all these devices, all these hands near her face is too much to bear.

'All right. So, is it the make-up? Sit here, angel, just breathe with me, in and out, slower, there, there, you don't need to move a muscle. Someone will come here right now and sort this out for you.'

Zanna's soft hands feel cool against her burning skin. She doesn't want this face. What did she do to deserve this face? It's turning on her and tearing her apart. She worked so hard for the old one and wants it back! Hands begin to flutter around her, wiping and clearing. A bottle of sugar water gets shoved to her lips. She's not meant to eat sugar, it only aggravates inflammation in the body. Don't they know that? She spits it out. Water takes its place. Holly surrenders to being cleaned and the panic begins to subside. By the time she's opened her eyes a change has taken place. Nobody says it, but she can tell by the way the crew awkwardly makes way for her and Zanna to walk out the door to the taxi idling outside. She has gone from being a person worth hearing to being a crazed victim. Her panic is contagious, and nobody wants to touch it.

'Oh God, Holly. I'm so sorry. I pushed you into something you weren't ready for yet. You were doing so well, I honestly thought you were ready,' Zanna whispers.

'No, no, it's fine, Zan, really. I don't know what got into me just then. My face just got so painful, and with all those wires and bright lights, I felt claustrophobic and freaked out.'

'Was it something that Olivia said? I'd briefed her in detail before the interview and told her that some questions might be triggering.'

What questions?

'No . . .'

'Let me put it another way. When she tried to ask you whether the attacker would strike again, you darted off the set. Is there something you're not telling me? Do you have reason to believe he will be back?'

That scalpel, still scabbed with her blood, slicing through her picture.

'No, I've told you everything. You don't know what it's like to have another human being look at you with such hatred. He meant to kill me that day. I'm sure of it.'

Burnt, broken faces, crackling and creasing beneath her spine.

'OK, well you can trust me with anything. Remember, I've kept quiet on more celebrity divorce announcements and drug busts than I have shoes in my cupboard.'

Zanna's phone starts buzzing. She answers, listens for a moment, narrows her eyes, 'Yes, yes. Wow, OK are you sure? Yes, I'll ask her right now, I'll get back to you later.'

'Who was that?'

'The producers of the show. Turns out a surgeon from St Mary's Hospital called in just after your live interview. He's pretty certain that the guys who fixed your face botched it up.'

'*What?!*'

'Yes, he says that he could see redness, inflammation and unnatural scarring.'

'But I was caked in make-up!'

'Well, he's an expert apparently. He wants to help fix it ASAP. He even has a gap this Friday afternoon.' A gap, like he's quickly going to bandage Holly's wrist. Could it be Jack? It must be. It's all too easy to trust.

'What's his name?'

'Dr Eugene Warner. I've heard of him before. An old stalwart in the industry, and renowned plastic surgeon. I've arranged for a good handful of my clients to put their faces in his hands. He's very skilful and, most importantly, very discreet.'

Zanna's network of privilege never fails to surprise her. There is an intricate market out there where anything can be bought or sold, but only among the already-blessed. She pulls up a picture of him on her phone. An old, studious-looking man frowns back at her. Not young. Not him. It doesn't stop her from wanting to shout at the taxi driver to stop the car so she can run.

'I'll think about it, OK? It's all been a bit much to take in today.'

'Yes, yes, of course. Still, I would give it serious thought, Holly. I'm worried about you. You haven't posted as much as you usually do over the last few days, and today is the first time you left the house wearing something other than yoga clothes.'

'I'm always only wearing yoga clothes.'

'Yeah, but you wear your nice ones. Not your ragged around-the-house yoga clothes. If you need a break to get over this, it's fine. I don't know, it's just a feeling. If you need to talk . . .'

She stops her there. 'Thanks, Zanna.' Thankfully, the taxi is pulling up outside her apartment. 'I think I just need some rest. It's been a big day.'

'Hey, Holly?'

'Yes?'

'None of this is your fault, you hear me? I know it's obvious but I feel that whenever a woman goes through some sort of trauma she needs to hear it over and over again. It's not your fault. No matter what you have done or think you have done. Not on that night, not ever.'

No matter what you have done . . .

The shaking consumes her so violently her legs threaten to give in. She knows. She must have known all along. Holly smiles back as best as she can, before turning around and running inside before Zanna can spot the heavy, messy flow of tears stinging her face and crawling into her scars.

Safely ensconced in blankets, she balances her MacBook on her knees and googles her symptoms: warm, swollen skin, slight yellow pus seeping out of the wound. The chills and sweats that plague her late at night. Searching her random symptoms online has always been a soothing habit that she likes to entertain. Usually she just stops at a basic diagnosis but sometimes she goes deeper into one of the hundreds of forums where people discuss and compare their symptoms. To her, these places are some of the lone-liest on earth. And if they are indeed home to the loneliest on earth, then it's good to be in the company of kindred spirits.

According to a quick search, she definitely has an infection and should see a doctor immediately. Dr Eugene Warner is not hard to find on the Internet either. She likes his warm, lined face with its big ruddy nose. He would look more at home on a farm than in an operating theatre. He seems like something firm she can hold on to. Maybe he's even some-one who can take control and stop the fever that threatens to consume her life.

If he really can fix her face, she might not have to be ugly again. She knows what that's like, and she remembers wear-ing it as a second skin. Ugliness doesn't always lie in how you look, but it also thrives in the negative spaces of all that is missing. It is the lack of a smile from a stranger, the absence of a look from a man passing by, the way the barista at the coffee shop doesn't feel a need to impress you. Obscurity is pervasive and persistent. She escaped it once, but if she's not careful, it may not let her go this time. For now, she will cling on to the small hope that Friday holds a turning point in her story, and that Dr Warner will perform a miracle and pull her back to the person she was before.

Chapter 23
Tyler then

Now that he knows, he sees signs everywhere. Holly's every post is drenched in newfound clarity. She is blatantly, profitably, maintaining a lie.

It takes everything in him not to throw himself off a bridge, swallow some pills, end the noise in his head for good. Because he could have stopped this much earlier. If only he had been the doting boyfriend he made himself out to be, he would have actually given a shit and examined Holly's profile to begin with. Instead, he wrote Holly off as another frothy wannabe supermodel using Instagram for exposure. He dismissed Frankie's interest in her as an annoying extension of her fascination with reality TV and fashion magazines. He'd got so used to editing that aspect of her out. If he'd seen the signs from the start, he could have done something before it was too late. Frankie wouldn't have died.

The black cab drops him outside Paddington station an hour early. This is deliberate on Tyler's part – it gives him more time to watch the trains and the people go by. It is a silent, ever-moving painting that is soundtracked by the science podcast he has blaring on double speed through his headphones. The board of destinations always excites him. Each city flickers with the potential of pure anonymity, with the chance of having everyone leaving him the hell alone. Today, however, he is en route to one specific destination: Exeter, Holly's hometown.

Holly's younger years are strangely undocumented. While she had apparently lived in Exeter her whole life, there was no online history of her time there. If Tyler hadn't seen her on TV interviews, he would doubt she existed at all. It was as if her life only truly began when she started making smoothies.

Four hours later, he steps off the train and paces down the high street. This isn't the perennial greyness of London city, swarming with suits. Here, he stands out. The feeling of youth is everywhere, in the throngs of students running for the train, in the unlikely piercings and full sleeve tattoos. Tyler's mind goes where it always does, down a lonely path of imagining how Frankie would like it here, what shops she would go into and what they would have talked about. He makes his way to Topshop, where the bio on Holly's website says she used to work.

It is not difficult to break the disconnected circle of sales assistants. Tyler has a smile that could charm anyone.

'Anything I can help you with?' asks an attractive girl with skin like brown velvet.

The lie slides off his tongue, smooth as butter, 'You can, actually! It's my little sister's birthday and I want to surprise her with some summer dresses.'

'Oooh, lucky girl!'

The girls flutter around him, holding up various floral and striped options.

'What do you think? Is this her taste?'

He makes a show of examining the print and cut of the dress. The cheap high-street fabric gives him an unwelcome rush of gooseflesh. Thank goodness he left his Tom Ford at home and opted for a simple band T-shirt and jeans instead. The scent of his money would have been stronger than the combination of these girls' stale perfume.

'Absolutely!'

He splurges a hundred pounds on a few identical dresses. The girls chatter excitedly as they ring it all up, the perfect time to mine for information.

'So, ladies, how long have you been working here?'

One girl with a bitter black-lipped mouth and greasy hair, who is clearly the manager, speaks for them all, 'I'm embarrassed to say I've been here for over five years, while these two started, like, a year or two back.'

'Ah – so you would definitely know the famous Holly Evans then?' An uncomfortable look passes over the manager's face, so brief he almost misses it. Her sidekicks stare at him blankly.

She edges towards him, friendliness disappearing fast, 'Who are you exactly?' The others, sensing the shift in mood, scuttle into the bright depths of the store. The sudden rise in defensiveness surprises Tyler. Surely anyone exposed to Holly's lies would feel as outraged as he does? What exactly is she defending?

'Relax, I'm not a journalist or anything, but I have been directly affected by Holly's story,' he says quietly. As customers float in and out, attended to by the shop assistants, he whispers the heartfelt story of how Holly's medical advice resulted in the death of his one true love. By the end of it, she is looking at him adoringly with sad, wet eyes. She shares her name – Andrea – and tells him to wait for her at a nearby pub.

By the time she arrives, he has found a bottle of tolerable Merlot and some bar snacks. He likes how impressed she seems, how his presence makes her stand a little taller. They snack on peanuts and discuss the weather until she is ready to talk.

'I was friends with Holly once, but I always knew there was something off about her.' Andrea says this with the authority of someone who is always first to discover an indie band or a new, secret gin bar.

'How so?' He leans forward, making her feel like the most important woman in the world.

'Well, she was always just a bit secretive, you know? Even when I worked with her every day and spent most evenings with her, I never felt like I could quite pin her down.'

'Was she as secretive about her cancer?' he ventures.

'Well, I do have an eye for detail, that's why I make a great manager. Nothing goes unnoticed,' she says proudly. 'When Holly started chemotherapy and everyone else was caught up in sending her flowers and feeling sorry for her, I started picking up on little things. She had these glassy, faraway eyes the whole time. You know what I mean? That deeply happy look you see people get when they fall in love. There was not a trace of fear. I know a few people who have had cancer or gone through a trauma, and they always focus on the details. They bore you with the gore of what they're going through. Not Holly. When it came to any physical details beyond the caption of her Instagram posts, she would go surprisingly quiet.'

Tyler's heart is pounding now. Excitement and rage pulse through his veins. He asks her, voice shaking, 'Do you think she was faking it?'

'I know she was now. While I had my misgivings, I still wanted to give her the benefit of the doubt. After months of endless chemotherapy and health drama, she just didn't pitch up for work one day. I thought the worst, of course – the way she was talking about her illness, it seemed possible at that point that she could just die in her sleep.'

'But she didn't.'

'No, and we never saw her again, not face to face anyway. The truth came out soon after that.'

Tyler would have given anything to see the look on Holly's face when her world came crashing down. The humiliation in her eyes as she realised the game was over.

'How did it happen? Did someone catch her in the act?'

'Well, nothing dramatic happened if that's what you're asking. Her father came to visit me as I was locking up the shop one evening. He explained that the hospital had called to discuss Holly's "psychological situation" after some sort of "incident". He's usually such a proper man, but that day he was all over the show, asking me questions about what exactly she had told me.'

Andrea's eyes avoid his now, and she starts playing with the bowl of nuts in front of her.

'He told me that day that she may not be sick with cancer, but she's sick with something else, a mental disorder he couldn't explain just yet. He made me swear to secrecy.'

The anger is rising in his chest again. His teeth clench as he asks, 'And how exactly did he do that?'

When someone is hiding the truth, always follow their eyes. Tyler learnt that as a little boy when he used to mine his father's platitudes for clues on his mother's health. Back then his father's eyes would dart to the sound of crying from her bedroom, wild with worry. Today, Andrea's eyes betray her for a split second as they flit to the sparkling black Audi parked outside and the Marc Jacobs watch glinting on her wrist. Tyler doesn't let her speak; he doesn't want to hear it.

'He paid you off, didn't he?'

She looks down and gulps the rest of her drink.

'That's none of your business, is it?'

Tyler slams the table with his fist, wine splattering onto his wrist.

'Considering that somebody I loved died because nobody cared enough to out a con artist, I would say yes, it actually *is* my business.'

Andrea's lip quivers. 'Don't you dare make assumptions about whether I cared or not. Do you know how it feels to care about a friend, to buy into their story and then find out it was all a lie? I felt like a fucking fool, a loser. How could I have not followed my instincts? Instead, day after day, I showered her with attention and supported her as she started to build her fake empire.'

She's more confident now, defiant, 'So what if he paid me a lump sum to not say anything? Someone like you wouldn't understand how tempting that is when you're a few years out of uni and haven't made anything out of your life yet. It's hard enough getting an internship, let alone a job. Some of my friends had struck it lucky through their parents' connections but I wasn't keeping up. It felt like everyone else was all over social media flaunting their Kate Spade handbags, new cars and spa weekends in the countryside and I had none of it.'

He wants to punch her in the face. 'You know how much more money you would have made selling this story to the *Daily Mail*?' Stupid, simple woman.

Her chubbiness suddenly looks more childlike than jaded, the gothic make-up more a costume than a lifestyle. 'It's more complicated than that. Holly's dad is – how do I put this? – influential. He employs my dad and my uncle, he donates to my mum's charity every year. Living here, you're part of an ecosystem, a family, and you can't turn your back on family, even when someone does something so wrong.'

'So your integrity is something that can be bought then? That doesn't sound so complicated to me.'

She stares at him with so little emotion it sends a shudder through his body. 'Tyler, you also need to understand women in order to understand this. I may have been angry with Holly, I may have even hated her, but that only made me want to watch her even more.'

Chapter 24

Holly

The girls are coming. She can smell them getting nearer. She can hear their whispers approaching her door.

Since the fateful BBC incident, Holly hasn't done any more media interviews, but Zanna thought it would be a good idea to nurture a relationship with the people who are on her side. The #JusticeforHolly girls.

'I know you feel awful, Holly, but there are some incredible people out there fighting in your corner. Trust me, just an hour in their company will make you feel a whole lot better,' she said.

Her good intentions only make Holly feel more frantic. It will take more than some positive social interaction to make her feel as if this is all going to turn out fine in the end.

Today feels like a test. Can she still pretend to be the person she was? The past few weeks have changed her. The nights spent going over all the things she's done wrong are mapped in her red, fragile eyes. Her uncertain, stilted voice hints at all which has been taken from her. The illusion has been broken, and as it shattered, so did her strength.

Will going through the motions miraculously change her back? She's been preparing the lunch since yesterday. There is a selection of raw nut cheeses in the fridge, as well as a jar of basil pesto. She has made seed crackers to accompany it, and a big bowl of vegan pad thai. She's just filled two jugs with her signature green juice recipe, and has checked the coconut and berry cheesecake in the freezer. It was touch and go when she bought the ingredients at the market. Somehow her card was not declined – not just yet. She's jittery, like she was the first time she prepared her recipes for her editors and she wasn't sure they would be good enough to publish.

Of course, they were. She was on the cusp of a wave as people started discovering how incredible vegan food could be. Watching the editors tucking into her raw chocolate brownies and Greek-style tapas board was the most inspired she has ever felt. She felt so lit up that day, like she could illuminate the whole room. For a time, it felt like her backstory was her only ticket to standing out, to feeling this way forever. But that day, she forgot about the cancer – she had the talent all on her own.

There is a pounding on the door. The girls are here, looming behind a flustered Zanna.

'Hey, lovely, sorry we're a bit late. The traffic is heinous out there! Anyway, meet Brooke, Candice and Nicole. These three have been total digital superstars in their own right and part of the amazing group of women behind the epic campaign to find your attacker. I don't understand the half of it, but you're lucky to have such incredible ladies on your side.'

It takes Holly everything she has not to run to her bedroom and hide. Her interactions with fans always used to feel so imbalanced as their wonder at her real-life beauty was always so palpable. Now she is the one who feels unworthy, the one who feels the need to explain her appearance.

Brooke, the obvious leader, steps forward first, grabbing hold of Holly with an unnaturally soft hand. She's wearing the same Adidas by Stella McCartney floral tracksuit Holly posted on Instagram once. Deliberate. In her eyes, Holly instantly recognises the hunger of a person who wants exactly what she has. She's seen it so often in the lithe women who come to her book launches and tag her in their recipe pictures. As much as her fans adore her, so many have that slight female edge which says that, if they had the same opportunities, they could have done better. Shame sticks in her throat. She has never thought about this so clearly before. She's always thought of their ambition as flattering, never sinister. This new-found cynicism is another way her attack has coiled its filthy roots into her brain.

She won't let it. She refuses to let some sick anomaly erode her belief in the goodness of humankind. These girls are angels in a world of online jealousy and attack. Zanna's right: she's lucky to have them on her side.

'It's an honour to meet you, Brooke.' She smiles.

'No, no, it is a massive honour to meet you! Although, I'm not sure you remember but I actually did meet you just last month at your breakfast event. I was the one in the audience who told the story about how your eating plan balanced my hormones, remember?' That thin smile, that barbed accusing tone. It brought back a moment in her walk with Jack. That moment when his tone turned sour. Her hand unconsciously travels to her face, touches the scars she should have so easily avoided.

'Oh, the breakfast event! Of course!'

The day of the breakfast was, in fact, a blur. Although Holly has built a following fast online, replying to comments and thanking people for their compliments is different from engaging with them in real life. She is naturally an introvert, content to style pictures of food behind closed doors. Any personal interaction beyond her smartphone has to be forced. That day fear pulsed behind her eyes, and lodged in her throat. Surely they would notice she is not as assured as they were? Surely they could read all her lies on her face?

But these events, as Zanna always emphasised, allowed people to connect with her recipes and see how down to earth she really was. She got through the breakfast event with the unnatural help of some quietly prescribed anti-anxiety pills. Publicly she only backed natural supplements, but privately she needed something stronger to face the room of expectant faces. In the fog of her mind, every word she said and person she met had soft edges that melted into each other to form one marbled memory.

Holly pushes Brooke's hand aside and moves forward to hug her. The other two move in and soon she is enclosed in the gentle mingling of floral perfumes. It feels so good to be loved, to be in the warm embrace of others.

The girls are obscenely beautiful. Their faces are rosy and flushed, probably from a recent yoga class. Their eyes are framed by perfectly groomed eyebrows and eyelash extensions. Their obvious effort with their appearance stokes the paranoia in Holly's chest that she looks as bad as she feels. She'd spent an hour holding a heat pack to her face this morning, but it only made the scars more inflamed. Are they holding in their revulsion at her appearance? Should she draw attention to it or behave like everyone else and just pretend it is the same as before?

'Um, should I show you guys around?'

She doesn't want to go there, she can't let herself go there, but her eyes do it for her. They glide over their three identically taut stomachs as they pull off their coats. They settle on their round, hard arses, undoubtedly earned through a daily regimen of squats. She eyes them like a prospective date, assessing and evaluating. A voice in her head screams *they are better, they are hotter, they are so much thinner than you are right now*. This is what it is to be a woman, always leaving your body and looking down on it, weighing up your flesh in comparison to everyone else's.

No, no, *stop*. They've done nothing to offend her besides having the perfect, normal life she had a week ago. And they must have demons too. No matter how adjusted a person seems, there must be some disorder under their skin if they are willing to dedicate most of their day to worshipping a random girl on the Internet.

'Here is the lounge area, and then the kitchen – my pride and joy – and my bedroom is down the hall.'

They linger in the kitchen, of course, picking up jars and powders while conferring excitedly about their favourite ingredients.

'Where did you learn to cook, Holly?' asks Candice.

'I taught myself actually. It was just a process of experimentation with the ingredients I like.'

'And striking out the ones you couldn't have?' Brooke asks. Holly realises with a jolt that she has forgotten to move the rainbow of pills she takes every morning with her breakfast, currently on the top shelf. She prays Brooke doesn't look up.

'Yes, exactly. I've always thought that restrictions actually help your creativity grow in a way.'

She's performing now. Her hands arch unnaturally as she desperately tries to be the girl connected to the smiling face on the inside of her book jacket. Though it's only her familiar face that has actually gone, the rest of what made her unique and relevant has also disappeared along with it. Now, she's guessing at what it means to be normal.

The girls nod at her in unison, seemingly unaware of the toll this is taking on her. She forgets that all they know is the flattened version of her on their screens. They don't know the difference between the old Holly and the new. In fact, they probably created a fictional Holly in their own imaginations months ago. What would the woman who matched those filtered selfies be like? So much better than her, no doubt.

There's an unspoken conversation going on among the girls. They think she doesn't notice it, but she does. Holly sees it as they dish up their food, placing minuscule samples of her cooking on their plates. Don't they like it? Hasn't it lived up to their expectations? Oh fuck, girls like these probably make her own recipes better at home. As always, the fear that she has somehow included some ingredient recently been maligned as non-vegan creeps up.

The discrepancy between her own personal recipes and the way they live on in the lives of her followers is something she has never got used to. Today, it makes her feel uneasy, on the brink of being exposed. Zanna looks over to her, giving her a firm nod and a thumbs up. That woman can detect the scent of Holly's imposter syndrome from a mile off. She nods in return and manages a weak smile. She'll be strong, if not for herself, then for her friend.

Brooke clears her throat again. Out of all the girls, she appears to want something out of this meeting the most. It burns behind her eyes. 'So, Holly, I know this is painful for you, but we wanted to ask a few questions about your attack?'

'It's fine, Brooke. I'm getting used to talking about it now.' There's an unconscious edge in her voice. The strangeness of the situation suddenly hits her. What right do these women have to take ownership of her tragedy, of her endangered life?

Brooke looks brightly towards Holly and touches her own unblemished face. Smooth, thin cheeks without an ounce of extra fat. The way girls cut each other is different and, sometimes, so much worse.

'OK! Well some of my questions might be a bit different. Some of us have studied the safety of women in digital media. See, from what we have researched, trolls don't select people randomly. They go for targets that represent something or someone in their lives that causes them distress.'

There's something in the half-smirk on Brooke's face that makes Holly want to get up and run. It's finally happening. It's here.

'So, you think there was something about me that made this happen?' she asks, her bitterness dribbling like saliva, stinging the split corners of her mouth. Zanna stares at the girls sternly. Holly feels a rush of love for her friend, who she knows will blow this interview apart if she has to.

'No, no, we're very against the idea of women "asking" for anything. We just wanted to know a little bit more about your story.'

Suddenly, they all appear a lot older than she first thought. People always write off the pretty girls, the thin girls. But these are the ones who are the most strategic, managing their bodies and the world around them until it bends to their will.

She should never have agreed to this.

'OK, sure. Well, ask anything you want.'

Brooke looks to the other girls. Candice whispers something in her ear, 'First, we'd like to know a bit more about your life before the blog. Were you happy? Did you have a close group of friends?'

Andrea. It's a door at the end of a dark passage she doesn't want to walk down.

'There isn't much to say really. I lived a boring life in Exeter and managed the Topshop on the high street. I lived with my mum and dad, and had a few acquaintances, but I was closest to my colleague and best friend Andrea. For a while, we did everything together but eventually we grew apart.'

That's not all, that's not all.

'Is there anyone there who would have ill feelings about you?'

What do they know?

'Not that I know of. I mean there was the usual girl stuff, you know? Fighting over boyfriends, and what not.'

The usual, you know? Your best friend shouting insults at you as you tried to explain yourself.

'Was it a hard decision to leave?'

It was the only possible decision. If she'd stayed any longer, her secret would have been exposed.

'Yes, of course. But it was time for me to grow up, wasn't it?'

Nicole, the quietest girl, speaks up, 'D-do you have any particular bad memories of your time in Exeter?'

'No.'

Her suitcase standing at the door. Her father in another room, refusing to come to say goodbye.

They're closing in on her. She turns desperately to Zanna. They haven't had their berry cheesecake yet, but they need to leave right fucking now.

Thankfully, Zanna steps in. 'Hey, girls, I'm so glad you could make it. Holly and I both wanted to share our appreciation for everything you're doing in the search for her attacker. I think our girl is getting a bit tired now, though, aren't you, Holly?'

Hold back the tears. Don't let the wolves see them. 'I am, yes.'

'Could we wrap this up with a fun group selfie?' The kiss of Brooke's smartphone camera feels like a burn.

The girls hug her in turn. As they walk away, Brooke turns around one last time.

'Hey, Holly, how old are you again?'

'Oh, twenty-eight?'

Nobody knows her real age. Holly has made up figures on the spot before to seem younger, or more mature, depending on what the person opposite her wanted. Why did she have to sound so unsure? Why do these girls matter to her so much? But then, girls like these always have.

'Twenty-eight? That's so weird, I'm sure I read in your book that you're twenty-five.'

'Oh, you know how publishing processes are: so many eyes, and typos still slip through.'

She could have imagined it, but she is sure Brooke just rolled her eyes. 'Yeah. Sure. OK, bye, Holly. Well, it was a privilege to meet you.'

As she turns to leave, Holly catches Brooke's eye. There is something in her pitying smile, a sinister glimmer in her eyes that is batted quickly away by a flutter of her eyelash extensions. There has been a shift. Brooke is no longer a fan but a leader, no longer enthralled but powerful.

Chapter 25

Tyler

It only took a few months of dating for Tyler to realise that Frankie was not good at mundane life stuff. She could secure millions in investment, but she struggled to open the packaging of her sandwich at lunchtime. As for those childproof pill bottles, God, he'd be bent over heaving with laughter as she tried to get the lid off. She let her car tax expire and always missed her doctor's check-ups. But, how could he chastise her for it? She lived in the mystical complexity of her mind. She didn't have time to concern herself with the little things.

Her driving was another issue entirely. It was if she had learnt to drive in a country in the throes of a civil war. Swerving, ducking, speeding and taking chances, she was always driving for her life. A few weeks into their relationship, he noticed her eyesight was so bad that she had lost all depth perspective in the dark. It was too soon to interfere, but he gently suggested she go see an optometrist. Frankie's only vice was a stubborn sense of pride. She didn't book an appointment. She simply stopped driving at night.

He should have pushed her harder, but it's hard to see looming danger when you're so close to it.

Yet how could he stay angry with his beautiful girl? Their quiet evenings together, spent drinking wine and talking through the small events in their day, introduced a calm he had been craving since the death of his mother. Suddenly, somebody cared about what he had for lunch that day and asked how his patients were recovering. Living within her love was like finally reaching the surface to gasp for breath after swimming underwater for too long. He told her he loved her one morning after sleeping over at her apartment.

'I love espresso so damn much,' said Frankie, as he carried their coffee to bed.

'Well, I love you.' He smiled.

'Oh, darling . . .' She grabbed his hand and kissed him until their coffees turned cold. In that moment, he knew that one day their ringed hands would hold one another in this same bed. Husband and wife, family, preparing to reach into the morning.

Another night, her apartment, five months later. He was distracted that evening, scanning the titles on her book-shelf and picking up her eclectic selection of ornaments. There was always more about Frankie to discover. Always the scientist, he needed to decode the source of her magic. She waited until they were reading in bed and he was drift-ing off, breathing in the rose scent of her hair.

'So, I went for a check-up today . . .'

'Uh-huh.'

'For my eyes . . .'

'Finally! Hallelujah! You know I would have gone with you, right?'

'Yeah, yeah. It's OK, it was just a check-up.' He was wide awake then, stoked by a rush of possessiveness. She should have asked him. He's her partner now and he's a doctor.

'So, what did he say?'

'Well,' she laughed nervously, 'it turns out that I've got a brain tumour.'

Nobody should ever feel the way he felt in that moment. His mind grasped for an explanation, a way out, but he could feel everything they had falling, falling down an endless black hole. He knows how this ends. He's been here before, sitting on the cold floor outside a locked room, trying to block his ears so as not to hear the screaming inside.

He tried to turn to face Frankie but she clutched him as hard as she could, as if wringing out their final normal moment. Worse still, her laughing turned hysterical.

'It's a big fucking tumour pressing on the base of my brain. The size of an egg, the doc said. Can you imagine?'

'Frankie, look at me, we need to talk about this seriously. We need to discuss your options. I'm a doctor, I can help you.'

She laughed her light, airy giggle and wrestled out of his arms. 'Not yet, sweetheart, there's so much life left to live!'

He should have intervened then. He should have learnt from the example of his father and taken control of the situation. Tyler and Frankie were a team, and sometimes one member of the team doesn't know what is best for them. He likes to think he tried.

He remembers pacing around her apartment, weeks later, begging, cajoling and raging.

'Frankie! This doesn't have to be the end! Look at these academic papers I found at the hospital – there have been cases *just* like yours where the patient has gone into remission after several rounds of aggressive treatment!'

'But at what cost, Ty? So I can spend my days vomiting, losing my hair and becoming completely dependent on my family, on you? You know how much I value my independence. Can you imagine what torture that would be for me?'

'So you don't want to get well. Is that what you're saying?'

Tyler had only seen Frankie angry once or twice and even then, it was mild. After barely being together for six months, they were still careful in what they revealed, wary not to get too raw and scare the other away. But today it pulsed through her body, white-hot and indignant. She glared at him, eyes narrowed.

'I never said that. I don't understand why we are so quick to believe that poisoning our bodies with man-made chemicals is the only solution to curing diseases! I've seen what chemo does to people, Ty, and I just can't do it. You come here brandishing these studies like they're the solution. Well, there are other studies that show how people have treated cancer through diet, medicinal marijuana and other natural therapies.'

Tyler sees a new future unfolding before him, one that looks all too similar to his past. Why won't she let him help? Why won't she let him love her?

'Studies, you say? You mean like Holly Evans's diet dressed up as pseudoscience?'

'You don't understand, do you? Tyler, I am making an educated, personal decision here. The fact that you think otherwise is insulting. You know what? I actually think it's best if you leave. We're both not in a place to discuss this.'

He shouldn't have left that day. He should have pushed harder. At that critical time, he had the authority to do something and he didn't use it. But before he could blink, her parents had swooped in with the offer of her old childhood bedroom in their house. He couldn't compete with her mother's cooking and a lifetime of comforting memories. Soon there was a cab waiting outside filled with her bags, and he was walking out of her apartment for the last time.

Even today the memory makes him seethe. He taps his news app as a distraction. The search for Holly's attacker is still making headlines. He doesn't get it. Syria is being bombed to pieces, Burundi is on the verge of genocide, yet the UK is obsessing about a few swollen scratches on a famous girl's face. It is amazing how prettiness and the scent of fame makes a person's media real estate go up. It's all about location, location, location. Location in the right place of society, where people are deemed special enough to be interesting. Nothing has changed since he last checked. The online map is still being populated each day, yet he can't find himself in any of the photos. This wasn't even an intentional move on his part. Truly privileged men like him, men who have grown up steeped in money, have the gift of being grey. Conspicuous consumption is for the tacky; true prosperity doesn't wish to be seen. So he slunk through London that night invisible, with nobody giving him a second glance.

He chuckles over his cortado. He could blow this shit wide open in a few seconds if he wanted to. He could make fools of these hysterical women, and of Holly especially. Perhaps he should send these girls a few incriminating photographs to show them the type of person they are really dealing with. Maybe they can help him when the moment comes to ruin her flimsy life for good. He's been ready ever since he returned from Exeter months ago, and read the sentence on her medical history that stoked his anger into a raging wild-fire: NO EVIDENCE OF DISEASE.

Yet there is something inside that is stopping him. Perhaps it's because revealing everything all at once would be too crude. Timing is crucial. Like the perfect wound, it has to happen when it will hurt the most. He wants a long, slow meaningful courtship of her ruin, not an easy one-night stand. He wants to stand in the distance and observe her falling apart. Isn't that what she forced him to do with Frankie?

Chapter 26
Holly

A new white bed. A new hospital. Another nuance to Holly's failure. It's not natural to move backwards, she should be healing better than she is right now. She has an audience of thousands to console. It's time to move on. Even her mother seems to think this, as is clear by her tired voice sighing over the phone,

'You really need to summon the strength to get over this, darling. You can do it, I know it.'

In her voice, something else, that clenched fear that she's starting her old tricks again. The intimation that she is the one who brought this on herself. Prickly as she is, her mother remains the only person in her family who calls.

'I'm trying my best, Mum. You know that the guy hasn't been caught yet. Everyone seems to be forgetting about this.'

Everyone forgets, and nobody knows the way he circles her, swooping every now and then, a flash of evil.

'Yes, but you've always had such a strong mind—'

'Jesus, Mum! Please don't go on about the toilet-training story again!'

'First of all, sweetie, please don't blaspheme. It's not attractive. And secondly, no, it's another story. Do you remember when you were a little girl and found out that Father Christmas didn't exist?'

'Yes, Mrs Folkes told us all when we were ten and some of the parents were really angry with her.'

'No, you actually found out years before that. I remember it so clearly. We all lived in that house in Buddle Lane. You were a few months short of turning six and had written an elaborate letter to Father Christmas asking for a pink bicycle. Your father and I were so excited to get it for you, but in the excitement of finding the right one, I left my car door wide open, with the bike resting on the back seat. I was unpacking the groceries in the kitchen when I saw you run out and look right at it. You even ran your hands over the handlebars. Then you whipped around, ran back inside and didn't mention a word of it. When Christmas time came, you acted like you had never seen it before and insisted on writing a letter to Father Christmas to say thank you.'

A sinking feeling. Holly knows where this is going.

'Why do you think I did that?'

'Well, as I said, you have a strong mind, and you wanted to believe. You blocked out everything you didn't want to see.' She can feel the bitterness crawling from her phone and into her bones.

'OK?'

'So, do that now. Focus on the good and pretend this evil man is far away, because, let's face it, he probably is by now.' Her heart clenches as she hears her father shouting in the distance, and the breaking of glass. 'I've got to go,' her mother whispers. 'I love you, darling.'

The conversation wasn't as encouraging as Holly wished it would be. If anything, it has unsettled her even more. What did she expect? In contrast to the fanfare of her attack, she faces today's operation by herself. She's not sure yet if this makes her feel freer, or more alone. Perhaps it's for the best. Her face has been raging against her for days now. She'd rather not see the impact of the diagnosis reflected on someone with a full range of expression.

Still, whatever the diagnosis is, it comes with the promise that an expert will fix her. She just wants someone to knock her out so that she can wake up to her normal life again, the one where she knew who she was. This seems to be her best shot.

Holly always expected to return to being invisible, but she thought time would be the one to do the disfiguring. Her beauty was never a thing that felt real. She wore it like an expensive dress she had bought in a sale, paralysed with self-consciousness and a sense that she was somehow undeserving of it.

When she was twelve years old, she had curly black hair hacked into an awkward bob, with braces slammed into her round face. While other girls were softly budding and being taken to dark corners of the playground, she was never chosen. The only time she was referred to sexually was when SHAWN FINGERED HOLLY was etched crudely into the desk in the library. Shawn was one of the slow kids, who was frequently bullied. Accusing him of touching Holly was just another way of punching him in the face. She couldn't even find the heart to get too upset about it, not when she was being punched for real at home.

At eighteen, a shift started taking place. Her features were changing, refining. The coarse curls crowding her face had relaxed into waves. While she was still slumped and awkward in posture, her proportions were blatant enough on their own. Narrow waist, full hips, large breasts. Contrary to what magazines would have girls believe, you don't need the right clothes or make-up to hook a guy. You just need to feel right under his hands. She started lying down often and gratefully, being moulded, appraised and approved of by rough, teenage hands.

Now, after countless Brazilian blow-waves and boxes of peroxide, she has blonde mermaid-hair, with a fantasy body that she has stretched and pulled around its original curves to become effortlessly slender. Years of juicing and her raw food diet have refined her doll-like features, and her bright, brown eyes appear large and wild within the frame of her delicate cheekbones.

Looking the way she did never fixed anything, but it made her life easier. Now, she is not just scarred, but she has been marked by a tragedy she did not choose. The thought of being in an operating theatre again makes her want to scream and run out of the door, but it could make everything normal again. It could quell the fear that the empire she has built is about to fall apart.

Holly Evans, you're a fucking fraud.

The words taunt her. They stick to every thought. She'll do anything she can to make them go away.

'Well, hello there. This must be the famous Holly Evans!' A tall, clumsy-looking man walks in. He runs his hands through his wiry hair, something he must do often as it is standing out all over his head. His face is chubbier than in the pictures – those must have been taken over a decade ago.

'Dr Warner?'

'Call me Eugene. It's a pleasure to meet you. My daughter is a big fan. She's got us all drinking your Green Monster shake!'

'Hah, that is an evergreen classic.' She tries to wink but her eyes no longer feel part of her body. Everything feels disconnected, loose, as if she has been reassembled in a rush.

'Evergreen, clever. I'm glad you're in high spirits this morning. Today is going to be a really good day.'

'Is it?'

'In my opinion, yes. When you first came in for surgery at the other hospital you were losing a lot of blood. The previous doctor didn't have time to fuss around with the stitches. I just need to go in there and clear things up. Ideally it would have been nice to have a consultation before the surgery, but as soon as my colleague saw your face on the news, he brought your case to my attention.

As soon as I saw you, I realised we didn't have much time. It's best to act now while the scars are fresh, yes?'

His touch is warm and gentle against her face, like a father's. Not her father, but like she'd imagine a father to be. Her arms ache to hug him.

'Will I look . . . ?'

'You want to know if you'll look yourself again? Not right away, but if you are patient and take your antibiotics, you should heal nicely in a couple of months. And then, of course, it may be six months until you get the full movement of your facial muscles back. Judging by this inflammation, I think you need to be a bit more religious in taking your medication. Am I right?'

'Maybe a little right,' she laughs. It's not that she's deliberately not taking her medication, it's just that her throat closes on her after so many pills. It feels like a fist pushing down her throat.

He crouches down beside her. 'Listen, Holly, this is serious stuff. I don't know who did this to you, but he managed to hack through some of your key muscles and nerve endings. I want you to be able to smile again, and to keep on doing all your positive work. You have the world at your feet, so let's work together to keep it that way. Do you believe in me?'

She wants to cry with relief. 'Yes, I believe in you.'

'Poor thing, you've been through so much. I'm sure you've been in and out of hospitals countless times with your . . .'

Don't look back in the file. Please don't look.

'Yes, but it's OK. I can be brave one more time. Let's get this done.'

He pats her shoulder. 'You're a remarkable girl. Now lie back and relax. I'll get a nurse to administer your pre-med. The worst is over now. It's time to get you on the path to the good stuff again.'

Chapter 27

Tyler

Two hours. That's how long it will take to operate on Holly. Two hours of staring at that familiar blonde hair and those skinny legs. The little tart always loved to show them off.

Fifteen minutes until he has to scrub in. But first he needs to make a quick phone call to the *Daily Mail*. It's time. Finally. He's glad he's waited, planned. It's almost too easy, but he knows Frankie would be proud of him. He's done it all for her and soon she'll get justice. Soon everyone will know what Holly's done.

'I'd like to speak to your newsroom please?'

Sirens blare outside the hospital while he holds the line, listening to the inane background music and fidgeting in his seat. Finally, a tired presence comes on.

'Hello there, yes, I'd like to provide an anonymous tip. I am a doctor based in London and lost my fiancée to cancer last year.' He still chokes whenever he says it out loud. 'While I agree that Holly Evans's methods may successfully prevent or even halt the development of cancer, I have never in my long career met a late-stage cancer survivor that has been cured through a one hundred per cent natural approach. I went looking for Holly Evans's medical file, which confirmed my suspicions. She faked her entire cancer journey. Not only is this catastrophic for the brands she represents, but her promotion of alternative cancer treatments has resulted in the loss of lives, including that of my fiancée. I had the medical documents, as well as a written explanation, couriered to your offices this morning.'

The buzz leaps in his chest as the reporter starts talking quickly about getting the story out there as soon as possible. He fizzes with the knowledge that the photos would have just been delivered to the #JusticeforHolly girls today too. Months before he and Holly met that night in Starbucks, he has photographed her slinking through the city. The images reveal a woman who is the exact opposite of who her fans think she is.

Everything is colliding so beautifully. Holly's carefully constructed world spiralling out of her grasp. Not only will the world turn on her, but so will the followers who loved her most. Soon she will know what it's like to lose what is most precious to her, and soon she will know what it feels like to have nothing.

Five minutes to theatre. Two hours in surgery. One hour in intensive care. That's how long it takes to ruin a life.

Chapter 28
Holly

Holly's tongue feels thick and swollen in her mouth. She tries to talk to the nurses but her words sound like someone else's voice. She turns her head from side to side as they wheel her to the operating theatre. Walls, beds, windows are luminous and sparkling with white stars. She is an acrobat balancing on the edge of consciousness. How she loves this feeling! How she wants to hold on to this in-between, this 'not here, not there' bliss. She hears jagged peals of laughter. It's her, not her; it's the joy inside her finding a way out, like vomit. A nurse with wide, cartoon eyes smiles down on her. 'Ssssshhhh.'

'Sssssh!' Holly giggles back.

She is under the blinding white light. Everything is too reflective, too clean in this room. It hurts her eyes. She tries to cover them but her hands feel so far away, so filled with lead. The tools, the knives have been casually arranged next to her bed, like a new box of crayons on the first day of school. She tries to stop herself but, no, there it is, there's the scalpel, glinting in the bright light just like it did that night. The memory burns behind her eyes – that heart-stopping feeling of fear, suspended in time.

The scream comes from something that doesn't sound like her. It's going into her face again. Panting claws her throat. She's too weak. Once again, there is nothing she can do to stop it.

A voice from another world, 'The patient is showing signs of distress.' A tall woman appears, her face wrinkled and grave. She is patting her arm. For a second Holly feels as if she is the woman and it is her hand, touching her own arm. She is everyone and no one, everything and nothing. She feels heavier now, like she's being pushed into the ground, far, far down until her body is scalded by the earth's core.

A face above her. A smile. Familiar. Good-looking. Cold eyes. 'Well, if it isn't my favourite patient.' No. *No no no no.* How could he be here? Zanna said she knew Dr Warner well. Holly had *trusted* her. But there's no mistaking it. It's him, swaying above her, his fingers grazing the tray of sharp objects. 'What's wrong, sweetheart?' he whispers, still smiling. 'Don't you want me to fix you?' Nobody notices, the nurses preoccupied far away in another corner of the operating theatre. She's screaming now. Bucking her body like a dying animal while he holds her down again. Slurred words crowd the room, but she's too far gone under the pre-meds. Nobody can understand her. One last surge of adrenaline pulses through her arms as she scratches desperately at the nurses, the doctors. 'It's him! He's the one! He hurt me!' They're holding her down, struggling against the bite of her words, the clamping of her jaw. A dark mask is secured on her face and held down. No, no, she can't breathe. Can't anybody tell she can't breathe? They all want to kill her; she's sure of it. This is her punishment for everything she has done. Words, not her words, floating above her, coiling into her ears like smoke, 'Oh, Holly, how should I hurt you today?'

Chapter 29
Tyler then

Frankie's on a mission today. She's unstoppable. Her blaze of curls shimmers as she paces out the door of her parents' place and towards her car. She's lost in her phone, fighting with Google Maps to give her the best route out of London for this time of the morning. Tyler's heart jumps in his chest – she shouldn't be doing that while walking, she should watch where she's going.

Not that she listens to him anymore. Despite his views on the matter, she has been planning this trip for weeks, a visit to the so-called 'Dr' Ray, some quack dispensing questionable medical advice from his hideout in the forest. It makes him feel so helpless he could scream, but love is about compromise, and he just has to hope that her common sense will prevail before it's too late. His breathing quickens as he pulls open the door and jumps into the passenger seat.

'Frankie, this is batshit crazy.'

'Tyler! I didn't expect to see you here...' The glint of rage in her eyes both terrifies him and spurs him on. Doesn't she understand that, no matter what his thoughts are on the matter, he will always be there for her?

Who is this new, manic woman who doesn't turn to him for comfort anymore? Her eyes are always distracted now, flitting over him and looking just past him. Even though she touches his hand sadly as she drives, he knows that she doesn't really need him there, not in an essential way, not in the way that matters most.

The majesty of the city crumbles and is replaced by an intense emerald landscape that hurts his eyes. He doesn't like the country and has taken refuge in cities ever since he and his father packed away the magic house decades ago. Doesn't Frankie remember this? Doesn't she care?

'Babe, please slow down . . .'

The road jolts in a sickening curve to the left and begins to darken. He wishes she'd let him drive but ever since the sickness came, she's become infuriatingly independent. It's all to make some sort of point, that she's still well enough to be part of this world, even though he can see her hands shaking against the wheel.

The sky is crowded with pine trees overhead. The woods she is searching for are so close he can smell them. It's fine. They will get there and she will do whatever crazy hippie shit she has planned and he will talk some sense into her on the way home. He keeps setting deadlines in his head, dates and days when he will say, 'Right, enough of this fucking nonsense.'

The problem is the so-called science. In the realm of the sick, there are doctors and then there are the almost-doctors, the better-than-doctors, the conspiracy theorists alive with their particular brand of treating the ill. Some promote an alkaline diet, others latch on to Indian medicine after one trip to Goa. They use crystals, essential oils, vibrations, massage, roots and berries to channel their elusive power. Their most potent ingredient, hope. Their deepest flaw, the conviction that theirs is the only path. Humouring this façade is enough to set him alight from the inside. His ever-present rage, the one that only Frankie can calm, is back.

Sticking out of the bushes is a hand-painted sign. Frankie swerves violently to make the gravelled entrance.

'Oh, thank God, we're here,' she whispers to herself more than Tyler.

'Are you sure this is the right place, sweetheart? It seems pretty uninhabited to me. We can always turn around and go home – you're looking rather pale.'

Her lips glow white against her freckled skin. She turns away from him, gets out of the car and once again loses herself in the alternative reality of her phone.

'Let me message him and tell him we're here.'

Ray, the name suited to a charismatic preacher with slicked-back hair and a Ferrari bought with his congregation's monthly tithing. But no, this Ray is a natural healer slash herbalist slash opportunist. From what Tyler could gather from Frankie's previous excited rantings, he had been interviewed for Holly's blog and she had recommended him to her readers as the person to visit for treating any illness naturally. Holly had gone to him personally, Frankie said, and she credited him with helping her beat cancer. Something about this struck a note of discord in his mind – he has seen incredibly limited data on cancer sufferers who have survived based on a natural diet alone.

As she stands in front of the woods, her red hair tumbling over her shoulders and the bones of her back jutting out like wings, it strikes him how suddenly fragile she has become. When did the muscles in her calves wither away? When did the back of her jeans begin to sag? The urge to gather her up in his arms and carry her home is physically painful.

'Wait, I can see it! Come on then, let's go.'

The air screams with silence as Frankie's BMW crunches over the ragged road. She is humming with happiness.

'So, tell me again, what exactly do you hope to get out of meeting this Dr Ray?'

'I'm here to heal, Tyler. The more I read about Holly's journey and the stuff that Dr Ray says on her blog, the more I see just how disconnected we all are from our bodies, you know? We just push and push ourselves to achieve, always edging the goalposts further away, each time believing that if we reach them we'll be happy. We ignore our bodies when they tell us we feel tired, and we pop another headache pill in the hope it will go away. I've been sick for a long time, but it's only recently that it's been given the name cancer.'

He wants to shake her. He wants to say, 'Does this mean you were sick during the happy times we had together before you found out? Does this sparkling new perspective that cancer has given you eradicate everything that has come before it?' He's jealous of it – the cancer – for colonising her body, and now her mind, for taking her away from him bit by bit. He sighs, and says instead, 'Well, I hope you find what you're looking for.'

Frankie turns and stares out the window, the woods holding secrets only she can decipher. 'I will, I always do.'

Dr Ray's cabin looms at the top of the hill, glowing from within like a real estate advert. He is standing at the door, in cotton shorts and a Liberty printed T-shirt despite the autumn chill in the air. His hair falls in greying blonde waves on his shoulders. Seemingly endless cats swirl around his feet. The bastard is so wealthy, he doesn't even have the decency to hide it.

'Hello there! Am I finally getting to meet the radiant Frankie in person?'

'Yes! Oh my gosh, it's so crazy, right? After all these months of emails . . .' She bounds out of the car, leaving Tyler to close the door behind her. He's been reduced to an afterthought, a slave.

'And this is?'

'Tyler,' Frankie mumbles.

He moves forward and grabs her waist. 'I'm Frankie's boyfriend.'

'Boyfriend? What a lovely surprise, Frankie!' Tyler can feel his cheeks burning red. After everything he has done she cannot even mention him in an email? For the first time, he feels like he is not welcome here, in this complicated present.

The two share a loaded look. 'I'm sure Frankie would be nowhere without your support,' Ray adds. There's something sinister about the way he says it. He sees them to a spacious lounge area with luxury linen furniture. Wide glass windows reveal the tangled forest below. Dr Ray has silently appeared beside him. 'I was an architect in my former life before I was led to become a healer. When it came to this place, it was important to me to build it as a statement of my intention. If I want to live more in tune with the earth, my building has to be in tune with it too. We're all one.' His eyes flit to Frankie. 'Come through to my office, Frankie.'

Tyler tries to relax but it's not to be. It's just not fair, the two of them sitting together, conspiring over her illness. When did cancer become a room that he, a surgeon, isn't allowed to enter? After what seems like an eternity, the door opens and the two emerge flushed and secretive. She's clutching a hessian bag heavy with herbs in one hand and holds a large rose quartz in the other. Tyler doesn't miss her hand slipping into her purse and pulling out a stack of notes. Survival is expensive. Dr Ray holds both her hands earnestly in his and says something he can't quite make out. They both look towards him and Frankie nods quickly.

'See you in six months!' she says brightly as she pushes the door open. The sun catches Tyler's eyes, causing them to water. He rubs them like a petulant child as he follows her to the car.

'So, what did he have to say?' he asks on the drive back.

'It's OK, Ty. You don't have to do this. I know you don't believe in this stuff.' Her voice is different with Tyler. All the warmth she held for Dr Ray has been drained out of it. Her words come out slower now, tired.

'No, it's fine, babe. Just tell me what he said.'

'You sure?' A spark of warmth, her hand doesn't bat his away.

'Yeah!'

The only way he can force her to love him right now is by pretending to be someone else. 'Well, he just spoke about how any illness in our body is something that has roots in our mind. A sickness or cancer grows from a negative thought we have about ourselves, or worry. It has roots in deep self-criticism and a lack of self-worth.'

'I don't understand. You're one of the most confident people I know.'

'On the outside, maybe, but I have my fair share of feeling undeserving.' Her eyes vacantly survey the road ahead, consciously avoiding his. 'Why do you think I put so much pressure on myself to achieve? Anyway, it comes down to a bit more than emotions. There is a lot of evidence that shows us that chemotherapy can actually make us sicker and suppress the very systems our body has inbuilt to fight cancer.'

He tries to hold down the sarcasm in his voice, 'So what does he suggest you do?'

'Well, he gave me some herbs, some meditations and some crystals to balance my chakras, and he echoed a lot of

Holly's advice. I need to cut out dairy completely and cut out sugar, for real this time. No little treats or cheat days. I need to have three green juices or smoothies a day and eat completely raw. This will bring about more radical changes than one round of chemo can promise.'

'Wait, so you're not going to even try chemo at all? What about what we discussed the other week?' What about what *he* discussed, more like. Frankie had shut him out and refused to listen to him. She wasn't thinking rationally anymore.

'*Leave it*, Tyler. Just honour my choice. I'm not fucking stupid, OK? Why should I waste my life feeling sick as a result of something that is not guaranteed to cure me? You of all people should understand that radiation for my type of brain tumour carries a risk of taking away my sight, and even my memory. What is the point of getting better, if the thing that cures me erodes who I am?'

Tyler responds in a slow, sing-song voice now, playful yet poisoned with rage. He hates himself for it, but can't control it. 'So, you are going to dispute decades of medical science in favour of drinking . . . I don't know . . . fucking carrots and kale? Have you *ever*, in your selfish, cloistered life, considered that this decision doesn't impact on just you? That by following some glorified diet you are not only damaging yourself, but others? Fuck. You know, I thought you were intelligent, Frankie, but you're as loopy as all the other girls.'

'Get out of the car, Tyler,' she whispers.

'Out here in the middle of nowhere?'

'You are not welcome here. Get out.'

He grabs her wrist and looks deeply into her mesmerising eyes.

'Make me.'

The sarcasm is boiling up now, swelling up through his throat in angry, hooting laughter. This is how that day is immortalised in time. Lines of wood rushing past in a blur of green and brown. The heavy, clinging scent of eucalyptus oil seeping out of the bag that had fallen over on the backseat. Tyler laughing manically, poking Frankie with a rough finger, while she cried soundlessly over the wheel.

They never drove along that road together again. She never made her next appointment. In less than six months, Frankie was dead.

Chapter 30
Holly

Holly jerks against the restraints cutting into her wrists. Something liquid dribbles down the side of her mouth. Her tongue strains to taste it. Blood. She's trying to open her eyes but they're stuck together with sleep. What she can make out sways back and forth. The memory of what she saw before she passed out burns as instantly and completely as acid. Those eyes that drew her in, smiling coldly at her as he clutched a knife in his hand. She needs to tell someone. Her lips won't budge; they feel like someone else's. Her throat – raw from screaming – stings as she tries to form a sound. There's a black shape in front of her, quickening towards her bedside, grabbing her arm. Oh God, no, please. Someone help, please. Something hard and round being pushed into her mouth. No, no, no, no.

'Holly, for heaven's sake, stop fighting and drink the fucking water.' The dark blur begins to take shape. It's Zanna, lion-haired and sunken-eyed, holding a water bottle with shaking hands. The female warrior is gone, and has been replaced by a defeated shell at the end of her bed.

'What? Have you never seen me without make-up before? Wait . . . don't answer that . . . I'm not sure you're supposed to be talking.'

The water feels gloriously cool against Holly's throat. She glugs until she can't take any more. Her tongue loosens and touches her lips and the insides of her cheeks. Two little slits at the corners of her mouth seem to be responsible for all the blood. Other than that, her face feels painless under her bandages. She doesn't need to see the result to know with intuitive certainty that the infection has been calmed. But why the uncontainable panic? What about the eyes she stared into in the minutes before she succumbed to the anaesthetic?

Dr Warner steps inside the room, trailed by two nurses. His posture is as grave and fretful as Zanna's. Something terrible has happened. She can feel it crouching in the corner of the room.

'How is our little fighter feeling this morning?' His voice seems harder today. He won't look her in the eye.

Fighter? What went wrong? Why won't anyone tell her?

'Sorry, Doctor, is she supposed to talk?' Zanna asks.

'Yes, the sooner the better really. We need to restore mobility to those muscles as soon as possible. Now, tell us, do you remember what happened yesterday?'

Arms, she remembers arms pulling her down, her hands grasping to get free. He was going to kill her. She knows it. Dr Warner's tired face is covered in raw scratches, a study of her own injuries in miniature. The sleeve of his shirt slides back to reveal a row of bruises. Was it her . . . ? No, it can't be? She wouldn't, would she?

'I, I remember seeing my attacker. He was a surgeon; he was right there above me holding a knife. I was trying to get away.'

He shakes his head sadly. 'Holly, that just isn't possible. The only other doctor in the room was my assistant, Dr Tyler Wells, who has just got back from conducting facial reconstruction operations for an NGO. He's up for a prestigious award for his work in the field and hardly ever leaves this hospital. He's not your attacker. Do you believe me when I say this?'

Tyler Wells, she tries to remember the name but already feels it slipping away.

'I . . . I don't know. I was so sure. His face, it looked the same. I thought I was going to die in there.'

'But you didn't, see? All we did was provide you with the best medical care and fix up your injuries – just in time I might add. It will take a while for you to smile the way you used to, but in a few weeks, the scarring will be a lot more . . . manageable.'

Manageable. That doesn't sound like healed, or like a path back to who she used to be. The disappointment seeps out the corner of her mouth, a pathetic whimper.

Dr Warner's hand glides over his scratched jaw. 'I'm glad we could assist you and I hope you get well, but in many ways this might have been a mistake on my part. You are clearly a very troubled girl and, well, I thought you were . . . somebody different. We all did.' He places a card next to her bed. 'Yesterday was tough on us, Holly, on me and on my staff. You were in a compromised position and could have done yourself real damage if we hadn't controlled you. You won't be seeing me again, unfortunately. I have passed you on to another doctor for your check-up but please, please call the number on that card and make an appointment with the psychologist there. It appears you have a lot to talk through.'

The nurses undo her restraints as he slips out, a lone, hunched figure. She twitches her wrists expecting a rush of relief but it doesn't come. How did she disappoint him? She knows what she saw. The memory of that face is clearer than the first time. But why doesn't anybody believe her? Why didn't he kill her there and then? And even if it wasn't him, what did they think would happen if they put her in a room with a scalpel again?

'Zanna, I promise you: it was him.'

Zanna holds a hand in the air, silver bangles jangling down her wrist. 'Holly, please. Not now. I have enough of your lies to deal with, I can't cope with another.'

'Excuse me?'

'Seriously? Are you going to play dumb with me right now? I thought you were my best client, Holly – thoughtful, charming, funny and strong. Hell, I actually thought we were friends. You were always one of those clients who would make me go home and think, "Well, at least one of the celebs I represent tells it to me straight." You in your slouchy jumpers and cosy cooking, all homely and salt of the earth. But you are just like the rest of them. Centring your entire existence on a *fucking lie*! Performing for an audience you created.'

'Zanna, I . . .'

'Please. Just don't. You won't believe the shit storm I'm dealing with right now, let alone the impact this is going to have on my career.'

Please, no, it can't be.

Zanna throws her phone against the bed. A headline screams out the white screen WELLNESS DARLING'S EMPIRE BASED ON FAKED CANCER.

'Well,' she says. 'Is it true? Or should I say, is it all *not* true?'

'I, I don't understand.'

'Let me spell it out for you, then. An unnamed source has accused you of killing his fiancée through your irresponsible eating plan. Thanks to you, she decided against chemotherapy and followed your "healing plan" to the letter. Well, she's dead, and he smelt a rat and went digging through your medical records. Nobody knows who the hell he is but the records are legit, and they show no evidence of cancer. Ever. Every single person in the world will soon forget about your attack and remember you for faking cancer. *Cancer* of all things, Holly! Jesus Christ, my grandmother died of cancer. Tell me this isn't true.'

That's when she realises, killing her is too easy. He wants her to suffer, just like his fiancée did.

'Zanna, let me explain.' The shame twists in her stomach. Nothing could be worse than this feeling, of disappointing someone she loves once again. The image of her father's thin mouth and her mother's disappointed, downward gaze burns in her skull. Zanna is moving further and further away from Holly; she can tell by her crossed arms and furious glare. No matter what she does, this brokenness will always lie between them, a wall with jagged edges.

'What's to explain? You either had cancer, or you didn't.'

'Everything I believe in is true, the diet, the raw philosophy, whole foods. But the cancer . . . it's complicated, medically. I can explain everything.'

'Oh, you've got to be kidding me, Holly! I don't think you get how big this is! There are legitimate, authorised documents doing the rounds online that show that you never had a trace of cancer in your body. "No evidence of disease." My phone is ringing off the hook. Your sponsors want to pull out of supporting you, and your publisher has released an announcement saying that it will recall your book until the matter is cleared up. But it's not going to *clear up*, is it?'

That day when she left home for good, her mother hugging her stiffly, her father so angry he couldn't even talk, Holly thought she had seen the worst. Anxiety, fear and shame have been her loyal companions, following her from Exeter to London, circling her in the shadows as she drugged herself to sleep. It seemed a worthwhile price to pay for her fame, her success. Now, an unfamiliar emotion prickled at the edges of her consciousness: regret. What carefree life could she have lived if she had never uttered the word cancer?

'Please let me just explain to you, Zanna,' she begs. 'You'll understand I promise.' What she means to say is 'don't leave me, please love me'. She's never seen Zanna cry – her expressions range across a wide spectrum, from bemused to bitchy – but now she seems close. She ruffles her dirty hair and gathers her things.

'Listen, Holly, I've always loved you, OK? But I just need some time to figure out how to get my head around all this. In the space of twelve hours you have had a psychotic episode, assaulted your doctors, and been revealed as a fraud. There's a hashtag doing the rounds of people waiting for you to wake up and react to your allegations.'

'What?'

'Yep, #whenHollywakesup is trending in the UK.'

'Fuck. Zanna, please stay. I don't know what to do!'

'I can't do it, babe, not tonight. I need to go home, sob quietly with a tub of ice cream and watch the Kardashians for a while. At least the Kardashians never lie. But until I decide what I'm going to do with you, follow my advice: don't touch your fucking phone, don't read anything, and whatever you do, don't share any comments with anyone. Until this situation calms down, you need to behave as if you don't exist. You understand?'

She whirls out the doorway in a fury of stale perfume. Thanks to Zanna, Chanel No.5 always smelt like promise; it was synonymous with her growing success and their blossoming friendship. Now, mixed with the acrid stench of sweat, it's taken on an added note of fear.

Holly's fingers graze her bandages. Twice he has touched her, violated her. Did his hands weave her new stitches or wrap the bandages tightly around her face? He could have got rid of her there and then, and put both of them out of their misery. He wants something more. A sudden violence in her wants to pull the bandages off and rip the stitches out. She's a lost cause now.

This time, Holly's private room is marked by the conspicuous absence of flowers. She quivers in her hospital bed alone, with the bare surfaces staring blankly at her as her only audience. A sound. A creak. Her body jolts into motion, jumping onto the cold floor in nothing but her backless hospital nightgown. The sound comes nearer, just voices and the wheel of the cleaning trolley. She needs contact with something out there. Against Zanna's advice, she reaches for her phone, hands shaking.

When she received her first negative comment online, it haunted her for weeks. It was so silly at the time – some follower (with her account set to private) – called her chunky and asked if she should really be advising others on a healthy lifestyle. The words taunted her late at night, just as she was trying to get to sleep. No retort she ever thought of felt good enough. She felt sullied, and nothing had the power to wash the dirt off.

She used to find comfort in the knowledge that it is impossible to live online without offending someone. Who knows why people say the things they do. That means nothing now. When thousands of angry comments mention your name, the shame bubbles under your skin. It's not about them anymore, it's about what is wrong with her.

The comments on her Instagram are predictably vile. What sickens her more is not the content, but the volume and extent of them. The #JusticeforHolly girls are at the forefront of the army, posting emotional clips about how betrayed they feel, adding several hashtags so as many people see them as possible. Rage makes her hands shake – it's all so nauseatingly strategic. She can feel their footprints on her body as they step higher on the social media ladder. Somehow, they found pictures of the times she occasionally craved a pill that didn't taste of ground herbs. This violates her more than any insult ever could. They must have been watching her all along. That day they came to visit, they let her humiliate herself, showing off her recipes and lifestyle, when all the while they knew the truth. This must have been what she saw in Brooke's smile. This was the ammunition fuelling her smirk.

The more she checks, the more the hatred keeps coming. A catastrophe in slow motion. Death threats, rape fantasies, nobody deserves to bear the brunt of such imagined violence. Not even Holly. Some followers have taken the time to write abusive comments on photos dating back three years ago. The pictures taken in hospital that mention her cancer are particularly bad.

Don't do anything.

It's not too many, no, maybe fifty at the most where she mentions cancer? She wasn't that wrong, was she? She deletes them all in a fever. She has to get rid of the helplessness screaming beneath her skin.

Not that any of the vitriol has affected her followers. They've grown in the thousands since she last checked. Usually she would post a sweet little clip of her blowing a kiss over a green juice saying, 'Wow! 650,000 followers! Thanks for the love, you guys!' Now she feels a new rush of rage, and wishes she could film herself pouring a green juice on the ground, pulling her middle finger and saying 'Fuck you!'

Fuck you all.

Strange, but so liberating to whisper under her breath. The loving, glowing circle of followers she once had has morphed into an ugly mob overnight. The reality of it tastes bitter on her tongue: if there is one thing everybody loves more than a goddess, it is a goddess in ruins.

Chapter 31

Holly then

It starts with a lump. She feels it before bed while standing naked in front on the mirror. It is hard as muscle, unmistakable.

She lies in bed that night, breathless and restless. Reading doesn't help, nor does trying to think of something else. Her grandmother died of breast cancer, so did her aunt. At the back of her mind, she always expected one day it'd be her turn. Now, her fingers find their way to the lump until she has memorised its size and shape. She thinks, *here it is, the moment everything changes*.

The next day she skips breakfast and rushes out of the house before her mother can ask any questions. She holds her breath on two buses, wishing one of the bastards sitting down could give her their seat. She's a sick person now, she needs it. *I could faint right here*, she thinks, *then they would all be sorry*.

The bus arrives at the Royal Devon Hospital without incident. Without an appointment, waiting to speak to a GP takes hours. Hours she doesn't have, as she looks at the clock. It's already 10 a.m., the time she usually unlocks the shop. She feels the vibration in her pocket, over and over again. She ignores it. Let them wait.

Later, she arrives at the shop dead-eyed and quiet. Nothing will be the same again.

'Holly! Where the fuck were you? Do you know what trouble it was to find another key? And we already had customers outside the door waiting for the new Ivy Park merchandise!' Andrea, the store's deputy manager, fumes before her. She could have got Holly's job last year, but Holly got the break instead. Any mistake now takes a lifetime to live down.

'I had an emergency, OK?'

The other shop assistants circle, feigning disinterest. They smell a brawl and know which horse they're backing. The stronger one.

'Actually, Holly. It's not OK. Tell us where the fuck you were. We have a right to know.' Come to think of it, Andrea should have been manager. She is edgier, more in touch with what the cool girls want. Her hair is dyed pink this month – she flicks it now for maximum impact.

'Ands, I said leave it. It's private.'

She stands still.

'No.'

So she gathers them around and in their tightly spun circle shares the devastating news.

Holly has breast cancer. The very first lie. It came out so simply when they were standing there wide-eyed and speechless. It was like they wanted to hear it. Telling them that she had a lump in her breast that may or may not be cancer was more confusing, less dramatic. It didn't feel quite bad enough to earn their sympathy.

Their arms fold around her. Their tears soak into her shirt. Andrea tells her to go home, please, take some time to process all of this. For the first time, she feels like the only girl in the room.

She has to have surgery to get the lump removed. This is a small, harmless procedure that involves cutting out the mass and a biopsy to confirm there was no evidence of cancer. It seems such a feeble solution, so she tells her new friends a different story, just slightly embellished, one that makes them gasp.

'You have to have surgery and chemotherapy?'

'It seems so. They will remove what they can but it seems like this is an aggressive form of cancer that is spreading rapidly.'

Who would have thought the terminology would come so easily? Years of eating microwaveable dinners in front of *Grey's Anatomy* and *Chicago Med* have given her a looseness of tongue when it comes to medical terms. She's said it aloud before she's even had time to think about her own lie. But now it's out there, it feels so natural that she can feel the tumour spreading through her. She grabs the counter next to her to steady herself.

Excitement and fear cause the same physical reaction. A pumping heart, a quickness of breath, difficulty in concentrating. The closer time inches to the day of the operation, the more uncertain Holly is as to which emotion is taking over. All she knows is that she doesn't sleep at night, but wakes up earlier and doesn't tire of serving customers throughout the day. Everything is imbued with fresh meaning.

She glows with the warmth of the coven of concerned women who have surrounded her with their attention. Her chest pains, her sleep, her eating patterns, even her digestion, all matter. Her audience expects something of her, so she begins to perform. Her everyday actions have new gravity. When she's alone, she imagines what her actions would look like in their eyes. If she leaves her phone alone for a minute, there is a message or a call waiting. 'You OK, hun?' She is part of something now, a tribe.

She and Andrea hang out most nights. They have curry evenings, go to the pub or just cram onto foraged chairs in somebody's garden with the other girls from work. This is the secret world she was missing out on all along. Now it is presented to her on a plate as a 'distraction'. After years of obscurity, people start to see her and listen to what she has to say. Holly always felt like an alien but it turns out she's read the same books, watched the same shows and listened to the same music as all these women who once ignored her.

It's not often women receive affection so openly and readily. From nursery, love always requires an exchange, usually involving giving something up. Starve yourself to be skinny and gain admiration. Hide your real opinion and earn new friends. Give away just enough of your body to be classed as sexy, but not a slut. These are the tricks that other women innately know, but not Holly. She has only understood how to get love when she got sick. Women are loved most when they are weak.

On the day of her operation, it feels as though the whole town is holding its breath. She walks through the quiet weekday streets, her coat trailing behind her. Her overnight bag is hooked over her shoulder, containing cute Beauty and the Beast themed pyjamas, a gift from the Topshop girls. It's a clear and crisp day. Everything feels hyper real, while she feels as if she was made of air.

As she walks through the automatic double doors and up the stairs, leafing absent-mindedly through a brochure on diabetes, every motion feels iconic, like the beginning of a new life. A nurse calls her to the front desk and gives her a few forms to sign and directs her to the ward upstairs.

A few hours later, snug in her hospital gown, she turns the camera on herself, showing the operating theatre sign in the background. She pulls a thumbs up and gives a radiant smile. Click, click, post. Her Facebook and Instagram friends burn bright in support. She feels radiant beneath the glow of it.

When it is over, nobody comes to visit. This is expected, as Holly has asked for no visitors, not even her parents. She is still smarting from her father's intimation that her 'unhealthy lifestyle' triggered the tumour in some way. Even when the girls beg and plead to bring her some flowers, she remains stoic. This is traumatic enough as it is, she tells them, she would rather face the hard parts alone. What she really wants to avoid is a group of girls fussing next to her bed, hysterically shrieking the word cancer.

The second lie: Holly's tumour was always benign, the doctor calls it a fibroadenoma. So confident is he in his diagnosis that he tells Holly that, while they would test it to be certain, she can rest assured it was not malignant. There are no cancer indicators in her blood to suggest anything wrong. The removal of her tumour was a precaution, nothing more. But there is always a very slim chance still, right? The doctor could be wrong.

The next week, she returns to the hospital to get the rest of her stitches removed.

Her ribcage still aches with every step, even though the only evidence of her operation is a tiny, bandaged cut on her left breast. As the doctor pulls out the last of the stitches, he calmly confirms that his diagnosis was correct. There's no evidence of disease in the lump they removed, Holly is perfectly well.

She walks in a daze towards the elevators, towards a new life where her lie has come to an end. The sign to the Children and Young Adult Oncology Ward catches her eye. Just one look, she thinks, just to see what her alternative future would have been like. The pastel walls are soft and welcoming. Everything is quiet except for the gentle ticking of machines. Hairless, grey-skinned girls and boys float through the wards like ghosts. However, all Holly sees are the colourful bursts of greeting cards and gifts. All she hears are the soft words of comfort from nurses and family members. Jealousy pulses through her. The doctor has not only removed her tumour, he took away all of this as well.

She walks downstairs on shaking legs and sits down at the hospital café. She asks for a carrot juice and a large Greek salad. Watches the people go by. She reaches for her bandage, still excruciating to the touch. It doesn't have to be over. Not just yet. Everybody can still love her. Everybody can still hang on to her every word. She shuts her eyes and makes a decision.

Chapter 32

Tyler

The heavy brown doors of the hospital swing open and release Tyler back onto London's streets, heart pounding and mind buzzing. He did it. He really fucking did it. Potential fizzes in every direction. Bankers pace to the nearest bar; tourists squint at the tube map as they try to find the route to Covent Garden; goths crawl their way back to Camden. The city will be alive for hours yet – the question is, where to go?

Or rather, how to find a place where he doesn't see Frankie. He wanders into Paddington station, grabs his usual from Starbucks and sits on a bench to watch the passengers go by. Train stations remain the only places where he feels completely relaxed. Everybody here is between destinations, anonymous. He could be just like any of them, on his way home to his chaotic den of a family. He can picture it for a second – Frankie with her hair piled on top of her head, passing him a screaming toddler as he walks through the door so she can grab a glass of wine. These so-called stressful moments, the ones people merely survive through, write self-pitying Facebook posts about and take for granted are the ones he craves the most. They were violently snatched away from him, and he doesn't have any of it now.

He stopped at Liberty one day and left with a tasteful slip dress by Alexander Wang, short enough to show her legs and loose enough to hide her bones.

'Put it on,' he cooed, pushing the package into her hand. He wanted to see her face illuminate the way it used to, back when they were happy. All he got in return was a weary, blank stare.

'Isn't this a bit austere for my taste?' she said thanklessly.

'Frankie, it's a timeless classic.'

'For the one thing I don't have. Time.' Ah, she was always so sharp. He smelt vanilla, rose and vomit as he enfolded her weak body in his arms.

'Please, baby. Just put it on,' he said softly, kissing her perfect ears.

'I don't want to,' she whispered. The cancer had made her like this – weepy and prone to petulance. 'I'm so tired.'

He unbuttoned her silk pyjama shirt slowly. 'Don't worry, I will help you. A new frock and a sunny walk will do you a world of good. Even Holly would say so.'

She was a vision in that dress, and as they walked down the street together, his hand clutching her arm, they looked like the couple everybody wanted to be. Him, slim and solemn in a tailored suit, and her, a thin sliver of light, quivering with energy. Women leered at Frankie as she walked past, wishing they too could be that skinny. If only they had known what had happened to get her there. Don't worry, ladies, you're always one terminal illness or unspeakable tragedy away from your goal weight. He wishes that time in their lives could have lasted forever, where she was so vulnerable and pliant, resting against the heel of his hand. Needing him.

Hanging around Paddington was a mistake tonight. Every woman, man, child walking past him makes him angry. 'I fucking hate the lot of you,' he whispers.

Seeing Holly one more time and knowing that the truth was out there wasn't enough. He actually thought it would be. Just one more chance to fuck with her muddled little mind. Seeing the panic in her eyes did nothing either. The buzz from last time would not be sated. Even when he sat drinking coffee in the canteen and saw the news headlines, the buzz only dulled slightly. The world hates her now. He's got what he wanted yet he still feels hollow, like he needs just that little bit more. Would he only feel at peace if he was able to bring Frankie back? Where is the feeling of release he needs so badly?

The neon destinations on the departure board in front of him shift and shimmer. Where to now? If only his next move could appear on a board, like Twyford, or Cardiff Central. Everything is gloriously uncertain. There is only one thing to hold on to. There are always new ways to hurt.

Chapter 33
Holly

The hatred is incessant. It hits from all angles, over and over. The ferocity of people's imaginations is astounding. There are so many different ways they wish Holly would suffer and die.

It's all too much to process. Holly just can't make sense of it. She lines the facts up, one after the other. Yes, what she did could be conceived as wrong, but doesn't everyone lie in some way on social media? People leave out their Friday nights alone, the pictures where their arms look fat or their face looks rounder than they imagine. That's not reality, they say. Then they take a filtered selfie from an angle so high they may as well use a crane.

Holly wishes these outraged masses could have seen her in the beginning, shoving thirty bananas in her face a day and chewing on raw kale, all in a hysterical attempt to see some results. Foregoing bread, sugar, alcohol, meat and then nuts and grains. They weren't there the day all her efforts finally fell into place and she began to glow. Yes, there were some lies, but the passion she felt for her diet was always true.

She knows she had her reasons, but now there is a lethargy, a sickness setting in. The only thing to do is sleep.

Aided by a fistful of multi-coloured pills, Holly passes out open-mouthed and motionless until her spit blooms into a rash on her new, fragile skin. She's untroubled by dreams or nightmares, and wakes in the same position she fell asleep in. Her heavy blinds have been pulled down, so there is no knowing what time it is.

Fuck you all.

She doesn't understand this defiant new person settling into her skin. Anger darts through her veins as she reads every insult. The fear of being hated was the silent driver of every picture she took. It made her slap on extra make-up to appear pretty enough; it stopped her from saying anything too political; it made her post pictures of cuddly pets and hugs with fans. All to appear squeaky-clean and pliable. That's the problem with the Internet these days. Everyone is locked in an evolving social experiment in cooperation, a delicate dance between fitting in and being noticed. Now that there is a mob out there baying for her blood, she's beginning to realise that maybe it wasn't hatred that she feared the most. It was being forgotten.

Her new phone lights up. It's only Zanna. As in, it could only be Zanna. She hasn't even given this number to her mother, who can't seem to tell the difference between a concerned friend and a journalist.

'Well, I'm ready to hear your warped fucking sob story now.'

'Um, wow, OK. I'm free whenever.'

'I'm outside, and I've got fresh spinach and coconut water, if that's still your thing.'

'What? Uh yes, of course it is.'

Holly opens the door so there's only a small crack and Zanna slips in. The entrance to her apartment smells overwhelmingly of egg and urine. Any gifts from former sponsors and brands are conspicuously absent. A slap of blood stains the wall.

'Meat eaters took to your wall the other day. Apparently, your fake little life turned people off animal products and they've had enough of your lies.'

'That makes no sense.'

Zanna shrugs. 'Does it have to?'

They try and make small talk but it's impossible. What has Holly done besides binge-watch multiple series and sleep on various surfaces indoors? As for Zanna, she is swimming in her baggy Balmain T-shirt and a vein pulses threateningly on her pale forehead. Both are barely holding on. Seeing her so disempowered causes a physical ache in Holly. She's responsible for this, and she has no idea how to make everything go back to the way it was. Once again, regret crawls along the surface of her skin. She'd do anything to scratch it out.

'Can I offer you anything, Zan?'

'The truth please. Neat, no mixer.'

'OK, yes, the truth. But anything else?'

'Just a glass of water.'

She's making this as difficult as possible, but Holly tolerates it. Zanna has the right to a mild tantrum. At least she is here.

'Well, your face is looking . . . better . . . at least.' Better is not the word for it. Her skin is uneven and red, and her features a warped replica of how she used to look. It's as if a child drew her face and while everything is there and intact it just looks a bit haphazard, a little off. Having someone see her, bandage free, makes her want to retch.

'Thanks. I feel like shit. Anyway, you're not here for that. The story is a bit complicated.'

'Yeah, I'm struggling to see that bit. I mean, surely you just get a blood test, receive a diagnosis and then you are confirmed with having cancer.'

'Your sarcasm is making this difficult.'

'Well, your pathological lying isn't aiding things either.' They stare at each other for a moment in fury, now strangers.

'I was told that I was at risk of cancer by a traditional doctor and needed to have a tumour in my breast removed.'

'OK . . .'

A tumour she had removed and tested, only for it to be found benign.

'After this, I walked away from normal medicine and managed my cancer risk with a holistic healer called Dr Ray. Because of this, there are no formal medical records that document my struggle with cancer, but it was present in my body. It just hadn't manifested yet. Why would I make this up, Zanna?'

Dr Ray, a guy whose website she found online. They spoke once over Skype, but other than that, she never saw him in person. She never dared.

'I don't know, Holly. To be honest, I can't tell you why half my clients do the things they do. I just manage the fallout.' She takes her hands. 'Please, please, tell me that you're not leaving anything out. Please, assure me that if I was to call this – Dr Ray – he would repeat everything you have said word for word?'

He may struggle to recall who she is.

'Oh, Zanna, of course he would. This has all just been a horrible misunderstanding.'

Zanna sways back and forth, tugging her hair repeatedly. 'Fuuuuuck! Holly, this is so bad. So, so bad. Risk communication is my thing, you know. If you'd just told me I could have put a strategy together, and worked with you. I'm just so broken that you wouldn't think to trust me with this.'

It doesn't really matter if everybody hates you, disappointing your only friend is far worse. For a second, a flash of a thought enters Holly's mind, of breaking open the razor next to her bath, and pressing its cool edge against her neck. Nobody would miss her now.

'Zan, do you hate me?'

She slams both hands on the table.

'Fuck, Holly! It's not always about being liked! And I really don't know right now. I think you're naive, stupid, and batshit crazy. I think you have a loose relationship with the truth. But no, I can't hate you. I know you too well.' She sighs and slumps back on the couch. 'Besides, I actually believe your ridiculous story.'

You shouldn't.

Holly tentatively reaches over to Zanna, touches her arm.

'Oh, Zanna, thank you! I don't know what I would do without you right now!'

She pulls away, still burned. 'Yeah, yeah, whatever. Now for the important bit. Is there anything else you feel you need to share with me right now?'

'No,' she says calmly, looking straight into her eyes.

Once a liar, always a liar.

'Are you really sure about that?'

'Yes.'

'No little misunderstandings where you think you are completely innocent but everyone else thinks you're a little psychotic?'

'Definitely not.'

'OK, perfect. Now I'm heading to LA to help another client on her press tour for a week. Try to stay in the house and don't do anything else to make people hate you, OK? Literally, don't move a muscle from where you are. Lock that camera away. Don't go online. I'll have a good think on how to get you out of this mess.'

Chapter 34

Tyler

'Would you like to see our wine list, sir?'

It's the one Friday he's not on call, and Tyler is celebrating with some daytime drinking among the bloggers, suits, and embalmed housewives at Brinkley's. He sneaks into the leafy conservatory for some peace and quiet. It's not quite his style, but he's too restless to while away the day in the safety of his apartment. He's feeling on fire, like things are finally going his way.

The little girl with the dog bites has been playing on his mind the past few days. The sound of her voice whimpering in his ears while he rocked himself to sleep. Such a perfect, precious thing, yet he couldn't save her. Thinking about her parents was worse. He saw them leaving the hospital, all worn-out clothes and weathered skin. The type of people who never get a break, and now their only hope has been ripped away from them by the jaws of a dog. These are the people that deserve all the help in the world. He got their details from the girl's file and called them a few days ago to tell them he had given a statement to the police regarding the dog bites. Today, he found their Facebook group begging for donations to help them take the dog's owner to court. Tyler quietly transferred two thousand pounds into their account, a gift to them and himself.

'So, what will it be?'

'The Chateau La Lagune, please.'

'Marvellous choice. Special occasion?'

Why yes, Tyler wants to say, it is indeed a special occasion. There was a ripple of disgust when Holly left the hospital. Rumours spread like wildfire among the nurses about how she had violently thrashed on the table, how she'd even lashed out at cuddly Dr Warner, for heaven's sake. One of the kindest guys in the hospital – the closest thing they have to a saint. She bucked under his arms until his wedding ring had cut into her wrist.

She hadn't reacted well to the anaesthetic either, screaming and biting her way into consciousness as it wore off, only to swear at the nurses. Obviously, she pushed her jelly and custard off the tray, wailing for a vegan option. When the news broke that she was a fraud, the nurses got immense joy in force-feeding her several doses of dairy and gelatine. Not even Duchess Kate gave them such trouble – she had pizza on the eve of giving birth, for Christ's sake! The full monty with gluten, full fat cheese, salami and everything. Now, there's a model English woman if there ever was one.

It gave him a little frisson of excitement, watching others share his hatred for Holly. Look how *powerful* he is, turning all these people on her and turning Holly on herself. Yet, people are easily distracted and the appalling behaviour of one is replaced by the more appalling antics of another, especially in a hospital where people are being pushed to their emotional limits. Just the other day some new-moneyed brat had to be moved out of intensive care for screaming at his parents on the phone he had sneaked into intensive care and disturbing the other patients.

This can't be it. This can't be all the punishment she gets. People like Holly deserve to carry the full weight of society's hatred like a yoke cutting into their necks. We're too relaxed these days, too quick to forget, and soon, even the most despicable get to rebuild. And the people they destroyed along the way? Well, they get forgotten too.

Two young girls titter nervously at the table next to him. Their high hair and cheap, unblended make-up parody their natural loveliness. Their carefully coordinated clothes too, while acceptable at some distance, reek of that Chinese burnt-plastic smell that no fast-fashion retailer can ever quite steam off.

They're looking at him now. Being an obviously wealthy and handsome young man sitting alone with a glass of wine makes him prone to being noticed. While many women at this establishment have money in their own right, these two are the types that venture five tube stops too many to go fishing for prey. Because, while they may be faking their riches, there's an emptiness in them that makes them crave the real thing. To them, he is just a stepping stone. Even if he fucks one of them and never calls back, it still brings them that much closer. He should walk over with the candle from his table and set fire to their flammable dresses, or . . .

'Hello, ladies. Mind if I join you?'

Giggling, blushing. God, they really are too young. Two untouched salads and a bottle of sparkling water are arranged before them, like a still life celebrating restraint.

'What are you girls up to?'

The worldlier of the two replies, 'Oh, we're making a flat lay for our lifestyle blog. Our fans love them.'

'Ah! Are you two famous or something?'

'No, not yet. We've got, like, three hundred followers, but we only started last year.'

'What's your blog about?'

'Oh, it's, like, a pretty new concept. It's just about two young, ordinary girls who love fashion, beauty and having fun!'

The other pipes in, 'Yeah, we have these, like, really crazy snapchats of all our adventures. Hey, why don't you help us with this pic? Just reach in like you're about to steal a cherry tomato.'

They're so pathetic it's charming – two fame-hungry little clones desperately trying to stand out. Again, part of the toxic legacy that Holly has helped to create. This kind of toxicity is like the slow-burning, constantly polluting fumes of a radiation plant, sickening and deforming us without us even noticing it.

He should just bring it up into conversation as if it's nothing. See what the mindless public really thinks.

'So, what do you girls think of this whole Holly Evans scandal.'

'OMG! We've been glued to the whole thing. I mean, how shocking, right?' They rustle next to one another like little flowers caught in a gust of wind, more alive than ever before.

'Like, pretending you have cancer is really serious.'

He nods gravely, 'It really is. She must have hurt a lot of people.'

'Yeah, everyone is going mental! Just mental. And did you see the pictures her biggest fans put up? She wasn't even one hundred per cent into natural remedies like she claimed to be – she secretly took painkillers and antidepressants!'

Her friend gnaws on a lettuce leaf. 'Her recipes are still good, though. I mean, she clearly knows her shit. Like, I went on her detox once and I lost a stone.'

'Oh my God, babe, like you needed to lose a stone anyway!' Giggles. Blushes.

'Shut up! I was looking like a heifer! But yeah, I loved her. If she just came out with the truth and apologised, I'd still follow her, you know?'

All he sees is white. 'So it doesn't even bother you that her life was fake?'

'Well' – she bats her eyelashes – 'isn't everybody's life a little bit fake on Instagram? We all choose the things we want to put on show.'

Tyler imagines grabbing her by the pretty, pert ponytail and smashing her face into the table until blood seeps into her fat-free salad dressing. Don't they understand what makes Holly so despicable? He'll allow himself one more question, for fear of reaching down into his briefcase and doing something he regrets. Come on, Tyler, their blood isn't worth it. It isn't Holly's.

'Why do you think she got attacked?'

They look at each other, giggling. 'Should we tell him?'

'Yes, tell me!'

'We don't think anybody did it actually . . .'

'Yeah, we think that maybe she thought someone was about to expose her and she pulled a crazy PR stunt to distract everybody.'

He downs the remainder of his wine and tries not to sound too hopeful. 'That sounds pretty complex, don't you think?'

'Not really. I mean, she faked cancer. Why not fake her own attack? Maybe she has a loose screw and she just did it for attention.'

And there it is, the next move that's been bristling at the back of his mind. He'd begun the process already, carefully picking up the scalpel crusted with Holly's blood with a surgical glove, and placing it inside a compartment of the tote bag he delivered to the hospital. He liked the thought of it living so close to her, and the contortion of her face as she discovered it. It was meant to be a threat, a reminder of what they shared that night, but she probably hasn't even unpacked her bag yet. It was one of the many small gestures he has made over the past few weeks. But now, it can be part of something greater. All he needs to do is make one phone call.

'Excuse me, ladies. I just need to step to the gents for a minute.'

Before he slips out the back entrance, he finds a waiter and says with a smirk, 'Bruce, charge my bottle of wine to the two blondes in the conservatory. Oh, and get me an extra one for the road, please? See you soon.'

Chapter 35

Holly

Holly's body is becoming a problem. It rolls into white folds when she curls into a ball on her bed. Cellulite shudders on the back of her thighs as she walks from the kitchen to the couch and back again. Whatever muscle she had built during her regular boxing sessions is now hidden underneath layers of disgusting fat. Not that she's had occasion to, but she's pretty sure that she'd fail that ultimate female test of buttoning up her jeans.

What is she supposed to do? Leave the house and get mobbed on the way to boxing? Blindly walk into a confrontation with him in the street, scalpel glinting in his hand? Or should she do one of her elaborate home workouts in her cramped apartment, knowing he could slip behind her when she isn't looking, and wrap his fingers around her neck? Much as her workouts made great content for her feed, they were not the only way she got her body. No, that picture perfect arse was the result of an army of trainers and some focused fasting when she knew a swimsuit shoot was coming along.

When she first began posting on Instagram, she was rounder, and had fuller breasts and wider hips. But as her

followers grew, so did their expectations. Health on Instagram is a delicate balance of muscle and bone. Women chant
the mantra 'strong is the new skinny', a snarling reminder
that it's not enough to starve, you need to build superhuman
strength as well. Holly trained until she got a healthy amount
of 'are you anorexic?' comments on her pictures. Everybody
wants to judge, but nobody wants to take responsibility for
what that judgement destroys. At least they liked her. That's
the only thing that mattered then, that they continued to
like her.

Well, not this time. This time, she won't shrink herself to
give a tangible display of her suffering. She won't make herself smaller and smaller to be less visible. She won't become
that little girl weeping in her father's arms again. Her pain
cannot be minimised to make everyone else more comfortable. She's raw, healing, distorted from the 'acceptable'
Holly she used to be.

The world outside looks disarmingly still. Holly takes
a shuddering breath and pushes her fear aside. She won't
be trapped in this airless, lightless apartment for a second
longer, playing an empty game of house with the trinkets
from her old life. She needs the air on her skin, and she
needs comfort. And no matter how hard she used to sell
it, there is no comfort to be found in the crunch of a raw
carrot.

She wants that particular addictive scent of KFC to sink
into her hair. She wants to feel the crunch of bones under

her molars, and the tear of flesh between her teeth. Chips! How she wants hot, salty chips with ketchup drizzled over the top of them like a commoner, not in a neat little pot on the side.

Holly looks at her pink face in the mirror and holds back a sob. There is nothing to be done about it. Her skin is doing its best to patch itself together, but the strain of the effort has made her look as if she has gone through several invasive chemical peels. The muscles where he sliced through her are also forging new paths and, in so doing, have got lost. She tries to fake a laugh – hahahaha! – but, as predicted, only one side can break into a full smile. Her confused glands don't salivate when she's hungry. Instead, they send a message for sweat to pour down her neck. Right now, her neck is as wet as if she's just had a shower. Shower – something she hasn't done in days. Why would she need to when she barely moves during the day? Her long hair hangs limp down her back, its roots darkened with grease. It's OK. She'll just do it up in a bun and throw on a hoodie and tracksuit pants. This whole exercise will take less than ten minutes.

She swings the door open, bile rising in her throat. Dammit, her hands can't stop shaking, no matter how much she tries to tell herself that he is probably at the hospital, cutting somebody else open. Her eyes scan the corridor in front of her – no sign of him. There is no mob or mess waiting for her either. It's just past 10.30 a.m.

They must be at work or university. It appears that even the mob has to survive and make ends meet. The air smells of glorious, fresh rain. Rumbling clouds overhead suggest more on the way. She wraps her hoodie tighter around her chest, and coils her long hair under the collar.

Stripped of her arresting prettiness, Holly feels giddily invisible. The businessman who walks past her continues his argument on his phone. She passes a construction site, and the workers simply eat their pastries, staring into space. How limitless her world has become! No constant awareness of eyes digging into her chest, her lips, her arse. No need to look down in public for fear of meeting a pair of hungry eyes that read any contact as an invitation to slither into her space. What was she pining for during all those years of her supposed 'ugliness'? This is what true freedom feels like.

At this time of the day, the only people in KFC are bums, the elderly and the hungover grabbing a fry-up, smoothing the creases of the clothes they're still wearing from the night before. This, this right here, is what she's been missing from every juice bar and hipster café serving a sanitised brunch to the pursed-lipped, self-appointed elite.

She remembers one snowy morning, when London's lifestyle-blogging elite had gathered at a similar time in a new health food joint in Portobello. As usual, the PR had said, 'mid-morning is the only time we have where the café isn't as busy'. This was bullshit of course. A mid-morning launch was the easiest way of limiting the guest list to those influencers whose influence no longer required the additional income of a day job. PRs only ever wanted the high rollers, the ones that didn't need a leg-up in becoming known.

They all sat picking at the heaving harvest table, dragging modest plates of food to natural light where they would photograph better. Nobody really spoke at these events, apart from the ever-bubbly PR who was desperate to get everyone to stay a second longer. 'Don't forget the hashtag, ladies!'

One of the girls, a lifestyle-blogging stalwart who had just been announced as Karl Lagerfeld's muse for the latest Chanel campaign, walked in after the food had grown cold and most of it had been cleared. She pulled the waitress over with a sinister smile, and made her stuff her goodie bag with branded granola, coconut oil and Manuka honey. Things she could easily afford, but that the waitress would probably lose her job over. She spent the rest of the lunch on her phone, patronising her travel agent for booking the wrong seat ('I like business class, window seat, second row, not first. It's not fucking rocket science') on her direct flight to New York.

At the time, Holly was too busy making nice with the PR and covering the event to really acknowledge the source of her discomfort. Now she sees it plainly. People who exceed a certain status in life become despicable and bloated with entitlement. Even she had started caring a little less about the press invites that flooded her inbox, and got a little annoyed when the world didn't automatically fall in line with her magnetic field.

There is a bit of all of us in places like KFC, mired in grease and fat, scratching through dirty handbags for a few coins to buy an extra ice cream. We are all losers and deadbeats deep down, just longing for a way to distract ourselves with a little treat. Holly orders a large fried-chicken bucket, an egg roll, chips, and a strawberry milkshake. She settles in. Fuck the constant counting of calories and interrogation of ingredients in every single thing she puts in her mouth. It's time to re-tox.

How did one lie and one basic desire to share photos of her food warp into this massive, uncontrollable thing? She hates herself for being so careless, for being naive enough to think she had created something special, a tribe. *Fuck her tribe.* It was never about her after all. It was about the dream, a plastic version of her she would never quite live up to if they spent enough time in her company. Once again, she is the Holly that is never quite good enough.

Half the bucket is already gone, and she's been crying without realising it. She wipes her runny nose with her sleeve. She'd forgotten this feeling, the joyous anonymity of eating alone in a grubby corner of a fast food joint. Everything is simple and still. She hears the kiss of a camera. Looks up into the eyes of a mouse-like girl whose smile reveals a snaggle-tooth. Holly doesn't quite register what's happening at first, but there's a small voice in her head that says, 'It's always the nerds that have the darkest hearts.'

A familiar terror aches in her chest. *Wait, I'm not ready for my close-up yet. Oh God, not now.* How many shoots did she spend agonising over how to nibble perfectly into a seed cracker? How many times did she terrorise her mother over dinners back home in shooting and reshooting her smiling simply over a salad, trying to erase every imperceptible flaw? It was never enough to create recipes that healed people. She had to look pretty while doing so as well.

What for? Why do women always have to eat behind their hands? Picking at the leftovers of their children as they stack the dishes? Always erasing the traces of food (*is there something between my teeth?*), scrubbing it or exercising it away. Making sure that what goes into their mouth is clean, healthy, sanctioned, the correct diet for a good girl. Is it really so revolting to be hungry?

If the little mouse in front of her wants a show, she's going to get one. Holly grabs some chicken in her fist. 'Mmmm oh yeah, this is so fucking good. Oh, I like that.'

More phones are gathering, flickering. It's just fuel for the fire. When she's done with the chicken she moves on to the egg roll, taking a vicious bite out of it. 'Oh God, how I love me some factory-farmed egg in the morning! I can just taste the murdered new life!' Orange yolk runs down her face and congeals on her chin. She takes a greasy finger and wipes it. In her periphery, she hears giggles and gasps. 'Mmm, this is my best part.' She sucks her finger, staring provocatively into the flashing lights.

You've gone too far. This is too far.

Up, down, up and down. The pornography that is public shame. They came here for a train wreck. Well, here she is, in all her filthy glory.

Chapter 36
Tyler then

Frankie's illness introduces an urgency, a sense of recklessness. There is no time to lose when death is in the next room.

There are obstacles in his way – Frankie now lives with her parents and their relationship has its fair share of struggles – but he knows what he has to do. The hopelessness of this situation can be saved by a grand gesture. He still has the power to turn things around.

He smiles to himself as Frankie passes her days moving slowly around her home, going through the motions of cooking her raw meals and taking her handfuls of supplements. She has no idea about the surprise in store for her.

Frankie loves puzzles, so he gives her a clue each day.

The first, a tube map with a red circle around Warwick Avenue, where they first met.

The second, a bottle of gin, a reference to the gin and tonic she ordered on their first date.

The third, a dozen cupcakes from their favourite bakery in South Kensington.

And finally, nine bunches of red roses delivered to her doorstep, one for every month he had loved her, and a first edition of Patrick Süskind's *Perfume*. Inside the novel that sparked their romance he had inscribed:

Will you marry me?

Chapter 37

Holly

Holly doesn't hear the incessant ringing as she throws up the last of her feast into the toilet bowl. She wipes down her fingers and dabs some disinfectant on the stretched corners of her lips. There's something so soothing about hurting yourself and then making it all better again.

She steps into the living room bleary-eyed, and falls onto the couch, pushing aside the debris of old magazines and coffee cups. It's safe, here in her nest. The flashing phone and her bloated, cramping stomach are all signs that she's done something bad, but they feel as far away as the blurry wailing of sirens deep in the grey clench of the city outside. Shame, rage, despair, she just doesn't have the energy to summon these emotions.

She can't let the phone ring forever. If anything, the little red dots notifying her of missed calls and messages will eat her alive. After a deep breath of silence, the phone begins to wail once more.

'Hello!'

'Jesus Christ, I was beginning to think that you'd gone and offed yourself! Glad you could step away from destroying your public image to take the calls of your last supporter.' Sweet, spun-out Zanna, with a voice that while enraged, is still strangely comforting.

'Are you saying that you still support me, Zan?' Not that Holly cares at this point. Her old life is a notebook, and she is tearing out its pages and throwing them out of the window.

'That's debatable. This is bad, Holly, fucking bad.'

It's not funny. Really, it's not. But something bubbles in Holly's throat that comes out as laughter.

'Oh. My. God. Are you really laughing right now?'

'S-sorry Zanna, I know it's not funny . . . I . . . can't . . . breathe . . . sorry!'

'Shit, babe, you're worse off than I thought. Have you spoken to your family lately?'

She takes a deep breath in and out. Her father has called her once to give her a piece of his mind. She deserves all of this, he said, and while it pains him to see his little girl hurt, he can't help but think she is learning an important lesson. She is welcome back at home, he said, but his voice caught over the word welcome, making it sound less like an invitation and more like a threat.

'No.' She chuckles over the phone, trying to catch her breath. 'They hardly wanted much to do with me before and they want even less to do with me right now.'

'Friends?'

'I never really had *friends*. I had a few bloggers I met with once in a while to shoot each other's outfits. What use am I to them now?'

'So you haven't spoken to anyone since I left last week?'

'Nope.' The giggles are catching in her throat again like a cough.

Silence. A rustling in the background and muted voices. 'OK, Holly, listen to me. Holly, no, no more laughing. I'm really worried about you and I'm getting on the next flight back to London.'

'You don't have to do that!' Tears sting the corners of her eyes. No, she really does. Holly simultaneously wants to push her away and needs her to come right now.

'We're going to figure something out, OK? You've made some big mistakes but you're not a bad person, I refuse to believe that. We'll get you some help and I'll keep the mob at bay.'

*

Holly curls up in a ball, looking up as Zanna paces back and forth. She's organising Holly's life, as well as keeping the crises of her other clients' lives at a manageable simmer. She mixes honey and cinnamon into a bowl of oats and slams it on the table in front of her. She doesn't bother to mention to Zanna that honey is not technically vegan – she'd get walloped across the face. She relishes in the feeling that she has a mother, a proper mother, all over again. At least someone can think for her now, so she doesn't have to wear herself out wading through the fog of her own mind.

'All right. I've called in a favour with a top psychologist in Mayfair who has agreed to give you an assessment. If relevant, which I think it will be, he will publicly make a statement that you are mentally vulnerable right now and call for the press to leave you alone. Most importantly, he can get you admitted into a nice hospital for a little bit of rest.'

Hospital. Rest. The stench of disinfectant. The face of *him* looming over her and creeping into her bedroom at night. She holds her head in her hands and starts slapping her face.

'Whoa, whoa, hold up. If you carry on like this in public you'll be put in isolation. Listen, you don't have to go to hospital if you don't want to, but we need someone to explain your behaviour to the public.'

'I don't care about the fucking public,' she says through a mouthful of oats. And it's true. It's worse when only a few people hate you. You can picture their mouths twisting as they spew their particular poison. When the whole world seems to hate you, it's different. It's so overwhelming that the mind can't process it. It blurs into a quietly unnerving white noise. The only real impact is that you can never get to sleep.

'That's not true, Holly,' Zanna snaps. 'And if you really don't care, I'm just going to have to care for you. Now please, for the love of God, change out of that fucking hoodie. You smell like desolation and fried chicken.'

There is a banging on the door so loud that the door shakes on its hinges.

'Zan?'

'Don't worry, babe, it's probably just the cops checking in on you. Let me go and get it.'

Even with the pillow over her face, she can hear Zanna's hushed, high-pitched tones.

'What are you *doing* here? I said she wasn't fucking ready.'

'Come on, Zanna, you can't protect the girl from everything. Besides, don't you think she needs to stand up for herself a little bit, especially after her little show the other day?'

'She physically and psychologically can't right now. She is extremely vulnerable, and needs some time and some space. Can you imagine what it's like to look the way she does right now? Not to mention having everyone hating you?'

Hearing it in the whisper of someone so close to her sends a little pang down Holly's spine. It's really that bad, isn't it? She peeks her head around the corner. The intruder still hasn't left.

'Please, Zanna, just five minutes. I just need a quote and maybe a picture and then I'll leave you guys alone.'

'Can I be honest with you, Gill?'

'Always.'

'I think you're a fucking vulture. Holly has stated implicitly that she wants her privacy, yet here you are circling her apartment, swooping in for the bloodbath.'

'Well, she wasn't so concerned about her privacy when she gave her little erotic fast food performance and lost the last little shred of dignity she had left.'

It's not true. She won't let it be true. She was trying to be real, to remove the fake veneer of fame that had separated her from her family, that's all. All she wanted to do yesterday was to be honest and vulnerable, and through that vulnerability find a new way to connect. Holly throws the pillow to the ground and shouts, 'Zanna!'

'Just a second, Holly . . . Gill was just leaving.'

Her feet find their way to the ground and step over the piles of clothes and takeaway cartons.

'No, no, she can stay.'

She flicks her hair out of her face, to look straight into the wide eyes and parted red lips of the journalist.

'Holly, you know Gill is from the *Daily Mail,* right?' She says it like it's a clue, as if it's code for something, but Holly can't quite decipher it through the hum of her anger. She'll show this person who the real Holly is, and then everyone will see too and forget all the bad things that have happened.

'No, Zanna! I want her to stay. Come in, come in and I will make you some of my signature turmeric tea. I probably have some delicious black bean brownies in the fridge as well.'

She doesn't recognise the voice coming out of her mouth, and Zanna is looking at her like she's insane, but something about this feels important. Maybe if she just acts how she used to, and explains herself nicely, she can make this all go away. She thought she didn't want approval, but now that it is standing on her doorstep, she wants to hold on to it and squeeze it for all its worth.

'Thank you, darling,' says Gill, stepping into the apartment before she can change her mind. She can't help looking at Holly's face, her pretty little mouth hanging open. Holly winces. Sometimes, if she doesn't talk and use her slack muscles for a while, she forgets that her old face is gone. It takes a stranger to make her remember.

Her nerves make time elastic, shrinking it in proportion to her anxiety. She fills the silence however she can. Because of this, the interview is an awkward staccato of Holly making broad, positive statements. They don't say much, but she can imagine them as headlines:

'I still believe in the Internet.'

'I will rise from my shame.'

'Everything I did, I did for my followers.'

Gill, the nice *Daily Mail* journalist, dutifully writes everything down while chewing on an old, dry brownie. She doesn't question a thing, she only smiles and nods. Zanna, on the other hand, dramatically holds her head in her hands for the duration of the interview. She only removes them when Gill excuses herself to go to the bathroom.

'Are you done now?' Her whisper is more like a shriek.

'What do you mean?'

'Your actions make no sense, Holly. First you don't care about what anybody thinks of you, then you morph into a health-crazed Stepford Wife when a journalist from the *Daily Mail* shows up and start spouting absurd inspirational quotes!'

'I'm doing my best here, Zanna! I'm *helping!*'

'Well, tell me this. Does your "best" include keeping your room and bathroom tidy? Because I can bet that little snake is snooping around in there right now.'

A sinking feeling. Nothing is at its best. Since *the thing* happened, she has only done the bare minimum.

'Well, I wouldn't say I technically *made* the bed but there isn't too much lying around.'

Zanna looks deeply uncomfortable.

'Nothing incriminating? Like chocolates under the pillows or whole roast chickens under the bed? Condoms?'

'Who do you think I am?'

'It's not about who you are. It's about what *she* is. Out of all the reporters you could have magically decided to grant an interview, she's the worst.'

Holly turns away and buries her head into the *Harper's Bazaar* she's been rereading for the past few weeks. Doesn't she understand how infuriating it feels to be policed all the time? Every move she makes these days is subject to a committee. Nobody is on her side anymore.

'Hey, Holly, is this yours?' Gill has returned, looking worryingly smug.

She's holding up the tote bag *he* delivered to her in hospital. Holly notices that Zanna's eyes also travel to her black, chipped fingernails. There is something sinister about this journalist's lack of attention to personal grooming. In this industry, it counts as a statement, or even a warning.

'Yes, it is—'

What's in there? Some remnants of her codeine stash? A sugar-filled, egg-laden brownie? Holly tries to think what she has done this time, but it is all too muddled now. Nothing comes.

Zanna jumps out her seat. 'Wait, Gill . . . why do you have her bag in your hand? Did you somehow get lost in Holly's room on the way to the bathroom?'

'If she' – the cracked black talon points to Holly – 'has nothing to hide, then there shouldn't be a problem. Journalists always snoop, that's what we do. Just like liars. Always. Lie.'

She watches helplessly, in slow motion, as Gill digs into the bag and pulls out a scalpel. Not just any scalpel, but *the scalpel* that sliced her face, covered in brown, dried blood.

Chapter 38

By Gill Selbourne for the Daily Mail

Blogger Holly Evans orchestrated her own vicious attack. This follows the recent discovery that she faked the cancer that was the foundation of her wellness empire.

Earlier this month, the blogger ran into a local fast food restaurant in London, with long, bleeding gashes down her cheeks. She claimed that the attacker was a young man in his early thirties who had a vendetta against her.

However, during an exclusive interview with the fallen wellness celebrity at her London home, the weapon that sliced her face was discovered lying hidden in a kit bag, still covered in her blood. The weapon, a small scalpel, will be submitted to the police for investigation. If it can be proven that it is Holly's blood and fingerprints on the scalpel, she stands a chance of facing charges for wasting police time. This is in addition to the charges of fraud that may be held against her by the multiple sponsors she conned into financially supporting her fraudulent story.

On confrontation, Holly seemed genuinely shocked, which adds further fuel to the fire that she is mentally unstable. Just three days ago, shocking footage emerged of her eating fried chicken in an offensively sexual manner.

There are numerous signs that she is starting to fray around the edges. After the embarrassing video clip went viral, many noted that she has gained a significant amount of weight, and that her skin and hair were in shocking condition. She was dressed sloppily and is now blatantly going against her previously militant vegan beliefs. However, even those have been called into question, when previous fans who were calling for #JusticeforHolly discovered a series of incriminating pictures of her buying into the traditional medicine she was supposed to have shunned.

Across the country, cancer survivors, assault victims and former followers are speaking out against the now tarnished Internet star. In this world of fake news, fraudulent behaviour is more than manipulative, it is criminal. What do you think? Let us know what should happen to Holly in the comments page.

Chapter 39
Holly

There is nothing like waking up from the thick muddle of a codeine sleep. Holly took an extra dose last night to exterminate the last of any demons that may plague her on the path to passing out. Her empty bank balance. Her attacker's looming presence. The possibility of arrest. The shame clawing at her from all sides, that sharp-toothed, unrelenting shame. She wakes up with a fresh rash from where spit has pooled against her face, and a throat that is gloriously raw. It takes a few minutes for all the elements of her life to take shape through her codeine cloud. In those minutes she is happy, cosy and warm. Then, one by one, she remembers her face, the scandal, the scalpel.

She hasn't behaved very well lately. She may have been behaving badly for a while. Her sanity quivers in her precarious grasp. Yet for everything she's done wrong, she did not do anything to herself with that scalpel that night. She could never forget his winning smile, and the way they walked hand in hand through the city. How *real* that connection felt, how promising. She can't even mourn the disappointment of how things turned out, because her choices over the past few years have led her right here. She should have known that secrets make you sick, that they have a way of coming back to haunt you.

She rolls over into a position that helps her forget the uncomfortable reality of her body. There is one thought that still plagues her more than the others – what if she'd just said no to him that evening? As her father used to say, 'You don't have to lap up every scrap of affection from strangers like a dog, Holly. It's embarrassing.'

What would she be doing this morning? Not this, not this. She'd be replying to her Instagram comments with 'xoxoxo' and 'thanks so much for your support', not avoiding a spiteful slew of insults. She'd still be so thin, so fucking thin, with an arse that could fit in one hand. Sure, none of it meant anything, but that doesn't change the fact that it was all so wonderful.

So why didn't she say no? She'd never had a problem fobbing off needy strangers. It was those eyes that did it, so bright and earnest. It was something else as well, something deeper. She didn't say no because he was gorgeous and she wanted him to see her as relaxed and up for a good time. Saying no would have cast her as frigid, cold and unfriendly. Saying no would have shone a beam of light on the uncomfortable, pervasive reality that men are not always the protectors they are cracked up to be.

Her sheets are so dirty that they feel clammy against her skin. Buttery popcorn husks cling to the small of her back

– a shameful reminder of yesterday's late-night snacking. Despair is more than a feeling. Its most acute expression is found in cold tangible objects. A lifeless phone that doesn't need to be charged because nobody calls her anymore. The landing page for her online banking, which reflects two credit cards over the limit, and a whopping £23.50 in savings. Most worryingly, a bill from her apartment building, with a note requesting in clipped tones that she begins to pay the rent on her complimentary apartment. Before, it had been a perk from one of the retail giants as she was the spokeswoman for their insipid, nutritionally poor, 'health' range, but it appears that this support, like all the others, has now been withdrawn.

She walks into the lounge and regards the lifeless lump before her. 'I'm going to be on the street soon, Zanna, you may as well step out the door right now and count your losses.'

Zanna grunts and rolls up from her makeshift bed on the sofa. They had spent the whole of the night before panicking about Gill's sordid discovery. After three bottles of wine between them and a lot of angst and self-doubt from Zanna, they agreed that Gill must have planted it. The blood can't have been hers. It was obviously a set-up, engineered to sell papers and boost website traffic. Luckily for Holly, although the blood was identified as hers, the police were unable to lift any fingerprints off the scalpel, so while they are regarding her as suspicious, the weapon has been written off as circumstantial evidence.

Still, she is haunted by the idea that he watched her in the hospital while she was sleeping, before slipping the bag with the incriminating item next to her bed. She sensed his presence constantly over that time, shifting in the shadows, whispering in her drug-addled nightmares and crackling beneath her bedcovers. The idea of him so close to her, smirking as he laid down the next step in his plan is too terrifying to form into a viable thought. Or, darker still, the unmentioned possibility that Holly is losing her mind, that she did this to herself.

You always did have such a strong mind.

How did Zanna, this gorgeous, mysterious creature, become Holly's only friend? She's a lost cause publicity-wise, so she should have been the first to disappear. Yet here she is, gingerly pushing carob cereal around a bowl of almond milk, holding Holly's hand as she drowns.

'Holly, stop looking at me with your face all twisted like that. It's creeping me out.'

'My face isn't twisted. The scars just make it look like that.' She's joking, but inside she's screaming.

A hollow laugh, at least. 'Fuck you and your gallows humour. You're playing the "I've been mauled" card right now and you know it.'

'Well, it's the only card I've got left.' Out of every catas-trophe that has slammed into her the past few weeks, the reality of her face stings the most. Ugly to others, yet hide-ous to herself. She thought she would be better by now and not still battling to form a recognisable facial expression.

The frustration of it feels like an electric current pulsing beneath her skin.

'Correction: the only card you have with me. Gill's story is turning the hearts and minds of the world as we speak. The handful of people that didn't despise you, now do for sure. You're gluten-free toast.'

They laugh until they're both doubled over, battling to breathe. Holly's hangover, combined with the remainder of her codeine, is beginning to feel like an altered state of consciousness.

'Seriously, Zanna, why do you stick with me? I attract nothing but trouble at the moment.'

'That's the attraction, right there. Trouble, especially public trouble, is what I live for. Whenever there is a public scandal, I don't join the ranks of the outraged online or around the dinner table. I sit watching all the interviews, wishing I could be in the room with their crisis communication team deciding what to do.'

'Have you gone on my Instagram lately? Have you seen the news? There is nothing more we can do. It's all over.'

She looks over at Holly, bleary-eyed, beautiful. 'Baby, I'm the motherfucking queen of lost causes.'

'Then what do we do next?'

'I'll be straight with you, Holly, I was wondering that too. Luckily, I found something interesting while sorting through your hate mail.'

'Human faeces?'

'No, that was last week. This is far more interesting.'

She places a thick red envelope on the table. It is covered in stamps, including a sticker that says COURIERED BY HAND. On the front, in an elegant script, it says, 'For the Urgent Attention of Holly Evans.'

Holly pulls out the sheet of paper, which has a luxurious, velvety texture.

'Zanna, do you trust this?'

'Just read it.'

Dear Holly,

We have been so sorry to read of the recent attacks on you in the media. No matter which of these accusations are true and which aren't, we believe that nobody deserves to bear the brunt of a public shaming.

We are all human beings, prone to faults, petty lies and regrettable mistakes. Anyone who forgets this has forgotten their own flaws, as well as the compassion and empathy required to experience all the joy and sorrow of humanity.

We can't help you weather the storm. In fact, we know that the only thing that will aid it in dying down is time itself. We can, however, provide a safe haven, a place where you will live in harmony among people from all over the world who have experienced the serious consequences of online shaming.

We have created a beautiful retreat in a secret location, where our residents enjoy their daily lives freed from the constraints of their old identities. You can expect modest yet comfortable accommodation surrounded by verdant, beautiful scenery. You can take part in one of our wide range of activities, including hiking, climbing, canoeing and even studying an online course through correspondence. Our qualified psychologist is available to work through the impact of your trauma with you. Given your background, you will also be interested to know that we provide three humble meals a day consisting of fresh fruits and vegetables, grains, and sometimes fish. We are, however, happy to tailor our menu based on your dietary restrictions.

You are welcome to stay with us for as long as you need. And, if you do decide to take us up on our offer, we will arrange for you to be transported discreetly to our premises free of charge.

This may seem too good to be true, but trust in the knowledge that we have our reasons for providing aid to the publicly shamed. It is our utmost pleasure to use our resources to help you in some way. This is, indeed, our greatest reward.

If you would like to discuss anything, please find our contact details below. We will answer the phone as much as our mobile phone reception allows.

We hope to see you soon!

Yours in dignity,

The Scarlet Retreat

Zanna grins at her manically. 'Well?'

'It sounds like a cult to me. Are you sure it's not a bunch of disgruntled vegans who have hatched an elaborate plot to sacrifice me at the stake?'

'It isn't.' Her tone is firm, confident. There is something she isn't telling her.

'How do you know for sure?'

She looks away from Holly. 'I called them this morning while you were still sleeping. They are completely legit.'

Silence. Holly doesn't buy it.

'OK, OK. I know the owner from her past life.'

'You mean a past scandal?'

'The Queen of Lost Causes never reveals her secrets.' She laughs.

Holly wonders what Zanna feels about this particular lost cause, deep down and behind closed doors. Neediness closes in on her. She feels as if she is being pawned off. Why does *she* have to go away when the people outside are the ones threatening her, attacking her, and even planting evidence on her? It doesn't seem fair.

'It sounds a bit too idyllic. I mean, what if this is some elaborate ruse that the press have constructed to humiliate me? Like, "Survivor: Shamed Edition"?'

'No. Although that sounds like a wonderful publicity opportunity that I'm putting in my pocket for a rainy day.'

The note lies on the table, furiously red. It is at once offensive and compelling. She is one of the shamed now, part of the ousted who have been reduced to their sins.

Holly wants to believe the best – really, she does – but trusting first appearances has got her nowhere. It feels like she is breathing through a blocked straw, suffocating.

But what if it's real? Maybe a few weeks in a secret location is just what she needs. Maybe she needs some time to gather her thoughts without the constant background noise, the unrelenting throat-clenching terror that he might be around the corner, waiting for her.

'Zan – I need to sit down for a second. I can't breathe.'

She misses simpler times. When she used to write long stories about the latest turn in her illness or the latest superfood she was obsessed with. There, there, Holly, everyone would say, everything is going to be OK. She was the hero, propped up by pillows, with everyone online cheering her on.

'Holly,' Zanna says firmly. 'This is the best thing that's happened to you in weeks.'

'Is it,' though? An invite from what sounds like a leper colony? 'Cause that's what everybody wants right? To keep the shamed locked away so that it's not catching!'

Her speech is coming out as a growl. Froth builds around the corners of her mouth, until it trickles down her cheeks. For once, Zanna steps back. Panic flashes across her dark brown eyes. She puts on her calm voice, usually only reserved for Oxfam campaigners and mental people lurching out of the bus towards her.

'OK, Holly, do you trust me?'

'Yes,' she says, voice shaking.

'Do you agree that a lot of shit has happened in the past few weeks and maybe you're not in the best place for making decisions right now?'

'I guess . . .'

Zanna spins the envelope on the table. Holly stares into its ruby blur.

'Here are your options. If you stay here, you are going to be subjected to more questioning by the police and more bullying from your haters. You will need to be chaperoned everywhere you go. No matter what you do, or where you go, you will carry the stench of what has happened to you. As for your attacker . . .' she says carefully. 'He is still out there trying to get into your head. Even if you think you can cope with the fallout of what's happened, you are still not safe. Not yet.'

'So what do I do?'

'You let me make this call. Pack your bags and go. I'll be here at home on the frontline, making sure they don't destroy your name completely. I'll say you've checked into a wellness centre. And obviously I'll be a call away if you hate it.'

'What about Tofu?' She leans over and strokes her small, purring body. Cats are smart, and she has become increasingly skittish as Holly's life has unravelled. What will she do if Holly, her only flimsy constant, disappears? Will she run away? A burning sickness thrashes in her stomach. She's a no-good fraud, who lets both humans and animals down.

'I'll take care of her, don't you worry.'

Fresh tears sting Holly's cheeks. Before she tries to look after anything else, maybe it's time to start looking after herself.

'OK, fine, let's do it.'

A few mumbled phone calls later and Holly is booked on a train leaving from Euston. She lies dead-eyed on the bed while Zanna packs her clothes. In less than half an hour, she has a small suitcase with modest contents that include a pair of hiking boots, a raincoat, two pairs of jeans, three jumpers and a surprising number of socks.

It is so far from her old life, it's laughable.

'Zanna! That's the most practical, least fabulous selection I've seen you make in our whole time together!'

'Honey, there are some things fabulous can't fix.'

They hold each other tight. In that moment, Holly finds it hard to believe that there is no meaning behind the rocky course her life has taken. After all, it led her to her first true friend. Zanna pulls out the oldest clothes she has from the back of the closet: frayed grey tracksuit pants, a stained beige fleece top, old trainers and a ribbed navy beanie.

'There you have it. Your travelling attire.'

'No glossy wigs or Jacqui Kennedy sunglasses for me, then? Not even a spray of perfume?' Although awkward at the time, Holly misses the specialness of her first exit from hospital after the attack. Now it is a mere memory, reframed as an embarrassing mistake never to be repeated.

'Nope, that would be a male-friendly kind of mystery. To truly be ignored, all a woman needs to do is be ugly.'

Oh, she knows that all too well. 'And what about other women?'

'All you need to be ignored by other women is to be fat and/or lacking in style. This ensemble gives you both.' It's the first time in years that she has tried to be anything other than attractive. Every item of clothing she has chosen, every beauty product she has smudged on her skin, has always been in an effort to look sexier, more enviable.

Holly's not ready to go. It feels too much like a confession that she's not yet ready to make. It's also embarrassing to admit that it's been a long time since she travelled alone. When her fame hit, her trips were cushioned by well-meaning, over-enthusiastic PR chaperones, or Zanna herself.

Zanna looks her up and down, proud of her work. 'Listen, you're going to do great. All you need to do is sit on the train for a few hours and your chaperone will meet you at your destination.'

A panic seizes over her.

'Have you told them I'm vegan?'

She looks desperately disappointed. 'Does it matter anymore? I didn't mention it. The old Holly, with the crazy diet and complicated lifestyle, is dead and buried. If you want to keep parts of her, I won't stop you, but I will always remind you that it's not necessary. Just be whoever you want to be. Maybe it's time you figure out who that really is.' She looks down at her phone. 'Oh, your taxi is arriving outside. Come, let me help you take your things around the back.'

The most important moments in life happen too quickly. You wait endless hours for your world to shift yet when it does it all becomes an imperceptible blur. The taxi driver quietly deposits her outside Euston station. She rushes to the train without anybody so much as turning to look at her. Every person in her periphery feels like a threat. She is petrified that if she stops moving for one minute, someone will recognise her. And do what? Tweet a picture of her looking fat? Snapchat her putting away another distasteful meal? Report her? There is an undercurrent, a knowledge churning in her stomach that the police would not approve of her travel plans.

The blurry haste of the day has faded into an excruciating present. Her layers of clothing chafe against her dry skin. Sweat gathers between her breasts and in the persistent rubbing together of her thighs. In her seat, flipping through the pages of the latest *InStyle* magazine, the aching clarity of each moment burns into her bones. By the time the train lurches into motion, she feels brittle and empty, a twitching carcass left for dead that nobody can bear to get too close to.

Chapter 40
Holly

'This train is now approaching Windermere.'

The passengers shuffle towards the train door, adjusting their hats and scarves. There is a biting chill in the air that scrapes Holly's bones down to the marrow. She rubs Vaseline on her aching face. Even as the tide of passengers rushes from the platform towards the exit, there is a sense of calm about the place. It feels timeless, magical, as if her twenty-first-century problems may not have reached here yet.

Her suitcase catches on the ground as she drags it towards the exit. She unfolds the instructions Zanna has written down for her. A woman named Ayo will be waiting outside, and together they will take a cab to her new home for the next few weeks, a sanctuary at the heart of the Lake District. Could Jack have had something to do with this? He seems to have orchestrated every traumatic event in her life so far. But she trusts Zanna – she has to – and Zanna thinks this will be good for her.

She quickens her pace, hoping her shaking legs will hold out a few more steps. She's on edge. Every situation has the potential to disintegrate into a scene. After the KFC incident, she no longer trusts herself in public.

Hooting, loud voices close in on her as she tries to pull her bag up the staircase. She can smell the alcohol on their breath before she turns around to face them.

'Need some help there, love?'

Four men wearing matching Superman suits and a fifth shivering in a pink leotard and ballet tutu grin at her blankly. Holly takes a step back. She has always feared the manic sexuality that festers among men in packs. It's all smiles and unfunny jokes until it turns poisonous, or even deadly. Their mouths gape open and shut like fish as they battle to say something smart about her face.

'I'm fine. Thank you very much.'

'Johnny, don't listen to her. Take her bag up the stairs, lad! Will prepare you for life with the missus!'

The groom, a bloated pink figure with skin the same colour as his costume clumsily drags her suitcase towards the station's exit. Holly tries to snatch it back before they have more time to examine her. Too late, he is already clutching her arm with his chubby fingers.

'Excuse me? Yeah, you! Excuse me, love?'

There's something in his eyes. He knows. It's OK. Stay calm. Be polite. She looks over him, eyes searching for someone who matches Ayo's grainy photograph.

'Yes?'

'Don't I know you from somewhere?'

'No . . .'

Please God, no.

'No, I do, I do. That's it! I saw your face on the telly just last week!'

He's gesturing excitedly now, trying to call one of his buddies. If one of them is smart enough to take out their phone it's all over. The prison that she is so desperately trying to escape will root its bars around her once again. Only the view outside will be different. Desperation consumes her life like a fever and she finally appreciates the genius of Zanna's plan. She's not just going along with this anymore. She *wants* it, more than anything. She's not ready to go back home just yet.

His friends reluctantly tear themselves away from a group of pretty girls and Holly frantically tries to find her phone. There's a number that she's just remembered Zanna gave her to call when she got there.

'Lads, look! The girl with the bag – she's somebody famous,' shouts the lad. A scream threatens to escape Holly's throat. No, no, no. A strong hand grabs her hand and pulls her roughly.

'That's enough of that,' a powerful, lightly accented voice bellows. 'Why don't we all leave this young lady alone.'

Holly looks into the brown eyes of a dreadlocked woman. Her magnificent hair is contrasted by a sensible navy puffer jacket and sturdy shoes. She ushers Holly and her bags into a waiting cab.

'Good grief! Sorry about the rough welcome, darling. Hello there, I'm Ayo. Zanna has told me all about you.'

Just the uttering of Zanna's name makes Holly relax a little. She's brought a little bit of home with her after all.

Ayo smells of essential oils and her hair carries a smokiness that reminds her of the incense her teacher burns in the yoga studio. She's all soft edges and big breasts, the type of woman who is good to hug. There is another layer to her; Holly feels it shifting between her gestures. The person she was before and the person she is now.

The road curves around a breathtaking, vast body of water. A flock of geese break the golden surface as they swim, leaving trails of deep blue. It's sunset, or the 'magic hour' as she used to call it during her Instagram days. Nothing about the magic hour was instant – she used to spend hours searching for just the right spot for her pictures, and just the right light. How strange it would feel to just take a picture of this splendour with no forethought! Does a sunset even matter if its liquid gold is not captured and stored inside her phone?

'Go on, you can take a picture if you like.' Ayo smiles.

'Thanks. I've never been to the Lake District before.' Despite her fears, this feels special. For once, she is on a trip where she doesn't have to perform. She can simply enjoy the fresh scenery and watch a new place unfold.

'Seeing it for the first time is always magical. Sometimes I wish I could relive that moment whenever I start to take this place for granted.'

'Where were you before?' says Holly.

'Well, I'm originally from Lagos, Nigeria, but I studied in London and have lived all over the place. That's why my accent is such a mixed bag.'

The lake gives way to rich, emerald-green plains. There is so much space here! Already Holly feels like her thoughts have room to move. Everything feels far away – the crowd baying for her blood, a possible arrest, the attacker hot on her heels. She sends the picture of the sunset to Zanna, with the simple note, 'Thank you for always knowing what I need. I'm going to do my best for you.'

The sky darkens as they climb deeper into the mountains. The journey is long, but Ayo doesn't say much. There isn't anything awkward about it. Rather, her presence feels like a soothing balm, an unsaid confirmation that everything is in control. She imagines with a smile how she and Zanna must have been fast friends. They both have that added depth that most people do without.

The vehicle comes to a sudden stop.

'Sorry, Holly, we've got a short walk now.'

They push through the shrubbery and follow a small, cobbled pathway. The bushes soon clear to reveal a tall stone cottage covered in moss. Ferns drift in the evening breeze and bright pink heather lines the cottage's entrance. Everything is a green, connected, thriving mess. It's how Holly always imagined the secret garden to be in her childhood dreams.

The inside of the cottage is warm and alive with the sound of music and voices from another room. Ayo leads Holly upstairs, to a small bedroom at the end of a long passageway.

'I thought I'd give you the room with the most privacy for the moment. You are the newest here and you're going to want your space while you get used to things.'

'Thank you, Ayo.'

'No problem at all. I've also had a bowl of homemade vegetable soup left in your room – it should still be warm. I figured you're probably too tired tonight to eat with the rest of the guests. They can also get a bit rowdy! Oh, and let's get the housekeeping stuff out of the way. There is obviously no Wi-Fi, and you're discouraged from going to the Internet café in town, at least for the first few weeks anyway. Not that this is possible – all the Internet cafés are down the hill around Lake Windermere, which you'd need a car to reach.'

The panic in Holly's eyes is clearly apparent, as Ayo adds, 'And trust me, it's heaving with tourists over there, which is the exact opposite of what you need right now. Anyway, where was I? Just turn on the shower at full blast and the hot water will eventually come, and breakfast is at 8 a.m. sharp. You'll hear me ringing the bell, though.'

'Wow. I, um, don't know what to say.'

Ayo twirls her dreads and shakes her head softly. 'Don't say anything, love. Just go to bed. We'll have plenty of time to chat and get to know each other tomorrow.'

She gives Holly's shoulder a gentle squeeze and shuts the door. The sound of laughter erupts from nearby. Holly finishes the bowl of soup in a few minutes – she hadn't realised how hungry she was. She's no longer sure what her diet is, or what she likes anymore, but she knows she likes this. The shape of Ayo's nose and mouth plays beneath her closed eyelids. Her mind strains to piece them together, like the random notes of a song she once loved. The realisation is vague, but assuring. Ayo is no stranger. Holly has seen her many times before. The question is, where?

Chapter 41

Holly

He will know by now that she is gone. She felt his cold eyes watching her as she moved in and out of her flat. He will be searching, planning. She should have told the police before she left, while she still had a chance. But what would she have said? They wouldn't believe her now. Nobody would, not even her biggest fans. She shudders as she imagines the self-congratulatory expressions of the investigation team. If she told them the whole reason she was attacked in the first place, they would say what everyone is thinking, that she had asked for it. In her darkest moments, she thinks they are right. A familiar taunt fizzes through her mind, just as it did when she was fifteen and holding a pack of frozen peas against her swelling eye.

Nobody gets hurt without a reason.

But none of this has to concern her today. Birds riot and shake the trees outside. Holly wakes up without a codeine hangover for the first time in weeks. Everything feels a bit clearer, and a bit more painful. She has to try to get her head right and focus on the good things. She's nestled in the majestic Lake District and free from the confines of her apartment. Holly is walking a fine tightrope of sanity – no matter what, she can't look down at the chaos and outrage below her.

As Ayo promised, the bell resounds loudly above the birdsong. Holly can hear the creaking of footsteps. Talking. Does she even know how to *be* with people anymore? The only person she's seen for the past few weeks has been Zanna, and she's sure Zanna would agree that she hasn't exactly been value-adding company.

'Hey, Holly! Get here quickly before Tara eats all the toast again!' A slim, dark-haired girl no older than twenty-one holds her hands up, laughing. She looks strangely familiar. Holly scans the smiling faces at the table. This feeling of familiarity is not limited to Tara, it applies to all of them. Every single person here is a public figure, or has been.

Holly's used to making small talk with celebrities and smiling for photo opportunities at events, but this feels different. Free of make-up and tailored clothing, they all seem like they are at a summer camp. Still, she unconsciously touches her face, aware of her diminished place among the beautiful.

On the table in front of them is a colourful spread of chopped strawberries, raspberries, apples and bananas. At its centre is a loaf of fresh bread, with dollops of melted butter and marmalade. Holly's stomach cramps in response. The smell is too good to bear.

'Come sit here, Holly. Here's some fruit salad, some yoghurt and some toast. Oh, and try the blueberry jam. It's a worthwhile favourite.'

'Oh, um, I can't. Anything with gluten is like poison for my condition.'

The table goes uncomfortably quiet. Ayo says in a level voice, 'It may be over in London, but everything is a little bit softer in this mountain air. Maybe we can relax your rules a little for the first few weeks here, just to see how it feels.'

Dammit, she hasn't even spent five minutes in the company of these people and she's already established herself as the complicated city girl with a list of special requirements. She's not used to meeting new people under this relentless cloud of darkness. She used to be described as 'a breath of fresh air' or 'a ray of sunlight'. When she walked into the room, everyone's faces would turn towards her like a field of sunflowers. It wasn't just her good looks, however; it was that something extra, that intangible magic that made her Instagram light up and spread like wildfire. People drew close to her so that they could claim some of that magic for their own. If she were asked to pick whether to get her beauty or her magic back, she'd pick the magic. Every single time.

She expects them to look away from her, anywhere but her precariously healing face. Instead, all their eyes remain intently locked on hers. Ayo clears her throat, 'Let me introduce you to the crew. We'll get to know each other a bit better after breakfast, but you can get to know their names for now.' She gestures to the dark-haired beauty with big brown eyes peeking through a jagged fringe, 'This is Tara, who joined us from the United States and has been here almost as long as I have, but you'll hear more about that later. Then we have Verushka, a CNN journalist originally from South Africa. Finally, we have Alan, who also hails from London.'

They all hold out their hands in greeting, as if it's so natural to just reach across a table and touch another human being. Holly has been so isolated from people for so long that she realises how strange this is. How blindly trusting we are of each other. Although she could not feel more uncomfortable, something about this feels reassuring. She resolves to fake being normal until it happens on its own.

Maybe it's the change in altitude, but the food tastes different here. Every piece of fruit bursts with flavour against her tongue. The hot bread swells and fills the aching places. How freeing it feels to relieve food of its responsibility to transform and perform, and just let it soothe her. She panics a little as she swallows the last of her second slice of toast, and gulps down a cup of tea but she can't lose it now, not here. This is all she's got. She can't overthink it.

Holly follows the rest of the retreat guests down the stairs and into the living room. They walk in clear alliances that don't include her. Verushka and Tara giggle over a shared joke, while Alan and Ayo speak in serious, hushed tones. Two pairs with no space for her.

The words of her father ring in her ears. *What have you got that could possibly make others like you? Nothing.*

A fire crackles softly in the corner and a few chairs have been arranged in a circle. There is a glass of water at the centre of the room, as well as some biscuits and a box of tissues. Holly crosses her arms defensively. Places like this expect tears, sharing and long, needy hugs, all things she is not sure she's ready to give just yet. She takes a deep breath and thinks of how shattered Zanna looked the day she found out about the lie. She has to make an effort, if only for her sake.

Everyone else sits comfortably, excitedly even. Tara takes out a notebook and Alan turns off his phone. Ayo clears her throat.

'OK, now, before we open, I'm going to explain some things for the benefit of Holly and maybe as a reminder for the rest of you here. We open the meeting every time by going around the circle and saying our name, our real name, and a word that summarises what shamed us. So, I would say, "Ayo. Sex" for example. Now usually a word immediately comes to mind when you think about what you were shamed for, but that word can change. Your shame can mean many things at once or feel like different things every day. Contrary to what your particular band of Internet trolls may think, the moment of your shaming was and continues to be complex and multi-layered. Don't agonise over it, just say the first word that comes to mind. Nobody here will judge you.'

They whip around the circle in seconds. There's no friendly greeting to soften it. They just spit out their name and their so-called crime.

'Ayo. Sex.'

'Tara. Porn.'

'Verushka. Plagiarism.'

'Alan. Sex.'

Holly's eyes widen as she remembers Alan's sex scandal. God, it was embarrassing – she saw the footage all over the place! She stifles her laughter through a cough. Suddenly, all eyes are on her.

'Oh. Shit. I mean, it's my turn, isn't it? Well, um, hello my name is Holly.' Wait that's Alcoholics Anonymous. She isn't ready for this yet. 'Uh, Holly. I was . . . well, it's hard . . . I've been accused of something I didn't do. It's all really complicated and I'm kind of here because of the way people treated me and not because I *did* anything, if that makes sense?'

Ayo frowns, 'Holly, I specifically asked for you to say one word.'

'But I'm different from'– she gestures weakly across the circle – 'everyone here.'

The room feels stifling, almost angry. Ayo turns towards her, 'No, Holly. You are not, and the sooner you realise that, the better. In this space, we are all the same. We are all recovering from being shamed, no matter how good or honest we think our intentions were. Notice I didn't ask you what you did; I asked what you have been shamed for. So please, try again.'

This is harder than Holly thought it would be. She holds in the urge to run. If she can just last here for a few days, then she can sneak into town, call Zanna and get the next train home. Surely, she'll understand?

'OK, fine. Holly, lying. There. I was shamed for lying.' As soon as she utters the word, heat creeps up her face and makes her eyes water. Guilt.

Ayo beams in her direction. 'Well done, Holly. You've come out and said it in front of a group of strangers. How did it feel?'

Strange. Sickening. Like rubbing bicarbonate of soda and apple cider vinegar into a gaping cut.

'It felt fine.' She'll do what she must to survive this place. For now, it is her only hope.

'Don't worry. It will get better in time.' Ayo takes a deep breath. 'I have a reading on shame from the series of *Just for Today* meditations. We follow a similar twelve-step programme to organisations like Narcotics Anonymous – I was inspired by their compassion. Tara has agreed to do the honours today. Over to you . . .'

Tara's voice is deeper and fuller than Holly expected. There is a calmness in her speech that betrays her slim frame. That's what it's like. Whenever anyone is called on to read they become the sweet, striving soul they were when they read out their first word, fresh-faced and chubby-cheeked, free of the pockmarks and scars that living in the world brings.

'Shame can strike those who are successful, those who fail, those who are socially unacceptable and those who act too proud. It has the power to demean, control and regulate. It is a spell that can bring the strongest to their knees if they don't fit into what society has deemed normal. Our first step towards recovery is to accept our past mistakes and move forward, rejecting shame and embracing our flaws.'

The words leave a silence that curls around them. Everyone else appears serene, but the quietness makes Holly's skin crawl. How does she reject a feeling that has infested every aspect of her life? She doesn't want to accept who she's always been; she wants to be someone better. That was always the point. She feels like a house overrun with cockroaches – the only way to clear the filth would be to burn it down. Her thoughts are broken by a voice in the circle of silence. It's gentle Ayo. 'So, Holly, usually after we have done a reading, we go around the circle and talk a bit around what the reading has brought up for us. Is there anyone who would like to begin?'

Alan puts up his hand with the eagerness of a schoolboy. However, as soon as he opens his mouth he holds himself with the commanding manner of a parliamentary speaker. Holly remembers his voice from countless news bulletins and, more recently, from an excruciating public apology.

'I am struggling with this, Ayo. Surely public shaming can have its place when a person does something wrong? Look at me, for example. I cheated on my wife with a prostitute and was filmed performing all manner of sexual acts. This isn't the way a husband or a leader should behave. Don't I deserve the public humiliation?'

Holly stomach jolts as she pictures the insults and threats gathering on her phone, switched off and stashed at the bottom of her suitcase. Outside this calm room, the hatred towards her still exists. Her name remains a slur.

'I don't think that rejecting shame means not taking responsibility for your actions,' Ayo says. 'You apologised and were genuinely sorry, and discarding negative feelings of shame will help you move forward. In fact, this space exists to give you the space to do so.'

Tara holds up a manicured hand. Her pink nails are decorated with small, heart-shaped crystals. 'I think what Alan is trying to say is that it's hard not to feel like you deserve it sometimes. I mean, I consciously chose to make money early in my career through porn. At the time, I never imagined I would win a beauty pageant and someone would find the footage.'

Ayo shakes her head, 'Tara, firstly, you made a mistake out of desperation as a young, vulnerable woman, never mind how sick it is that our society feels the need to judge a woman's "purity". And as your reading said, it's about forgiving ourselves for what we have done in the past, no matter what others say. Are you getting ready to forgive yourself?'

Holly turns along with the rest of the group to look at Tara. Her hair hangs as a shield over her face.

'I want to say yes, and during the day when we're walking in nature and laughing I think I'm close. But the moment I try to fall asleep it holds me in a noose, choking me.' She starts crying again. 'And no matter how hard I try, a feeling sneaks up on me, even in my happiest moments, that I could take a knife, a rope or pills and just end it all.'

Ayo shuffles across and puts her arm around her. Holly's struck by how normal they look in that moment. They could be two friends who have just met and bonded on a yoga retreat. Nothing hints at the horrors that have brought them together. She is the only one branded by her shame, the only one whose sins have made her ugly and easy to isolate in a crowd.

'Does anyone else feel like Tara?' asks Ayo. 'Does anyone contemplate just ending it all?'

It's not so much the suicide itself that Holly fantasises about. She has no interest in how she'd die and how much it'd hurt. When pain consumes your reality it all becomes the same, just variations of the same tune. Whether the attacker is herself or someone else is inconsequential. The torrent of abuse all has the same destination. So she dreams about death itself, about that endless clean landscape uninhabited with feeling. She wants to swim in the negative space. If it was as easy as activating a switch, she would have chosen death weeks ago. She raises a shaking hand.

Holly looks up. Tara has lifted her hand, so has Alan, so has Verushka. Ayo looks at them all and raises hers too. In that quivering, exquisite moment, in the middle of paradise, they push their palms to the sky in a salute to the simplicity of death.

Chapter 42

Tyler

Today is a better day than most. He has just wrapped up a fascinating six hours performing a complex surgery, hammering bone and stitching up small slits of skin. He enjoys the harrowing operations the best, the ones that leave lesser surgeons awake and sweating the night before. His fingers tingle with the thrill of small, detailed work. The closeness of death wraps around his shoulders, comforting as a blanket. It feels warming to disengage. When everything is going well, the person is never a father, sister, lover or mother. They are simply a pathetic broken puzzle of skin and bones that needs to be brought to order again. When you get it right, it hits you harder and deeper than any drug. You reach the ultimate high – you spit in the face of death. When you get it wrong, well . . .

His visits to the café opposite Holly's apartment have been different. She didn't slink out the door at her usual times. He sat in the café one day until it closed and the waitress with the perfect eyebrows asked if he wanted to grab a drink (he didn't). He tried calling Holly's publicist for an interview opportunity and she shut him down, saying she is taking a 'well-deserved break'. Not that he needed any confirmation – he felt it, a dark, creeping feeling of rage. The little bitch was gone.

In her wake, she has left a legacy akin to the worst kind of cancer. As fast as it is removed, it takes root and grows somewhere else. All over the world, skinny white girls jut their hipbones towards the camera, preaching the purity of the latest organic food trend, prophesying warnings about toxicity. There are slight variations on the theme – the yogi, the dancer, the athlete, the model, the girl who seems to be drinking coconut water on a new island every week. Raw till four, fully raw, high carb low fat raw, vegan, flexitarian, paleo. They're all the same. They demonise food to justify their fear of feeling full. They look back with nostalgia to a simpler time that they never knew. These silly, silly little girls feed themselves with the adoration of others, and he has a responsibility to stamp it out.

As expected, Holly's scandal had resulted in a rash of inflamed, emotional opinion pieces about how she has ruined various lives. One writer blamed her relapse into anorexia on Holly, casually linking to her blog at the end of the story so the readers who reflexively shared her article could 'follow her recovery'. He ill-advisedly clicked on the link to find her so-called recovery is tentative at best. Her Instagram page is a claustrophobic catalogue of calorie counts of what she eats every day. It is all a vile exercise in attention seeking, an effort to stake a claim in the conversation and, in so doing, grab an elusive portion of Internet fame. It's all fruitless, like grabbing at air.

Tyler is the one who set this chain of events in motion. Only *he* can own the pain that Holly has caused. Only *he* wrenched his rage out of the comforting cocoon of the

Internet and into reality. Before he took action, everybody else was quite happy to fawn over her and laud her distorted outlook as an advanced form of reality. The injustice of it burrows into his nerves and makes him grind his teeth.

He happened to stumble on a call for people to testify against the wreckage that Holly had made of their lives. Not to testify in court, but to testify in the only trial that matters – the trial by media. He shouldn't have felt so driven to respond: that slimy reporter could recognise his voice; his employer could question his intentions; Holly could see him and squeal. Yet in the wake of all she has done, who would believe her? And doesn't he want to smoke her out of that hole she is hiding in anyway, and ensure she disappears once and for all?

Come out, come out, wherever you are.

More than that, the thrill of outing Holly has worn thin. He needs something more to feed on. It's not about her anymore; it's bigger than that. He needs someone to listen to his point of view and finally say, yes Tyler, you were right and Holly was wrong.

This desire has brought him to this path that snakes through the Royal Arcade and into New Bond Street. London is tentatively warm. His heart is a burning sun. He swings his arms and smiles at the tourists peering into the window of Louis Vuitton. He blares his favourite Kanye West song, 'Homecoming', through his headphones.

Even the stench of male cologne from the nearby Abercrombie & Fitch store cannot taint his mood. He greets the doormen at Claridge's warmly. Today he gets to set the record straight. He feeds the buzz with a trembling hand, in the hope that this will silence it for good.

Victoria, the correspondent for the entertainment channel, sits at a corner table, flicking through her phone. Two burly men and an acne-marked woman conspire over black coffees at a table nearby, feet crowded with big, black bags. They must be the film crew.

'Victoria?'

'Tyler! Thank you for joining me! And I'm so sorry for your loss. I can't imagine what this recent news is bringing back for you.'

Typical tabloid hack – trying to prise out the emotion before he's even sat down. If she were a real journalist, she would wonder if there was any connection between Tyler's career as a surgeon, his vendetta against Holly and and the identity of the man who cut her with a scalpel in the street. But she's just an empty-headed, overworked media whore who is too concerned with making good television to read between the lines. And by the way she is flicking her hair and focusing on his lips, he knows he's got her.

It is a fact that both thrills and enrages him – everybody wants to believe the guy wearing the white smile and the sharp suit, even if they can smell the stench of rot rising from beneath it. He touches her thin arm and holds her eyes. He'll give her a story she'll never forget. After he's done with her, the world will remember Frankie the way they should, as *his* girl, and his alone.

As the team sets up their cameras, he orders a tea with full fat milk and a scone with double cream. Victoria's pen scratches on her notepad, clearly noting he is not vegan, or gluten- or sugar-free. Tyler drums his watch. He has a consultation in a few hours and this is wasting his time. He wants to growl in the cameraman's ear to hurry the fuck up, and insult the woman setting up the mic until her acne glows red. He knows better, though, and he just needs to hold it in for a while longer.

'Ah, sorry about all this, Tyler, we're all ready to begin our chat now. Don't pay any attention to the cameras. It's just you and me. Let's begin with a little introduction. How did you first hear of Holly Evans?'

'My fiancée . . .' He coughs for effect. 'My late fiancée found her on Instagram. She didn't pay much attention to her at first – she was just one of many girls posing in bikinis in exotic locations, punting a diet or a project. But there was something warm and intelligent about Holly that she picked up on. She started off as a motivational figure in her life. When she – sorry, this is hard for me – when she got cancer that all changed. She became obsessed with Holly's diet and lifestyle, and took her advice to heart.'

'What did that involve?'

'Well, she had an aggressive, yet potentially curable tumour but rejected any medical treatment or operation in favour of a raw diet. This consisted of a juice in the morning, a smoothie mid-morning, another smoothie for lunch, several bananas a day and a salad of chopped greens for dinner. As well as various natural herbal supplements and monthly colonic irrigations.'

'Are you of the opinion that this was unhelpful to her potential recovery?'

'Absolutely. As a medical doctor, I spent years in medical school understanding how illnesses spread throughout the body and how the right treatment can address this rapidly. While I will agree that a diet free of dairy and sugar could possibly prevent the growth of cancer cells, there certainly hasn't been enough testing for us to lean on this theory entirely.'

'Did you clash over this?'

A slamming door, harsh words she didn't mean, a phone that kept on ringing, no matter how many times he called.

'No! No. I loved Frankie with all my heart and supported her through everything. We were soulmates – we had the kind of love you only find once.' The camera zooms on his broken eyes. 'I voiced my concerns, and pleaded with her, but it was only ever out of love and she knew that.'

Surely she knew that?

'She sounds incredibly special. Tell us a bit more about Frankie.'

'She was the ideal woman – beautiful, smart, kind. She was so strong and really successful. Frankie worked in finance, you know. She was high up doing investment stuff that I never really understood. She made anyone she spoke to believe that anything was possible. I loved how she always listened to me and how she made me feel.'

This is the problem with love, isn't it? As soon as you start describing it, it sounds inane and dull. Words cannot capture the magic; not even memory can.

'It must have been very painful to see her die.' Victoria stares at him wide-eyed. The camera crew moves closer still, getting a close-up of his face. It's time to give it all he's got, the money shot.

'It was the most unthinkable pain, beyond anything I have ever experienced. Combine this with the frustration that she was wilfully taking her own life and it becomes an acid that burns everything it touches. And it's not gone, and it will never be gone. How can I ever find any closure when she didn't have to die?' Tears fill his eyes naturally. He fakes many interactions in his life, but he's never had to fake anything when it comes to Frankie. It was, it is, it always has been, all real.

'Do you think Holly directly contributed to Frankie's death?'

'Absolutely. She took a lie and presented it as fact. She did this in such a forceful, compelling way that even intelligent women like my precious Frankie took it as fact. Holly doesn't understand that when you have thousands of followers and brand endorsements, people take what you say to be the honest truth. Nobody researches these days, and why would they, when they have found something they want to believe in? With that sort of following comes grave responsibility.'

'With great Instagram stats comes great responsibility.' He can see the headline for the insert whirring inside her mind. Tick, tick, boom.

'Exactly.'

'You mentioned that she was buried in an intimate family ceremony. Tell us more about the mood on the day.'

He knows what she's doing. She trying to get her viewers to identify with the pain he went through. She wants them to imagine themselves in the back pew, tearing up when they see his broken face leading the procession. The partner left behind. But he can't talk about that, not on television, where Frankie's parents and friends may see him.

'All I can say is that as a doctor, I would encourage all your viewers to only believe in the opinion of someone with a medical background.'

'Tyler—'

'I would advise a balanced diet rich in good fats, lean protein and dark leafy greens. I'd also highly recommend you take two days a week where you eat as you please. Honestly, just snack, eat burgers, and eat whatever you want to. It's time we all stopped taking ourselves too seriously and regained a healthy relationship with food.'

'That's really valuable information, thank you. But I think what we're looking for is a bit on what it was like to say your last goodbye.'

She won't let go of this, will she? Nosy, opportunistic little witch.

'I'm sorry, I just, I just can't relive that right now. It doesn't feel right. That time was sacred.'

'Yes, of course. I'm sorry, Tyler.'

'Are we done now?'

'Yes, of course, Tyler.'

She keeps saying his name – as if in its repetition he will forget that she is a stranger. The camera gets packed away and he finishes the rest of his tea. Takes a deep breath as he gets his head right, back into the space of the caring surgeon. He shuffles in his chair. There are several missed calls from the office. He's late again, and it may start to draw unwanted attention.

'I'm sorry if I pushed too hard at the end there,' she says in a low voice, as if they're friends now.

'Oh, it's not a problem. It's just something I find really hard to talk about in public.'

It's not that he is emotionally unable. He can't talk about it because he has no memory of the day. He can't remember the faces of Frankie's family as the funeral procession marched in, carrying the coffin that held her body. He can't recall the eulogy, or the song that they played in her honour. He doesn't know if they chose her corporate mugshot as the cover of the funeral program or whether they went with that free, smiling picture of her at the beach. These details still keep him up at night, shaking with ugly, growling sobs. The end of Frankie should have been a moment when the world held its breath, when London's choirs joined together to sing her favourite song, when rows of the sunflowers she loved so much lined the streets. Instead, it is just a blank space. Why would he remember anything? He never attended Frankie's funeral. He wasn't invited.

Chapter 43

Holly

Holly sits cross-legged on a bench outside the stone cottage, her pen hovering over a blank page. The sky is so clear that she can see all the way down the mountain and into the green valleys below. Today, Ayo has given each of them the task of writing their life story from beginning to end. It should be so easy, but Holly has no idea where to start. Where did the lies begin and the truth end?

She has a creeping fear that she is not progressing the way she is supposed to. Although they hold their 'sharing' meetings every day, Holly has not been able to speak. What would she say, that she faked her own cancer? That her lying hit a dead end, drove her crazy and caused her to binge on fast food? Sometimes she is so ashamed of her actions she wants to disappear off the planet; other times she holds on to tattered scraps of her innocence.

Maybe that's where she should start, back at a time when she was innocent, when she told lies because that was the only way to survive. The words appear on the page in a tangle, her handwriting excited and rushed. This feels like the beginning of a breakthrough. Better still, it feels like the pathway towards forgiveness. She's so lost in her story that she doesn't notice Ayo walking up and sitting next to her.

'How are you doing over here? That looks like quite an essay!'

Holly's hands unconsciously move to cover the notebook. It feels too raw to reveal just yet. 'Yes . . . I think I'm starting to understand my actions a little better.'

'That's wonderful news!'

She laughs nervously. 'I guess it's about time. I've been here three weeks and haven't exactly been participating as much as I should. That's what you want to talk to me about, isn't it?'

'Oh goodness, honey! You really need to stop beating yourself up. Everybody recovers differently. There's no map that shows you how to do it. You just have to push on through.'

Holly can't open her mouth and say anything. She knows that as soon as she tries to say a word, it will clog her throat and come out as a sob. This acceptance feels like a beautiful gift that she is unworthy of, especially considering everything she has done. Finally, she whispers, 'That makes me happier than anything in the world.'

Ayo sighs. 'I'm glad to hear it. We really care about you here, Holly. We know what you're going through, even if it feels like your problem is bigger than anyone else's right now. I can assure you that we're all the same. Once you start opening up to us, you'll see that there is no judgement here, only love. But . . .' Her face falls.

'What?'

'I have received some disturbing news. I usually make a point of telling my guests to disconnect from all media, especially anything to do with their shaming, but I have to make an exception in this case.'

Her heart sinks. There cannot be anything else to discover. 'Why?'

'Well, it might have legal implications, especially in the wake of that journalist discovering a scalpel in your home. Don't panic! It also might not, depending on what you tell me now. There is a man who has been doing interviews on international TV news channels, claiming that his girlfriend died due to following your medical advice. Apparently, she believed that you cured your cancer through only eating the recipes you shared, and now that your cancer has been disproven, he wants to press charges against you for consumer fraud.'

Anger jolts through her, making her knees shake. She didn't force anybody to believe her, did she? All she did was put information out there. Without that simple hashtag that started it all, nobody would have even known her name.

'The accusations must have been blown out of proportion, Ayo, you have to believe me!' A door opens in her mind, a quiet creak, and a shadow arches in to form a shape.

'Holly, we're not going to go into that. All I see here is possible evidence that you consciously or unconsciously led one of your followers to believe they could cure a terminal illness using raw foods.'

The birds are shouting all around her in a cacophony. The wind howls. She doesn't think she's crying, but her face is wet and her mouth tastes of salt. It can't be. It was never meant to come to this.

'I don't know what to say.'

'Holly, just tell me that you didn't make any definitive statements that your diet cures cancer. More importantly, assure me that you didn't say your diet cures cancer *in order to sell a product*. If you didn't, I am happy to keep you hidden here. But if you did, I have to send you home so you can respond to police questioning.'

'The police want to question me?' She wants to scream, run, take her chopping knife and find the heavy pulse of her jugular vein. How does she summon the strength to face this?

'Yes. I mean, after everything that has happened, it is all starting to add up a bit.' Ayo leans forward and holds Holly's face in her hands, 'But listen, girl, we've got this. Zanna is the ultimate pro and she can stall the questions for a little while. Just take the afternoon to go for a long hike and think if you ever said anything that could be construed as concealing the truth. Check in with me later and we'll take it from there.'

*

Holly turns left and heads towards the most remote trail. There's a reason hikers steer clear of this path, she soon discovers. It is steep, rocky and ridden with patches of slippery moss. These obstacles don't slow her pace. If there's one thing she knows how to do right, it's walk. Isn't that how she started in London, pacing the streets alone with a fistful of imaginary friends flashing inside her phone? Those were simpler days – she couldn't understand the shape of what she was building yet. She was just posting recipes and making connections, brick by brick. Every comment was thrilling, and she thought that the marketing reps sponsoring her products were her friends.

How did her experiment with her health, with the truth, become deadly? How did it accumulate enough weight to convince another human being that it was a cure?

For the past few years, every meal she faced in her life was an opportunity to prove just how pure she was, how healthy. Her skin, her body, her hair, her life, were all a result of a path she chose at random. The truth is that since coming to the retreat she hasn't seen the rapid decline in her health she expected to see, and she's been eating fish, eggs and all the bread she could find for the first time in years. Old Holly preached against the toxic qualities of gluten and would have been terrified of getting bloated after eating bread, yet she hasn't felt uncomfortable. Not once. Even without her daily wheatgrass shot and cleansing lemon water, her skin is glowing. There are no ingredients to make her calming evening turmeric and chamomile almond milk latte, yet she is sleeping through the night. Her legs are strong and lean from hiking, despite not practising the daily Ashtanga yoga sequence she swore by on her blog. Life somehow exists, thrives, outside the rigidity of her rules. Now, she finds out a life has ended within them.

She strains her mind for one particular lie, but it was all a lie, wasn't it? Every picture, every motivational quote, added up to convey a message. Hell, she even used the settings on her camera to filter every picture to look the same. Anything that didn't fit within those bright, perfectly lit frames was labelled as wrong. Who did she think she was? She'd only read one book on nutrition, and hadn't even studied anything after school. All she knew was how to style a good window display and pose for a photo. Looking at it that way, she can see it all for what it is. Disgusting.

The path thins and a canopy of trees imposes a sudden darkness. Within the howling wind, she hears the trapped cries of the thousands, millions, of people who truly had cancer. Their moans as they grit their teeth through another round of chemotherapy. Their desperation when they receive a scan that shows that, yes, the tumour has grown once again. Their sobs as they assure their families that they must find joy and live on without them. They rage and scream, haunting and taunting her. The dark door in her mind is blasted open, revealing the quivering tar-like truth behind it. 'I'm sorry,' she whispers, the stones and the trees her only witnesses, 'I'm so, so sorry.'

Someone died. A young woman trying her best to heal from a genuine terminal illness died on her watch. She knows what she has to do, and it makes her sick to her stomach.

Still, there is some hope. She remembers the raw shopping lists she painstakingly put together. She'd spent a whole week researching what exactly nutritional yeast was and whether it was a healthy addition to a meal plan. She had taken care. It can't be true that her innocent actions killed someone else. But if it is, it's time she took responsibility.

The weather is turning. Holly pulls up the hood of her raincoat and makes her way back to the retreat, running the last stretch and into Ayo's office.

'Holly, are you all right?'

'Yes, yes, I'm OK. But I need to ask you something. Can I see her?'

'Who?'

'The girl who died, or the footage about her. I did something terrible but I know I took complete care in all the nutritional plans I put together. If I can just hear what I have been accused of, I'll be able to fully shoulder the responsibility of what I have done.'

Ayo looks concerned. Something in her expression suggests she has been in a position like this before.

'Are you sure this will give you closure?' The rain pelts the windows outside. A storm is brewing. Holly wishes she could soar like the birds above the clouds and find shelter. Even this idyllic cottage in the countryside cannot protect her now.

'Well, something close to it. Maybe it will help me get my head around it.'

She wants to confirm the terrible truth she suspects, the beast lurking behind the door.

'You sure this won't be salt in the wound? It can be quite damaging to see how badly our reputation has been broken through shaming.'

Holly nods her head solemnly. 'I'm sure. I have to do it now or I never will.'

'Fine. I will get the clip and play it on one condition – that you watch it with the rest of the group.'

Her heart plummets. Once they all see the clip, she will be confirmed in their eyes as a monster.

'Surely that's more damaging to me?'

'Just the opposite, actually. No matter what you feel as you face your shame, we can help you share the load. You'll have the reassurance that you're not alone.'

Holly's not so sure. Her whole life has been driven by an impulse to edit the truth, only showing the things that are palatable. This stiff circle of almost-friends around her are the only people in the world who don't know how vile and messy it all is just yet. Can't she have this for a few moments longer? Can't she too have the freedom to decide whoever she wants to be? She takes a deep breath, the way Ayo taught her, holding it in until it swells in her chest. Sometimes, in order to survive, we must comply and conform.

Chapter 44

Holly then

Holly fastens the blue surgical mask tightly over her face. The blended cotton-like texture always prompts a rise of involuntary goosebumps. She pulls a hairnet over her bald skull and walks into the children's oncology ward.

'Well, if it isn't our favourite volunteer!' Nurse Carol steps out from behind the front desk and consumes her in a hug. That's what it's like here. So warm, so kind, everybody hugging one another like old friends. The nurses know how she takes her tea, what her favourite TV series is and who she thought was best dressed at the Oscars the other night. Not many people understand these little things about her.

'Oh, come on, Carol. You're not allowed to have favourites!' She blushes. It isn't a surprise, though. While many volunteers enter the children's oncology ward with high, happy voices and good intentions, not many can stand the tedious reality. The day-in, day-out assault of medication on the body and the range of unpredictable side effects it brings. Not every cancer sufferer is a 'fighter' in the way the world sanctions, sitting serenely in bed bearing their pain with dazed eyes and a stoic half-smile. Many lash out, cry and insult those closest to them. This has caused many volunteers to cynically throw their mask to the ground and storm out, but not Holly. She is a fighter too.

The patients like continuity. It gives them something to clutch on to as the world around them collapses. That is why she arrives at 10 a.m. every Wednesday. This is also when her family and friends believe she is at the hospital for her weekly round of chemotherapy: 10 a.m. Nobody can take time off work then and visit her, although some have tried to walk her to the ward once or twice. She's always batted them off with fierce sadness, telling them she would rather they didn't see her this way. It's their support that matters most of all. This is enough assurance for them as they stand and wave at her from across the road.

She walks over to Alice's bed first. Like the nurses, she too has her favourites. She's fast asleep, with her one hand reaching above her head like a child. At just fifteen, in some ways she still is. More patches of hair have fallen out, with only a few black strands left. It is so lovely how her beauty persists in the brokenness. A few months ago she was just a teenage ballet dancer hoping to make the school's production of *Nutcracker*, running down the school corridors with friends and filling her days with food and sport and gossip. Now she passes every second here.

As Holly reaches to touch her, she stirs.

'Oh, Holly, it's you.' She whispers. 'You've shaved your head again.'

'Do you want to touch it?' She bends down so Alice can feel the stubble of her shaven head through the hairnet.

'Whoa, that's so weird.' She giggles, but there is something world-weary right behind it. 'Why do you do it?'

She smiles softly at Alice, 'Because I want to show you that you can be beautiful and confident, no matter if you have hair or not.' Holly feels a bit choked up saying it out loud, realising her impact on this young girl's life.

'I feel beautiful already,' Alice says curtly. The edge in her tone is now unmistakable. Today is not a good day.

It's fine; nothing she is not used to. She'll just rise above it. Holly reaches into her handbag. 'I brought you some presents to pass the time. Here are the latest two issues of *Heat*, a new limited-edition lip gloss from Topshop and some glitter nail polish. Oh, and this cute unicorn cover for your phone.'

Holly missed all this. The trends, the sickly sweet teen perfumes and the candy-coloured make-up. When she was Alice's age, she never quite understood it. She felt like she had walked into an advanced maths class by mistake. Now, she gets it all. She knows what these girls want. She knows how to make them like her.

'Uh . . . thanks,' Alice mumbles. What is wrong? Does she have these magazines already? Does she prefer *Grazia*? Were the colours the wrong choice? Just like that, she is fifteen all over again, second-guessing herself after one sneer from a cool girl.

Her dad in her ear whispering: *Your friends don't like you. They just like how you follow them around like a pathetic little puppy dog.*

'Is everything OK, sweetie? Has it been a rough treatment day for you?' There have been bad ones before, where Holly has held her as she heaved into a bucket, pulling sheets of paper towels and smudging them across her face to wipe off tears and sick. She knows the lingo now that she shares the ups and downs.

'As if you would understand,' she sneers.

Holly looks around her to check for nurses, then pulls part of the curtain around Alice's bed shut. Something feels off about this. She can almost smell it, a rankness like meat that has been left out in the sun.

'Talk to me – what is going on with you? I thought we were friends?' How many times has she visited Alice in this ward? Eight? Ten? She's been coming here for over two months.

'I did too,' she says, reaching for her phone, 'That was until I joined Instagram. My friends thought it would be a good way to see what's going on out there in the world and feel like I was doing stuff with them. I looked up to you so much, so yours was one of the first names I searched.'

A loud ringing fills Holly's ears. It can't be. She couldn't have. Alice pulls up Holly's Instagram page on her mobile phone, showing a montage of illness. Holly showing her bald skull. Holly smiling next to a drip. Holly lying in . . .

'That is my fucking bed. Look, you can even see one of my posters! You lay in my bed and took a selfie while I was being helped to the bathroom!'

She's shrieking now, sobbing. The horror contorts her tiny pixie face.

'Alice, I can explain.'

'Shut up! Please! We're lying here, barely holding on and you came into our lives and what? Stole our stories? What kind of *sick freak* does that?'

It wasn't meant to go this far. It was only meant to be a few visits, enough to understand what the side effects of chemotherapy people were expecting her to experience felt like. Her initial lie had got out of hand and she needed the information to keep it going. But the stories were so emotional and the kids were so sweet, she just kept on coming back.

Alice is wheezing now, rage spitting from her blood-less lips. 'You win, Holly, you *are* sick. I have leukaemia, but I am not as sick as you are. At least I stand a chance of getting better.'

Holly tries to reach for Alice's arm, to feel once more the connection she did during all those visits. Surely she can get her to understand this was never about her.

'Get away from me!' she growls, primal and scared.

'Alice, wait . . .'

'I said, *get away from me!*'

The screaming gets louder and the nurses come pushing past Holly to soothe her. She pulls off her mask and hair-net, throwing them to the ground as she runs along the corridor, down the stairs, out, out and away from the pulsing hurt within its walls.

Chapter 45

Holly

Everyone is assembled in the living room, laughing and chattering. Ayo has laid out a spread of hot scones with dollops of fresh cream and jam. It could be the beginning of an afternoon tea. Holly stands looking in on the happy scene through the window, wishing she could stay here forever, without ever having to walk into the future. The second she steps through that door, she is responsible for snuffing out the evening's glow.

They don't even look up when she walks in, and for that she is grateful. In this strange place of broken lives, sad stories are painfully common.

Ayo nods at Holly and addresses the room. 'Hey, every-one. Hey! Good God – can we have some quiet please? Today our friend Holly was delivered some troubling news that relates to the reason why she is here. She has made the brave decision to watch a video clip of this news to decide what to do next. But before we do any of this, she's going to tell us her story.

'Before she begins, I want to say a few words on the distinction between guilt and shame. Most of us are familiar with what it is like to feel shame – this is a dirty, desperate emotion where we see our reputations smeared in the eyes of other people. You may think guilt is the same thing, but it is isn't. Guilt is how we personally feel about our own behaviour, when we recognise that what we have done is wrong. The difference is clear in Holly's case, where she is finding some things that she feels guilty about and some things she feels ashamed about. Through this process, she hopes to find a way forward and do the right thing. But let me step out of the limelight. Please give her a big, encouraging round of applause. You all know how daunting it was to tell your story for the first time.'

She examines the faces before her. Alan looks ruddy-cheeked and relaxed, fresh from a day canoeing on the lake. Tara looks desperately beautiful without her make-up and her beauty-pageant smile. Verushka smiles encouragingly, with the knowing look of someone who has been here before. In all cases, there is a clear line between what was bad about them and what was good. The rot doesn't run too deep. Nobody died as a result of their actions. Holly has nothing to lean on, no way to sugar-coat the truth.

This isn't a book launch where she can blush and thank everyone for filling the room to overflowing. It isn't a media event where she can preach about her latest 'obsession' with goji berries and kale. Who is she really? She reacted to every show she watched and every album she listened to in line with what others thought about it. This is what she learnt from childhood: to be safe, you need to fit in, you need to reflect what the other person wants you to be. Has she ever been a person, or just an echo? She grinds her teeth and begins.

'My story probably begins the first time I shared a picture, because that is when all this attention started. But for me its roots extend to before that. When I posted that first picture, I didn't understand social media much. I didn't get that one image could travel around the world and cause people to form an opinion of me based on a fleeting moment. Even though I didn't know the power of Instagram and how it would change my life, I always knew I wanted people to like me. It doesn't seem to happen often. I've never considered myself likeable or even pretty, so when my pictures started getting attention, I played up to it, giving people more of what they wanted.'

Ayo gives her a sharp look.

'But now, I know I must take responsibility for what I did. So I will say it out loud – I never had cancer. I had a benign tumour, but that was removed during a quick operation and only required one night in hospital. As my mother has always said, I have a strong mind that blocks out the things it doesn't want to see. I was fooling myself just as much as I was fooling everyone else. But let me start at the beginning . . .'

She looks around the room, expecting everyone to look shocked, but nobody even seems surprised.

'When I was worried about the tumour, I was getting support and love from my family and new friends like never before. When it was confirmed that my tumour was not cancerous, I couldn't bear to tell everyone and lose my new friends. So I made a decision to pretend that I had breast cancer and had to undergo chemotherapy. That way, everyone continued to gather round, and I continued to feel loved.

'This meant some uncomfortable logistics. I researched the symptoms of chemotherapy and faking them became part of my morning routine. I shaved off my hair, and eventually my eyebrows. I cut into my skin to make it look like I had a drip and I drank disgusting concoctions sometimes to force myself to vomit at work. At this stage I legitimately began to research natural remedies and ways to change my diet, mainly because my father blamed me for getting sick in the first place. As much as I was getting something from being sick, I was petrified of being truly ill. Finally, I found something that I loved! Even better, I was good at it. Although I started out with simple recipes, they felt good and my family and friends loved them. I didn't have any specific plans about all of this at the time. It was a simple little thing that was making me happy.

'I muddled on, pretending to go to chemo, and getting deeper into my new diet. I focused less on cooked food and more on raw vegetables, as I just seemed to be digesting them better. Besides, my skin was starting to look great and people were commenting on my healthy weight. I was like a little scientist, experimenting with different ingredients and combinations to figure out what worked best.'

And then, all of a sudden, going into the oncology ward wasn't an option anymore.

'When I came up with the Green Monster smoothie, it was my pride and joy. Something in the combination of peanut butter, banana, spinach and spirulina made me feel brilliant. So, one day, I snapped a picture of myself drinking it for Instagram. It was pretty cute, but nothing special. I mean, I hadn't curated it the way I do with any of the pictures I post these days. I added a few hashtags . . . I'd just started doing that. For that post I used #smoothie, but it didn't seem enough. I figured anybody going through chemo would enjoy it, so I added in #healing #radiation #cancer #survivor.'

Act like it wasn't planned, act like you didn't mean for this to happen.

'People started liking it, some started posting comments like "Get well soon" and "Stay strong". Then this girl from a reality TV show found it. I should have said something then, sure, but it felt nice to have these total strangers willing me to get better. Well, for some reason that particular recipe resonated with a lot of people.

'Suddenly I felt this thrill of getting noticed, and this pressure to perform for my audience. So I posted a raw pad thai that day. It was a recipe I was proud of after all. I'd say to myself each day, "Just this once, you can do it for a little boost during a bad day." But I started to need a boost every day after that. Those little comments blossomed into regular followers, friends even. I got a better phone, then

I got a proper camera. I started spending more time arranging my food and editing how I described it.

'Now I know I must take responsibility. Nobody forced me to lie. Even when the temptation is there, it takes a seed of darkness within you to reach forward and grab it, to succumb to it. For me, that seed was wanting, no *needing*, people to like me. I wanted to keep it at any cost, and it didn't take me very long to realise that the cost would be to haze over the truth. People needed to believe that I had cancer.'

A look from Ayo again, burning into the back of her skull.

'Sorry, *I* needed to believe I had cancer. If I didn't, everything I was doing would lose its meaning. There was too much at stake. And, you know, I kept telling myself, "Well, surely everybody fools themselves a little on social media. Surely nobody's pictures show who they really are in real life."'

Holly shifts on her feet. The practicalities of her lie, the pictures she has shared with the world flash uncomfortably in her mind.

'Nobody sets out to fake something as big as cancer. It starts out small, and gradually adds up. For me, it began when I omitted to tell people that my tumour was benign. I neglected to tell people my treatment was over, and that I was now well. In a way, the incessant new focus on my diet made me feel as if my problems weren't over, and that I still needed something else to be well.'

There is always something else you need to be truly well.

There is no turning back now. Here she is, facing up to what she's done and presenting it to others. Usually when you tell a story, you edit it for your audience. You focus on the parts you think they want to hear based on how they murmur approval or shuffle in their seats. Holly can't read her audience today. Everyone sits silently before her, eyes blank. In some ways, this is the first time she has pieced together what has happened herself. In arranging the events of the past few years one in front of the other, with no thought of editing them, everything is worse than she feared. She carries on.

'I felt like I needed to give my caring friends and my followers new stories to feed their interest. So I shared tales of infections, new tumours, new risks. I blocked out reality, and researched my new life online. Every single thing I said was medically possible and accurate, including the natural ways of treating it. The life I created became more real than any life I had half-lived before that. *This* was the real me.'

She sees it then, clear as if it were the next room. Her old home with its oppressive leather furniture and forced family pictures. The hasty repair jobs over the holes in doors where a fist had smashed through, the bleached bloodstains on the carpet. They tried to forget, but the house vibrated with anger. Yet it was boring, so boring that nobody noticed the scratches on her arms or her hacking cough when she was forced to go to school even though she was sick. Nobody considered her broken enough to give her a second glance. That was the real her, lying to keep the peace, fake-laughing at sexist jokes and cutting the anger out behind the locked door of her pink bathroom. All she ever wanted was to create a new Holly, one that people acknowledged and saw. She never expected that they would see so much.

She has promised to herself she wouldn't cry, but large tears slide down her cheeks. *Deep breaths, take deep breaths.* If she surrenders to the crying now, she won't be able to stop.

'I was found out, of course.' The telling of how or why is too painful to repeat out loud.

She hasn't touched this tender place in her heart for a long time. It is excruciating, and relieving all at once.

'I moved to London soon after that, and widely publicised the fact that I had "healed" myself of cancer. During that time, I consulted with a natural healer called Dr Ray, who believed I did have "cancerous levels of toxicity" in my body. He mirrored my belief that my nutritional approach was the right one. I leant on his opinions and promoted him heavily, because he justified everything I had done up until that point. From then on, I felt as if I was free to do the one thing I really loved to do: make up recipes.

'I blamed everybody else for my problems, I always have. When my face got cut, I was angry at my attacker, then I got so angry with my fans who turned on me. After everything I had built, after all the love and support we had given each other, they were so quick to turn on me. Things they praised me for in the past – my weight, my hair, the way I speak – suddenly became an opportunity for ridicule. It made me wonder if they ever followed me out of warmth, or whether I was just one of those people everybody loved to hate. I've never known the secret to being liked, you see. I don't have that intangible thing that others have.'

She takes a deep breath. 'Regardless of how I feel about anything and what was real or fake, it now turns out that someone out there, a young woman, took my advice to not undergo chemotherapy in favour of a raw, vegan diet and died. So, I guess that leads us to now. Ayo invited you here to support me as we watch this woman's partner describe her story in detail. I don't know whether to feel angry or sad or ashamed right now, and I don't know how I'll react. I feel like my mind is not my own anymore.'

She waits for the outrage and insults, but there is nothing but the sound of the rain gently falling outside. Ayo stands up and walks towards the TV screen, avoiding eye contact. 'There is no right or wrong way to react, Holly. The only thing you should try and feel is compassion. We are so often separated – by our ethnicities, class, sexual orientation, and our phone screens – that we forget there is a real human behind the image. Your fans only saw you for the sum of your photos. Try to see this girl for the living, breathing human being she was. She must have looked up to you a lot and would have liked that.'

The screen flickers on in a kiss of static. Already, Holly's blood congeals with humiliation. Only a few months ago she was standing on that otherworldly platform herself, blinking under the spotlight, blushing underneath industrial-strength hair and make-up. Those same presenters had gushed over how lean she looked in her black Stella McCartney dress and had sighed as they tried her raw Thai-spiced salad. Now they face the camera, eyes wild with glee. They never loved her dress. They never loved her hair. They never loved her freaking salad. Her hands are shaking. She feels Tara move over and put her arm around her shoulders.

'Today we have an exclusive interview with Tyler Wells, the surviving ex-boyfriend of a woman who tragically died after following the nutritional advice of fallen social media health icon, Holly Evans.'

Tyler Wells. There is a familiar musicality to the name, a feeling that she repeated it to herself sometime in the past, but why?

The story begins with the presenter introducing the person being interviewed. The camera pans on to his face. Holly's breath catches in her throat. Her muscles clench and her throat swells. She pants and wheezes, eyes squeezed shut. When she opens them, she's looking into his eyes again. They're green and clear, wet as moss. The type of eyes you want to believe, the type of eyes you follow out the door so you can look in to them again.

'Holly?' Ayo presses pause. No, this is worse. His face is frozen in time, his eyes still running the length of her scar, following her across the room.

'It's . . . oh my God, no . . . it's him.'

'Who, Holly?' Everybody is so close to her, she's suffocating. Why the hell did she agree to have these strangers here with her? 'Holly.' Ayo touches her arm. 'You're going to need to tell us what you mean.'

'He never told me his name was Tyler, he called himself Jack.'

A flash of memory, the lavender scent of freshly laundered sheets crisp against her skin. Tingling fingers and toes, watering eyes as the drugs wore off, leaving her cold and confused. The shame, the shame, as persistent and present as her pulse. Dr Warner's sad eyes describing the surgical procedure and how she lashed out at him and at his assistant, Dr Tyler Wells.

'*Who*, Holly?'

'The man who cut me! The man who did this!' She starts tugging her face, over and over, until one of the people in the room holds her arms back. It's one thing too many. Alan inches forward and pushes a brown paper bag in front of her face.

'Just breathe into this, Holly. It helps, I promise. You need to take deep breaths. You're safe here.'

Verushka, silent until now, says softly, 'Should we really be forcing her to do this, Ayo? She doesn't look ready.'

Something about Verushka's tone seems too patronising for Holly to bear. She pushes away the bag and grabs the remote. She won't let some slimy journalist say what she should and shouldn't do. If they were both in London, she's sure she would have spilled Holly's story in a second.

'I've come this far,' she says through gritted teeth. 'Let's hear what else he has to say.'

The interview set-up looks positively cosy, all soft cream linen and perfectly brewed cups of tea. She knows the interior – Claridge's. She took her mum there once, for a tense conciliatory tea the first time she came to visit her in London. Holly had just signed a deal with a smoothie company and felt as if she had finally regained control of her life. Not that her mum appreciated any of it, as she kept on asking if they could stop off at the Pizza Express on the way home because they served 'real helpings'.

Victoria, the journalist, purses her lips and tugs at her twinset as Tyler talks dotingly about his fiancée, Frankie. So that was her name. It has a familiar ring to it. It sounds like the type of person Holly may have wanted to be friends with, or be like. Something lights up in her memory, golden and alive, but then the moment is gone. All that is left is jealousy. Oh, to be innocent and untouchable. Oh, to be so smart. Oh, to be dead.

At one point, Victoria asks, 'What do you think attracted Frankie to Holly?'

'Well, she was the full package, wasn't she? With her long hair, clear skin and beautiful body, it's easy to see why women aspired to be like her. On top of that, she just seemed so damn nice. Everything she said was rooted in ideas that were wholesome and good. She took women back to a place where natural living was better. After so many fad diets, she was a breath of fresh air, a return to the source.'

Holly wants to punch the screen. The same smooth voice that gasped on 'discovering' that she was a famous blogger now speaks glibly about her, revealing how much he knew about her all along. What spark did she really feel that night? How similar attraction and fear can feel. How easily they can be confused.

His gestures are the same as the night she met him, that boyish curiosity, that constant motion. His fingers flick against the saucer of his teacup. His hands pick the salt shaker up and put it down again. Every now and again the camera catches his foot twitching beneath the table. It's as if he is interested and engaged on the surface, but inside he is rushing to be somewhere else. He holds a devil beneath his skin and it's pushing its way out. Not that Victoria notices. She can't seem to stray from his face. She's falling for him hook, line and sinker, just like Holly did.

At one point they zoom in on a photograph of Frankie, with her full name underneath it. Holly can't feel anything anymore. She doesn't need to search her contacts list to know that Frankie's phone number is there. She remembers her auburn hair, the way it bounced when she laughed, the way it fell in a curtain when she uttered a terrible secret.

Tyler is not the innocent victim he has made himself out to be. Holly knows this in her bones. At the very end of the interview, her instincts are confirmed. When Victoria asks about Frankie's funeral, something about his reaction is not right. After a twenty-minute special of revealing all about their relationship, he shuts down. Holly knows how it feels, to want to close everyone down. After all, she knows a lot about lying. The filming cuts suddenly, as if even more of his response has been edited out. This fills her with hope and a new sense of purpose. Whatever Tyler claims to have felt, there is a darker side to his story. Holly's heart beats a little faster – it's a side to the story he doesn't realise she knows.

He looked so smug, sitting there in his sharp suit with a perfect sob story. What would his perfect, unlined face look like if he realised she held the power now, that he had given it to her? Holly is so sick of other people – especially men – being the ones to punish her, the ones to decide what is right and what is wrong. So what if he wants to kill her? She's not going to cower this time. She's going to fight back.

Chapter 46
Tyler

Everybody loves Tyler and it's as boring as hell.

His Instagram following has multiplied tenfold, twenty-fold, thirtyfold in the past twenty-four hours. It's embarrassing really – all he has on it are some blurry pictures of Frankie on their first and only weekend away in Bath and some shots of a rare sunny day in London, the general banality of someone who doesn't think that anybody else is watching them.

He's done radio interviews, television interviews and is scheduled to record a podcast once his shift at the hospital is done. The podcaster, a high-haired, Vans-wearing lad in his early twenties, seemed perplexed when Tyler emphasised that yes, he is a real doctor, a genuine surgeon with patients that take precedence over whatever this is. He doesn't have the time to float around all day and talk about being Tyler Wells. That's what this influencer business seems to be about – talking your face off about everything you're doing but not really doing much of it.

Tyler should be happy. Not only did he receive an out-pouring of love and support after he told his story about Frankie, but the world wants to hear it over and over again. They want to see it from every angle until it feels like their own. They feel heartbroken for him and incensed that someone like Holly dared to exist. *Someone like Holly who is still out there, who still exists.*

During an interview with a local news station, they asked him to talk a bit more about his approach to food. It didn't seem like a big deal at the time, but subconsciously he must have known it was. Why else would he have flattened his public-school accent, letting all the air out? Why else would he take on the jarring, musical East End intonation of the nurses that take three different buses to get to the hospital? In his new voice, he leaned back and said, 'Well, it's about balance, innit? I'll eat my leafy green veggies and grains with the best of them, but there's nothing wrong with an ice-cold beer and a burger once or twice a week. Our body needs fats to survive, so as a medical professional I am very comfortable with adding slices of bacon to my diet, or some chocolate. Hell, even a glass of good, red wine has medical benefits. It's all a bit classist, yeah? Diets like Holly's imply that the Average Joe's way of eating isn't good enough anymore. It introduces an elitism to food that, in my opinion, is motivated by greed. Not everyone would agree with my thinking, but it's just the Wells way.' He laughed then, and chewed on a brownie for the camera. 'Why should our conversations about food always be about restrictions? The problem with so-called health experts like Holly is that they feed off the guilt of others. Well, it's time to let that guilt go.'

Now, there is an email in his inbox from a publisher, asking if they can meet to discuss a potential book on his and Frankie's story, and would he be interested in a spin-off cookbook about the Wells way? This attention doesn't feel earned – all he did was draw attention to Holly's bullshit. Should he really get a fucking medal for stating the obvious? Then again, why shouldn't he?

He walks into the operating theatre, washes his hands and cracks his knuckles before turning to the anaesthetised patient below him. It's a neck operation, a tricky removal of a benign tumour, which will require him to carefully slice through muscle and nerve. This level of critical work has a tendency to calm him. Not today. As much as the fine finger work consumes him, his mind still wanders, reflexively thinking of ways he can play to his growing crowd.

Seeing your days through the eyes of someone else helps define them a bit better. He remembers feeling this way when he first started seeing Frankie, the excitement of framing his day for her alone. Nothing seems fruitless. All the disappointments, frustrations and lost moments fall into an effortless narrative. You want to be what people think you are. The operation feels like white noise, something to do with his hands while he thinks about the Instagram photos he'll take later and what he'll say about them. He's really on to something here with this eating plan. Think of the people he could free from twisted, food-obsessed beliefs. What the world needs right now is a common-sense approach to diet, one that he is qualified to deliver.

Tyler leaves the hospital on a high. He's headed for Haché on Fulham Road to satisfy his craving for the Steak Catalan burger, a big hunk of meat topped with chorizo and chilli jam. Cooked red meat, sugar and fat – it's the beautiful antithesis of Holly's obsessive diet. Slowly, slowly, he will eliminate the space she occupied in the world.

His phone buzzes in his pocket. It could be another agent, another interview. Tyler's heart sinks when he sees the number. It's Frankie's father, calling for the fourth freaking time today. How many times does a person need to call before they realise that they are being ignored *intentionally*? Don't people have any sense of self-respect?

He puts his headphones on and puts his iTunes on shuffle. Tonight deserves a soundtrack. The opening chords of Bloc Party beat in time with his heart. Nothing could be more fitting. This was the album of his and Frankie's first month together. It was the pulse of the underground indie club they used to go to in a time before Holly. They were rough enough around the edges to fit in, to kiss messily on the dance floor and grab underneath each other's clothes in the stairwell. He'd do anything to go back to those times, to pace through the streets of London, Bloc Party on repeat, with no understanding of life and of her.

Her cancer became a part of him too, that's what she never understood. She pushed him away as it took over her body, but it had already slipped through her skin and wormed its way into his. It turned over his own cells, poisoning him and morphing him into something different, something darker. Its roots still tug at his heart and tighten around his thoughts. Now, he is older, burdened and bitter, a rushing, hunched figure pulling his coat tighter and tighter across his chest.

The music was meant to enhance his good mood, but instead it lets in a gust of cold air. And along with it, the buzz coats his bones. The interview, the fifteen minutes of fame, the diet, it's not going to be enough. He can try and be happy with it. He can even try to go along with it, pathetically playing to the press and thousands of nameless fans. But even now he can feel the buzz whirring and churning, forming a solid shape, a need. It's a need that smells like blood. This is so curious – Tyler encounters blood every day of his job. Now, the terms of engagement have changed. He wants blood to crust and darken underneath his fingernails and seep into his expensive clothes. Not just any blood, Holly's blood. He chases life every day, desperately clasping on to it. Imagine, oh imagine, the sweet release of letting a life that shouldn't be here slip through his hands.

God, he hates himself. Look at the fucking mess he's become. He used to have a plan in life. He was so solid, so *sure*. He was going to put in his time at the hospital until he became Chief of Surgery, marry Frankie and put their kids through one of those posh creative schools. She could have quit her job and stayed home at with the kids and floated over to the hospital during his lunch break, carrying coronation chicken sandwiches from that little place only they knew. Hidden in the wrapping he'd find some of that old school liquorice that she knew he liked. He had it all going for him.

This is all Holly's fault. Everything would have been so perfect if she hadn't set Frankie's mechanism of self-destruction into motion. Ha, set it into motion. That's a funny one. As if she simply touched one domino and the rest fell down. She incessantly came between them with all her perfect pictures, wholesome recipes and inspiring words. Holly's responsible for driving him and Frankie apart. If it weren't for her, this beast within him would still be sleeping, undisturbed.

He's almost at Haché now. As per usual there's a queue snaking around the corner, a mixture of wide-eyed tourists and bored locals. God, he wishes he could just walk into the restaurant all alone, order his burger and eat in peace. That's all he wants, just one day where the stupid, slow and annoying are kept locked away. That would leave nobody, allow him to walk the streets freely, unhindered by the weakness of others. Sadly, this is not the case today, so he scrolls through the latest news on his phone.

Despite the bombshell about Frankie's death, the news reports seem to be pulling away from Holly's story. Tyler hopes that this is in revulsion, but it probably doesn't run that deep. Column space is limited and there are only so many words you can write to describe someone as a fake.

Then you have to chase a more interesting story, like this one today about a little girl who has disappeared while on holiday in Marbella. You have to move on. To be honest, there's far more mention of his name today than Holly's, and the news is all good. Headlines swoon, 'Finally, the fresh face of nutrition we've been waiting for', 'Doctor says: go on, eat the burger' and, to his embarrassment, 'Hunky surgeon with a hot diet to match'. Soon, every last trace of Holly will be gone. Nobody will be hurt again, he will help heal his followers' relationship with food and everybody will move on.

'Good afternoon, sir. Table for one?' an annoyingly short waiter interrupts his reverie.

'Yes, please. And don't bother with the menu. I know what I want. One Steak Catalan burger please, medium rare, extra chorizo.'

'Ah, a man after my own heart.'

'Indeed.'

His phone buzzes urgently. Frankie's father again. He puts the flashing phone back in his pocket. If something is ignored often enough, it disappears eventually. His mind picks at the thought of why he is calling. Have they seen him on the news? What did they think of his interview? It's best left alone. He has no time for diversions. The last time they spoke, Frankie was dead, hair spread like a fan above her in her coffin. He hoped she was wearing the rose-shaped marcasite pendant he had given her but he never got to see. He hadn't even known what chapel they were using for the funeral, or if they used one at all. On that muggy, typical London day he had sat on the couch, downing Scotch from the bottle as his almost-wife lay unmoving, as his almost-father-in-law yelled over the telephone, 'STAY AWAY FROM MY FUCKING FAMILY, YOU HEAR ME? OR IT'LL BE THE LAST THING YOU DO, TYLER. STAY THE HELL AWAY.'

Chapter 47

Holly then

They meet at one of those sad cancer events where the music is too loud and the décor is too bright. Where the sick are ushered in like cattle to be subjected to the healthy's idea of what they need to do to feel better. Today, it is a fashion show, an awkward procession of designer sleepwear to help the audience survive in comfort.

Holly walks inside, head bowed. It's been a while since she's been among cancer sufferers and she's nervous. Her London life to date has been a far more comfortable series of raw food and vegan events. She was welcomed into a new circle where, for once, she legitimately belonged. Now, being back into this fold of cancer sufferers feels like a terrible mistake. She shouldn't have said yes to the invite, but the organisers' sad story about lack of funding, and request for Holly to be the keynote speaker broke her heart. It will just be one quiet good deed, and then she will slink back into the unlikely universe she has created. Besides, it's not like there are any media people present to recognise her.

'Hey! I *know* you.'

A wild-haired redhead strides over to her. Confident and strong in an easy, angular Cos dress, she doesn't belong with the other downtrodden women swimming in loose jumpers. Even Holly's simple jeans, cardigan and trainers now seem in poor taste.

She can't help but break a smile at her. 'Maybe you do. I'm Holly Evans.'

Her curls quiver in excitement and the stranger grabs Holly's arm, 'Oh my goodness, I *knew* it. You look even more radiant in real life, do you know that?'

It shouldn't matter. Holly should shake her off and go backstage to prepare her speech, but the woman anchors her somehow. She's the type of woman you want to look at a second longer, or rather, you want her to look at *you*.

'What is your name? And what brings you to a place like this?' They both regard the silver and pale blue draping, the twee banners, and the gel candles haunting every table, and burst into laughter.

'Oh gosh. I'm Frankie and this is my first time at . . . something like this.' Her voice softens. 'I only received my diagnosis last week and my doctor thinks I should, you know, hang out with like-minded people while I figure things out.' For the first time, Holly notices the bulging Boots tissue pack in her hand. She must have expected the event to involve a lot of crying.

'Yeah, because what better to distract you than a crowd of people even sicker than you are.'

Another laugh ripples through her. 'I'm beginning to find this whole "being sick" thing a bit of a strange state of affairs. Like I'm meant to play a role, you know?'

Doesn't Holly know it . . .

Her heart breaks for Frankie, standing at the cusp of a world she didn't ask to enter. Soon, nobody will care about her job anymore, her opinions or her nice Cos dress. They will only want to ask the type of questions that peer inside her body, that poke into her fragile skin. Everything she thought she knew about herself will be put to the test and proven wrong. A new cancer-self will emerge and devour it all.

In some ways, she's jealous.

'You're OK, right?' she whispers. 'I mean, you quit chemo and went for natural remedies and look at you, you're fine now? No evidence of disease?'

'I'm all clear,' Holly says reassuringly.

'Right. My new boyfriend is a doctor and he doesn't get my paranoia over the traditional medical fraternity. It's coming between us all the time. I mean, we've only been together for six months and he's acting like he has some sort of authority over my life path and what is best for me. He doesn't understand that ever since I was little I hated everything to do with hospitals. He won't read my research on alternative cancer therapies. Maybe if I tell him I met you in the flesh and saw how wonderful you looked he will believe me. You went the natural route and you are fine.'

She nods. 'Yes, Frankie, I am fine.' Something pushes, trying to free itself from her tongue. She could tell her. Now is the time she could open her frozen jaw and hawk it out, an ugly, writhing thing on the floor between their feet. But she couldn't bear to see Frankie's freckled face contort in disgust. She looks healthy enough, with a strong mind to match. Armed with this and her doctor boyfriend she will come out of this. Holly's opinion doesn't matter, her lie is of no consequence. Frankie will be fine.

The organisers, two sour-faced women wearing matching heart-shaped badges, gesture for her to come on stage.

'Holly?'

'Yes . . .'

'It was amazing to meet you, really.' Frankie shifts on her feet. 'Could I email you sometime? Maybe even grab a cup of coffee with you? I'm feeling a bit alone on this path right now.'

She looks like a little child, her small, innocent face framed by angelic curls.

'Of course, of course. Consider me your friend.'

Chapter 48

Holly

The air feels thinner now, but clearer. The sneering face that cut Holly now has a name and a story. Tyler Wells, surgeon, surviving partner of Frankie, a better girl than she could ever be. What Tyler does not know is that things are about to get a whole lot worse. If he wants to watch her from his pedestal, she has every right to watch him back. She has every right to reveal his secrets. Just as he has revealed hers.

After they finish watching the interview, she begged Ayo for access to the cottage's Wi-Fi through forced tears. The guilt was eating her alive, she said. She needed to contact some people, to make arrangements, to set things right. Ayo nodded then and held her tightly. She understood the power of making amends.

Now the phone warms her hand. The relief Holly feels is expansive, imbuing the room around her with a golden glow. Perhaps the people who go on retreats like this feel better afterwards simply because they are connected again, not because anything special happened during their isolation.

Isn't the magnetic pull of the Internet so strange? She knows everybody still hates her. She expects the thick, unending bile of vicious comments but she needs to log on anyway and scroll through the horror until she feels sated. They don't burn as much anymore. Nothing can erode her new-found feeling of redemption. She isn't the only one who has lied. In many ways, Tyler's lie is far worse. After all, it may have cost Frankie her life.

Now she has the opportunity to make things right. She'll show her followers that yes, she lied and she feels terrible about it, but she never meant to hurt anybody. It will take care and meticulous planning, but if she pulls it off Holly Evans will be reborn.

A quick search for his name on Instagram reveals him right up top. The Wells Way, the fat-filled, indulgent diet he was peddling on live television, has made him an instant star. His pictures are still amateurish. Poor lighting and blurry subjects. None of the sharp, clean lines that the professionals have. He's just winging it, throwing a garbled message into the ether and people are *in love* with him for it. She can tell from the hundreds of comments, from the way people talk to him like he's a friend. Holly should know. This is the world he snatched away from her.

Her hands shake over the phone. Her body pulses with delicious excitement. It's that feeling of messaging a crush to say hey, how's it going, would you like to maybe hang out sometime? She selects each one of his pictures, and touches her finger on the little heart. A fluttering butterfly-winged assault of like, like, like, like. Who cares what others think? She has a purpose of her own now. She needs him to see her name flashing on his screen over and over again. An uncomfortable reminder. He needs to know that she is watching.

Chapter 49
Tyler

Tyler runs through Soho, pushing past dawdling lovers and distracted tourists. He turns the corner where it happened, and feels a little tug in his chest. The mud and rubbish on the paving has long since washed the last trace of her blood away. There's no time to stop, to breathe the moment in. He's late, and the stain of his sweat has ruined his Ralph Lauren shirt.

Hawksmoor, his favourite steakhouse, is launching a new menu tonight. The restaurant glimmers with food bloggers and journalists who have been invited from all over the city. He stands outside the window, catching his breath. It still feels peculiar that this self-aware crowd now includes him.

The door opens to warmth and fire smoke. The ripe smell of steak and red wine hovers heavily over the crowd. A blogger he's seen in the papers with high, coiffed hair and a prominent chin paces determinedly towards him. She has an animal-like sexuality to her, the type of woman who would have her way with you then leave while you're in the shower.

'Tyler! Oh my goodness, I can't believe you made it!' She enfolds him in a musky embrace and fires questions at him. How is he? Is he going to the launch at the Savoy? Is he signed on for the media tour of that new four-Michelin-starred restaurant in the south of France? Once she has exhausted every angle of superficiality, she flits off.

It continues, over and over again. The unsolicited love of strangers. Their perfume and smoky blazers rubbing onto him. In this world, you don't have to do anything to be famous. You just need a whiff of approval from someone, an article in a magazine, an air of importance. Then everybody pushes themselves into your path, hoping you will give them some of whatever it is they imagine you have.

He goes through the motions. Greets the chef and the owners. Feigns interest in the cooking process. Asks the questions that he figures will impress them, the questions that will make him stand out. He can't get too emotional about it. Focusing on how unqualified these self-proclaimed foodies are to even talk about anything more than a bowl of cereal will get him nowhere. Why exhaust himself with questions of who is deserving or undeserving? This is all a game that he will do anything to win.

He takes out his phone, elevates himself above a slab of pink, salted meat with a deep glass of wine teetering next to it. Pink, blood red, burgundy. Focus. Zoom. A still life of everything Holly hates. A provocative prod in her side.

Look how easily replaceable you are. Look at all the different ways I can take your life.

He adds a few filters and sharpens the image. His skills improve every day. The little adjustments he makes feel less like a lie and more like an advantage. Though he dismissed Holly's online kingdom, he can't help but think that his is different, his is something real.

The likes come in immediately. Ten, twenty, one hundred. A few overwhelming comments. One direct message from a young woman intent on sending him several unsolicited nudes a day. He's read a bit of psychology. He knows that this pounding feeling in his chest is nothing more than a shot of dopamine, a physical reward for every like.

What the textbooks don't tell you is that some highs are better than others. One hundred, no, one thousand likes don't compare to one particular name flashing across his screen. Holly Evans, over and over again, telling him she has noticed. Telling him that she is watching.

The buzz is back. This time, languid and delicious. It flows thickly through his veins and coils around his bones. His small, petty statements of intent are replaced with a clear purpose. He is performing for someone again. He slips out of the restaurant, ignoring the tugging arms of fake friends begging him to stay for one more drink. He makes his way through Soho, down Broadwick Street and left onto old Compton Street. It is later than he expected. Restaurants are locking up. The bakers at the French patisserie are blaring trance music while pounding dough for tomorrow's bread. Even the sting that comes with walking past his and Frankie's favourite sushi place has dulled.

All the planning, all the nights of stewing in his sweat thinking of the ways Holly harmed him have started to feel fruitless. This spark of activity came out of nowhere, this glimmer of hope. He didn't have to bother chasing her as much as he did. All he had to do is wait for her to come to him.

Chapter 50

Holly

How many hours has Holly spent studying magazines filled with thin, beautiful girls, pondering the secret to being loved? How many times has she beaten herself up for not having that special, secret femininity that kept her make-up in place, her arse tight and her demeanour sunny?

When she shifted from ugly to beautiful, she didn't notice the pattern underlying each action. She didn't question the choices she made about what clothes she wore or the way she did her make-up. It was a case of priorities. She couldn't say she had cancer anymore but she could draw attention to her eyes, her waist, her hair. What she didn't realise is that all her attention was won by looking the same as everybody else, and touting a message everybody wanted to hear.

As she stands in the now-familiar kitchen at the retreat, she realises the secret once and for all. Compliance. Smile like you mean it. Compliment strangers. Have the expected reaction to trauma and pain. Don't diverge from the path for fear of being labelled 'other'. Sinister. A lone wolf.

She fries a handful of onions in coconut oil, adds masala, cinnamon and some fresh curry leaves. God, it feels good to cook again. She knows by smell when the onions are done, and adds some fresh chopped tomatoes and red lentils. This remains the only area of her life where she feels natural, and still in control.

Ayo and Tara chat contentedly to each other as they set the table, looking up briefly to proclaim, 'Holly, that smells sublime!'

'Thanks!' she replies. 'It feels so strange to be actually *cooking* food again!'

In many ways, she is healing. After the watershed moment of finding out about Frankie's death she has done everything right. She has delivered long confessional monologues in the afternoon meetings, cried furiously over the shame she feels, and spent time after dinner getting to know her new friends. Some of her feelings – anger, sadness, regret, self-hatred – are true, but they start to recede as she focuses on a more urgent plan.

It hurts, but a new emotion is breaking through the surface. Forgiveness. She can't change the choices she has made in the past, but she does have the power to do the right thing in the future. Every night, before she falls asleep, she dreams of seeing Tyler. The scenarios change. Sometimes they happen to be waiting for the same tube or walk into the same room at the British Museum. The best ones are where she is most triumphant: she has smoothed foundation over her new face until not one remnant of a scar is visible; her hair is freshly dyed caramel blonde, with wind-blown beach waves as laid-back as Frankie's; the muscle she has built hiking in the hills surrounding the cottage each day and practising her sparring skills against the retreat's boxing bag is visible through her black body-con dress. He stares at her, because no man wouldn't. He looks at her, and she watches his face fall as he realises she knows, as shame sucks him into its endless black hole.

'I can't believe you're leaving us so soon,' sighs Verushka. 'I was just getting used to your amazing cooking!' Over the past few nights, Holly has taken to cooking the retreat dinner as an act of service. She loves foraging in the garden for fresh herbs and walking in the crisp morning air to buy fresh vegetables at the market. For her, it is another form of redemption, of rebirth. If her new friends can forget her past and see the value in her cooking, surely the rest of the world can too?

'Don't worry, I'll leave you some recipes.' She smiles. As much as she would love to live suspended in this cosy moment, nestled in the warmth of this kitchen, laughing at Alan's awkward jokes and fighting Tara for the last slice of bread, it is time she took control of her own life. Her train ticket is booked, her bag is packed and Zanna is expecting her. It's time to go home.

Chapter 51

Tyler

Tyler's ringing phone has become a constant soundtrack to his day. It starts as early as 7 a.m. after his run, and keeps going late into the night. Some of the calls relate to his actual job, others are waves of journalists, all riding the 'Hotshot philanthropic surgeon tells of private anguish' angle. More still forge a new path, one that is dominated by 'The Wells Way', one that is solely his own. He doesn't have the time for any of it, but at least it's a distraction from the buzz, a distraction from the other missed calls, the ones from Frankie's father.

He's thought of blocking him, but that feels too final, an admission that there is bad blood between them. He'll lose interest eventually, surely. All this fuss will die down and the calls will dry up, his among them. Tyler isn't even sure what the exact cause of the acrimony is, although he has an idea.

It's not his favourite memory. There were better days. He'd caught the fear by then – it itched inside his skull. She didn't love him anymore; she didn't love *him*. The signs had been racking up, undeniable. Her eyes fled somewhere else when he spoke to her. She never wore her engagement ring. Hours went by before her reply to his message flashed across his phone and even then, it was lukewarm. He'd tried to spoil her with gifts delivered to her parents' door, but these went unacknowledged.

It didn't make sense. Tyler felt he had been the model, caring boyfriend. Did Frankie and her family want him to do even more than he was doing now? It just wasn't possible. No, it was something else, something outside of him.

A darker fear scratched at his nerves. Maybe she had found someone else? That would explain her sudden lack of care in his presence, the contempt that snarled at the corners of her words, the awkward gait of her mother as she answered the door. Luckily for them, Tyler was no quitter. He would do anything to feel illuminated with love the way he used to. Sickness can be healed, and love can be spirited back into life.

He crunched through the fresh snow lining the pavement, a little less confident than he had hoped to be. Frankie had told him not to come over, so he was about to surprise her. On the one hand, he was desperate to see her, to bury his face in her hair. On the other, he hoped he'd catch her in the act of betrayal that was gradually tugging her away. Even the fleeting glance of another man kissing her would be better than this slow torture.

He wouldn't mention the cancer this time, not today. Every time he tried, she coiled further into herself. Instead, he'd bought a new book that he thought she'd like, something to remind her of where they started, and to pass the time as she healed. It must have broken her heart to have to quit the job she loved so much, and he wanted her to see that he understood. He was desperate for her to know that he felt her pain as acutely as if it was his own.

He stood outside her front door for a few moments, fresh snow peppering his hair. There was no turning back. He pressed the doorbell hard and heard it echo inside. Footsteps then, louder and louder until the door creaked open and they were standing facing each other.

She'd grown thinner, puffy and gaunt all at once. Her eyes, still flashing so brightly, appeared too big for her pallid face. She leaned wearily against the door.

'Tyler . . .'

The speech he had practised so many times in his mind lodged in his swollen throat.

'Babe, I needed to see you.'

'That is not your choice to make! How many times have I told you that I need space right now? I don't have the energy to repeat the same conversation over and over again.' She sighed out the word 'energy' with an anger that, frankly, made her look ugly.

He felt a rage rising in return, unstoppable. The broken figure in front of him had asked for this, every excruciating moment of it. If she hadn't been so obsessed with her hippy-dippy bullshit and her pie-in-the-sky role model, she may have stood a fighting chance. He felt so fucking helpless, banished from comforting her, his educated suggestions thrown back in his face.

'And what conversation would that be? That you don't seem to think I'm a good enough doctor to help you?'

Frankie began to edge away from him, glancing behind her frantically. She was getting nervous, but he couldn't help himself.

'How many fucking years have I trained in medicine, Frankie, huh? How many late nights have I stayed up to study and pour over decades of research? For God's sake, everyone else thinks I'm a hero! Why believe me, though, when you can find some random stranger on Instagram who looks good in a bikini, and follow what she says?'

Her voice, once husky, came out like shattered glass. 'Tyler, please, I'm so tired. Mum, come here a second please? MUM!'

'Not tired enough to stop with your green juices, colonics and fucking fairy dust that you think will cure you.'

'This is why I said I didn't want you here,' she whispered. It reminded him of his father – *Tyler, you're not helping.*

'Oh, really now? Admit it, Frankie, I'm the only one who gives a shit about you! At least I say what everyone else is thinking! Your family is too fucking timid to stand up to you, but I'm not.'

She made herself smaller and smaller. He didn't want to, but she made him; she wasn't looking him in the eye so he was forced to do it. He grabbed her face in one shaking hand.

'Look at me when I'm talking to you! It's because you don't respect my opinion, right? You think I went to the best schools and university for nothing? You think it was easy watching my mum die, and now you? God, do you know how many people I have worked on that don't get the chance to survive? Yet you've thrown yours away!'

She whispered something inaudible.

'What was that? Sorry is your throat a bit sore now? You're going to have to speak up, sweetheart.'

Her eyes were on fire. He'd never seen such hatred in them before. It was her fault; she hated him so much in that moment that she was spoiling for a fight.

'I said,' she spoke slowly, spitefully, 'because it is my fucking body and I have every right to decide what I do with it. No doctor, no partner, no lover has a say in the decisions I make over *my* body, and *my* life. That is something my *family* and the people who *really* love me understand.'

With that, time changed. He disconnected, retreated deep into his body, coiled in the red-hot rage that burned through his veins. He grabbed at her, but she lost balance and fell to the ground.

'Mum! Dad!' she cried urgently.

Shouting then, crying, firm hands pushing him onto the street and slamming the door. They didn't understand. He was just trying to help her, to change the ending to the story.

'Don't you come back, you hear me?' Frankie's father shouted into the cold.

He never looked back as he ran down the stark, white streets of London, muttering, 'it's her fault, it's her fault' like a madman, like a monster, like a man in love.

That was the last day he saw her. Frankie's condition declined over the following months and she let go. He often tries to imagine what those last days had been like. Did her family honour her wishes? Did they know the passage she wanted read at her funeral? Or that she wanted her ashes scattered across the Himalayas?

It's a funny feeling when someone you knew so intimately goes on and moves through their life without you. You feel tethered to them, yet as they move forward your reference grows further away. Soon it becomes little more than a mirage, a dream. He writes letters to her in his mind all of the time. Sometimes they say sorry. Most of the time they plead. 'Why, why did you force me to speak to you like that? Why did you make me break the beautiful castle we built?'

While he has to live with his mistake, he has a chance to make things right. The way their story ended was not his fault. Frankie may not be here to punish Holly for how she ruined a relationship and took a life, but he sure is. Hurting Frankie was an accident, but hurting Holly is something he will do with intention.

Chapter 52

Holly

It's the words that taunt her. Day in, day out, the frantic rhythm of imagined conversations. The things she will say when she sees him. Whether she is asleep, meditating or cooking in the retreat kitchen, it beats behind her eyes like a drum, a script waiting to be acted into life.

The tone changes depending on her mood. This morning, she lies tangled in cool bed sheets and reaches for her phone under her pillow. After looking through Instagram, Twitter and Facebook, she turns the camera on herself and examines her reflection. Zooming in and out, looking for flaws. The sun and fresh air have been miraculous, but not miraculous enough. Her skin is plumper and the scars look less angry, but they are still painfully visible. She blinks back tears – this might be as good as it gets. The anger and the regret are too heavy. She can't carry them anymore.

Today the script in her head has morphed from one of rage to one of apology. Holly feels Tyler's hurt, his loss, acutely. She needs him to know that he did something wrong, but she did too. None of this was ever meant to go so far, and they are both victims in their own way. Maybe it will all end if she's the one to say sorry first.

'Hey, Holly.' Tara hovers outside her room. 'Are you ready to go?'

In the fever of her imaginings, she almost forgot that today is the day she leaves the retreat. Ayo was meant to be the one to drive her to the station, but she had to leave the day before to attend to some undisclosed business. In her soft, elegant fashion, Ayo never mentioned the nature of her trip, but everyone knew that it had to do with the event, the shaming, that brought her here in the first place.

This is the funny thing about online shaming. It all happens on the Internet, so people think, oh it's just little sparks, they won't hurt you. But those sparks build into a raging wildfire that leaps off the screen and into your own life. It becomes tangible, bringing practical, visible consequences with it. Like police statements, an empty bank balance, a need to go and identify criminals in a line-up, weight gain, weight loss, night terrors, the clenching of your muscles till they become smaller and smaller in the hope that then nobody will see you. Whoever first said, 'sticks and stones may break my bones, but words will never hurt me' never had an Internet connection. Holly is both sad and relieved Ayo isn't here. Without seeing in Ayo's eyes how far she has come and how much she has healed, it may hurt less to leave.

Holly walks through the house one last time, struck by how a place that was so unfamiliar a few weeks ago now feels like home. How strange to have entered this house when she was so filled with self-hatred and to leave now as a different person, a person she actually likes. She finds Alan and Verushka sitting outside in a small patch of morning sunlight, sipping coffee and having an animated discussion about the state of the global economy.

'Well, I'm off!' she says brightly.

'Oh my goodness, let's hug quickly so I don't burst into tears!' Verushka says. 'This feels like the end of an era!'

'Don't worry.' Holly smiles. 'You'll be seeing me again in a few days for your special assignment in London. Zanna will give you a call to talk through all the details.' To think she is about to see Zanna again! Tonight, she plans on cooking her a three-course surprise dinner to say thank you for everything she has done.

Holly and Tara arrive at the station early. Not ready to leave the comfort of her retreat friendships yet, Holly buys them a cup of steaming hot chocolate each and suggests they watch the trains go by. She imagines Ayo quietly slipping on one with her small suitcase, a meditation book on her lap, headed for an unknown destination. She realises that she has, selfishly, never pictured Ayo's life before the retreat. She's always been this soft, magical goddess who spoke in a calming lullaby and floated along the halls of the cottage. She *belonged* there. If pressed, she'd guess that Ayo was a nursery school teacher, or a massage therapist. She has the open quality of a healer.

'Tara, do you know Ayo's story?'

'Hasn't she told you? Ayo was in politics back in Nigeria. She sat in Parliament and was an outspoken feminist.'

'That seems a long way away from here. Did she have to leave Nigeria because she was shamed?'

Tara is quiet for a long time, so quiet Holly is not sure whether she offended her, or if she simply didn't hear her.

'Oh well, Ayo told me the story once and it was quite vague. I'd only been at the retreat for a week and was struggling to sleep. I just felt so disgusting, you know? Whenever I closed my eyes I could see myself the way others saw me – this grainy footage of a desperate young starlet trying to be sexy.'

'You're not vile, Tara. It's easy for people to judge others; it helps them forget that they too are human.' Sometimes Holly is surprised by her own eloquence, by the assured voice of this new person she has become.

'I know that now, but at the time I felt stained with shame. I was sitting in my room on the first night I came here, trying to stifle my sobs. Ayo must have heard me, because after about half an hour she came into my room all wrapped up in that kimono that she loves, with two cups of hot masala chai. That's when she told me.'

She looks around, as if she is somehow still around to hear her.

'As I said before, Ayo was a highly respected female polit-ician with a strong stance on several contentious government issues. You could say she was a fighter, always on the side of the everyday guy and girl on the street. This meant she was anti-corruption, pro-choice, pro-female empowerment, etc. This made her a favourite with the global community and the people, but not so popular with the ruling elite.'

Holly tries to imagine Ayo restrained in a pencil skirt with her dreadlocks piled on her head. It shouldn't be so hard to imagine strength nestled within her softness but she struggles to form a clear image. Tara goes on.

'The political struggle on her home soil became too much, and she became too much for Nigeria's politicians. So they shipped her off to New York to fulfil the coveted but faraway role of Nigerian ambassador. This was the beginning of a beautiful time in her life filled with inspiration, rooftop parties and long walks in Central Park. Over there, well, she felt free to be her true self and she fell in love. She met the most compelling, intelligent woman, an expat from London, and they made a life together. They sounded like a total power couple and were a regular fixture at all the hot New York social events. The powers that be must have got wind of it, because they terminated her assignment and sent her to a less high-profile country, Germany I think.'

'What happened to her girlfriend?'

'Well, this is where things fell apart. They stayed together, and the girlfriend even started a company back in London to be closer to her. But obviously they were doing long distance and would send each other messages to spice things up – pictures, texts, whatnot. The thing is, unbeknown to Ayo, her phone was tapped the whole time.'

Holly feels tearful at the thought of her warm, wise mentor being targeted by others and her innermost desires being exposed.

'Who tapped the phone?'

Tara says, 'Ayo's not sure, because the first she heard of it was when it was published on the front page of a national newspaper. Deep, intimate, messages between her and her lover broadcast for all to see. Taking part in any sort of homosexual act is still a criminal offence in Nigeria, but because it didn't happen in the country itself, they couldn't do anything to her. All they could do was ridicule and shame her until she quit her job and vowed never to come back. This retreat is now her passion, because she understands the impact that public shaming can have on a person's life.'

'Is she still in touch with her girlfriend?'

'Sadly, they split up, but they keep in touch. Apparently she's a hotshot publicist to the stars now. She lives in London, so I think they still stand a chance one day, when the humiliation has subsided. Ayo has a picture of her somewhere – really edgy-looking woman, with an asymmetrical black bob.'

Holly drops her journal to the ground; her mouth goes dry.

'Tara. What's her name?'

'It's something a bit exotic, maybe Lana? No, that's not it. Anna? Wait, too plain.'

'Zanna?' she stutters.

'Yes! That's it! Her name is Zanna.'

Holly is overcome by a love so big it threatens to choke her. Of course, Zanna had been in love with Ayo. How radiant they must have been as a couple – Zanna as light and nervy as air, and Ayo, grounded as the earth. Each of them were so skilled, so capable. They must have felt at one point that they had it made. A public humiliation intense enough to break them, no wonder both of them built careers that ensured, in their own way, that others would be spared the eternal impact of shame. Holly's plan for Tyler is cemented in her mind. She owes it to both of them to do the right thing.

Chapter 53

Tyler

It would be easier if, when someone leaves, they were spirited away, leaving no trace of their existence. Yet humans are messy creatures that accumulate things over time. They leave debris in their wake.

After the strange men carried Tyler's mother out of their enchanted house, there was cleaning to be done. Tyler was no longer useless or of little help. His father marched him through the house as they picked up and threw away remnants of her sickness: strange congealed potions, rough brown pills, and fortifying protein shakes. Things which were meant to help but were now rendered without a purpose. Her spirit was gone, so things just became things, no matter how closely they lay against her skin. Tyler bundled the sheets that still smelt of her into his small arms, and sobbed into what was left of her scent.

Frankie left her own debris in her wake. When Tyler returned to his apartment, remnants of his and Frankie's time together haunted him. A ticket stub from a band they had seen together. An almost-empty jar of moisturiser. A pink cardigan she hadn't really cared for. He grew obsessed with returning these lost items, but no matter how many times he knocked on her family's door, nobody answered, even though the smoke trailing out the chimney hinted at a fire burning inside.

Today, he distracts himself to keep his mounting feeling of despair at bay. While he may be helpless, at least his picture got more than 1,500 likes today. In his Inbox, a message from Holly:

'Hey Tyler, I just want to say I know you are the one who did this to me. I know everything.'

A few minutes later, a new message.

'I'm not angry anymore, and I'm not scared either.'

Silly little girl. Does she really think she can play with fire? He could say so many things, but he holds off his reply. Let her wonder. Let her remember who has the power here. Yes, he is the one who is about to start working on his own recipe book, where his message will hopefully reach women like Frankie and stop them from falling for con artists like Holly again. He can't wait to experiment with cooking – slicing and carving prime cuts of meat with his favourite knife. He always did make an unbelievable, garlicky lamb shank roasted in red wine and thyme. What sweet justice that would be! He hums a light little tune through his gritted teeth. People are finally paying attention to what he has to say, they are buzzing around him like flies at a buffet. Even Holly cannot resist edging nearer.

Chapter 54

Holly then

It's a hopeful, sunny day in London, and Exmouth market is bustling with people on their lunch break. Long queues form in front of the food stalls selling doughnuts, paella, gourmet burgers and tacos. Holly's mouth goes dry as she spots Frankie's thin frame in front of a stall aptly named, 'The Veggie Guy'.

'Holly, you made it! You're just in time. This guy over here makes the best salads in London.'

Frankie slaps a dollop of hummus over each pile of vegetables, grabs some plastic forks and leads them to a nearby park. As she follows her, Holly can't help but admire her confidence. She would never ask a stranger for lunch in the park – it feels so intimate. In fact, she almost didn't come, but she was curious about why someone as obviously successful as Frankie would want to spend time with her. She was also encouraged by the prospect of making a new friend.

The park is packed with a jarring contrast of people in business attire and shirtless builders. At 1 p.m., everyone needs a break in the sun. They find a small patch of grass with some shade and settle down, Frankie chattering excitedly all the while.

'What I love about you is that you have taken charge of your illness, you know? You haven't sat back and let a bunch of medical specialists tell you what to do. You have done the research and made a decision based on what is best for your body.'

Holly looks away, afraid Frankie will catch the panic in her eyes.

'It hasn't always been this easy,' she says. 'My family doesn't understand my new lifestyle at all.'

Frankie laughs too loudly then, and Holly notices her fists are clenched.

'Oh, tell me about it! I knew you would be the only one to understand this! Remember that doctor boyfriend I told you about?'

'Of course!'

'Well, life with him took an unexpected turn the moment I told him about my choice not to undergo chemotherapy. We hadn't been going out for very long, but he turned intense really quickly. I won't lie, I enjoyed the attention, but when I got sick the attention felt smothering. He was obsessed with looking after me, and with changing my mind about not having medical treatment.'

She's acting more amused than outraged, the way most girls do when a man has hurt them deeply. Better to rewrite the pain into a fun story to share with friends instead of acknowledging the cruelty that lurks beneath the words.

'I couldn't take it anymore so I broke up with him. Around the same time, I moved back home with my parents so they

could look after me. But he couldn't take no for an answer –
he started small, with constant phone calls and texts. Then
he began to drive to my parents' place at all hours of the day.
I thought maybe he'd get it out of his system but he's still
at it. Just last week, he proposed to me! And I feel horrible
because, a few months ago, I would have said yes. That level
of attention from a man is so hard to come by; I felt like I had
met my soulmate.'

Holly notices the cold sores clustering around Frankie's
lips, the torn skin at her cuticles and the new bones that
jut out her arms. She didn't just call Holly to talk about the
benefits of a natural diet. She needed to talk about this. She
edges closer and puts her arm around Frankie.

'You're not worried, are you?'

Frankie turns slowly towards her, still holding a determined smile on her face.

'Holly,' she says softly. 'Have you ever loved someone
who you think could kill you?'

Chapter 55

Holly

The apartment is all packed up, but Zanna has managed to stall the movers for just one more week. Holly finishes scrubbing her body raw in the shower, turns off the water and wraps her head in a towel. She stands for a moment, breathing in the rose-scented steam. It feels good to be back.

They knock as she's slipping on the borrowed black shift dress that still carries the scent of Zanna's signature Chanel No.5. She runs to the door and flings it open. It feels so freeing to no longer be petrified of what's outside.

'Are you sure you want to do this?' Zanna frowns. 'After this is posted and goes into the world, there's no turning back. I cannot guarantee or control anything from here.'

'I'm sure.' Holly edges closer and hugs her. Everything is going to get better soon. No matter what storm this video brings, she feels buoyant with the certainty that life is about to return to normal. She will remain in London and begin a new life. She hasn't spoken to her father yet and doesn't plan to – there is no need to be that Holly again.

Verushka adjusts the camera and sits in the chairs they have set up for their interview.

'I'm ready when you are!' Choosing Verushka to interview her was the easiest decision she has had to make in months. Nobody is stronger, tougher or more committed to telling the truth. No one deserves a second chance more than she does. Out of the context of the retreat, Verushka is calm, businesslike and every inch the sharp reporter. Holly, on the other hand, has chosen not to wear a smidgen of make-up. The world wants to see her broken. They want to see her insides. So she's going to offer herself up, raw and humbled. She takes a seat, and the camera starts to roll.

'Hi, everyone, I am Verushka Pillay, an independent investigative journalist. Here with me is Holly Evans who, for the first time since the attack that set off a series of events that brought her name into disrepute, will be telling her side of the story. Holly, what would you like to say to your followers, the media and the world?'

'Hi, Verushka. I want to start off by saying that I am not here to excuse or defend anything. All I come here with today is an apology. I invited thousands of you into my life to share my wellness journey. I represented myself as authentic while editing out the uncomfortable realities that didn't fit into the image I created. By doing this, I neglected to acknowledge the power I had to influence other people in their nutritional and medical decisions.'

Her eyes fill with tears. The worst is yet to come. She can do it. She has to do it.

'Would you like to share what uncomfortable reality you were editing out specifically?' Here it comes, the wave of shame. After this, nothing will ever be the same. Holly closes her heart and jumps.

'I can confirm that I never had cancer. I underwent surgery to remove a non-cancerous tumour. From the moment of that operation onward, everything was a lie.'

Verushka looks at her encouragingly. Keep going, keep breathing.

'Through the misrepresentation of my medical history, I earned thousands of pounds in brand endorsements, as well as the financial benefit of a crowd fund set up to help me pay for alternative treatments. It was never, ever about the money, though, although I see now that my financial gain is completely shocking. For this reason, I intend to pay back every cent to my sponsors.'

With a wave of nausea, she thinks of all the stupid purchases she frittered her riches away on: a new car she never drove, designer cruelty-free clothing and accessories, spa days in the country and unwanted gifts for her mother. Money is fluid like that: the faster it comes, the quicker it goes away. She grits her teeth and says, 'In addition to this, I will be donating a third of all my future income to Children With Cancer UK.'

She holds the gaze of the camera openly, earnestly. They need to see she means it this time.

'Holly, if you were well so soon after beginning your career on Instagram, why did you keep lying?'

'How do I say it . . . I think if you want to believe something is true and you lie often enough, the lie becomes real in your own mind. The lie took over. I was mentally ill and have been seeking professional help for this. I recently took some time to attend a highly beneficial retreat, which has helped me examine and take responsibility for my actions.'

'Such as the times that you posted pictures of yourself exhibiting clear symptoms of cancer, such as hair loss and bruising?'

Breathe in, breathe out. Let them see it all.

'Yes. I fabricated it all. I shaved my hair off, I harmed myself and I cannot tell you the remorse I feel as a result.'

'Do you realise you were faking a serious illness that shatters the lives of millions of people every year? That there are people with mothers, fathers, partners and children that sought comfort in your lies?' She has to hand it to Verushka – she's good.

'I do now, and all I can say is that I am so deeply sorry for the lives I have affected through my work. Every motivation I had for doing this was selfish but it was never meant to hurt anybody else. I thrived on the attention and the care I received from my friends and the online community. Unfortunately, I took it too far.'

Zanna stands behind the camera, nodding in encouragement. She's getting through it. She's almost there.

'Was your diet a lie too?' Verushka asks.

'No, I believe wholeheartedly in the vegan diet and stand by all the research I did into nutrition. I never felt healthier or more alive than when I was following my diet plan.'

Then, the clincher, the moment she would rather not remember.

'What about the recent story where a woman died following your plan?'

Holly holds down sobs and the urge to be sick. 'I can't speak for individual cases, but I can say that I have started investigating these claims and am doing everything I can to take responsibility for them. There is nobody to blame for the impact of what I have done but myself. I am filled with the deepest regret and take responsibility for any hurt I have caused. In fact, I have already been in email contact with Frankie's family.'

Holly notices Verushka and Zanna looking at each other with wide, worried eyes. This was not part of the script. She smiles at them encouragingly. It's OK. She knows what she's doing now.

She looks into the camera without fear of what it is capturing. Her skin is pink and swollen with fresh tears. Her hair, no longer blonde, is showing its dark roots. There is no more shield against the world – no fancy clothes or make-up to hide who she really is. If her old self could see her now, she would look away in revulsion at the ruined woman she has become. Yet Holly feels remarkably, blissfully reborn.

Chapter 56
Tyler

Tyler finds a corner table at the Ivy Café with good light. The sun hasn't set yet, and the room glows gold as he cracks his fork into the steaming top of his shepherd's pie. It's not as good as his mum's was, but it will do. He takes a quick picture, filters it and shares it on Instagram. As his phone flashes with validation, he hums.

Tyler of all people should know that when you share your life on the Internet, the people that follow you manifest as real human beings. They creep out the screen and into your space. Isn't that what he did with Holly?

Tonight, he's the one being followed. After posting the picture of his dinner, a bunch of banker lads jostle over to him and invite him to sit at their table. 'Top lad, this!' they say. They love his new diet, and they think his girlfriend was a belter. 'Time to find you a new girl, son!' they joke, while passing him another drink. The whole experience is uncouth and awkward and he can't will it away quickly enough. But this is his destiny now, to be strangely public, to be deeply lonely yet strangely loved.

It's early, but it feels like he has lived through a long, ragged evening. He turns into a back street to walk to the station, one lined with expensive houses that masked the looming council estate nearby. Poverty always made him feel uncomfortable. The footsteps behind him come as a surprise, as does a raspy voice calling his name. Probably another fan, eager to take a picture with him or ask that their nan's mac&cheese recipe be included in his book. This is what fame does, he thinks, stripping the innocence out of human interactions, leaving you to constantly feel like prey.

There, luminous in the shadows he sees her. She looks as worn as the picture of her that used to live on his fridge. Stripped of her old face, golden hair and usual pastel work-out gear, she looks weathered and dangerous. He feels a rush of self-pity. No, it's not fair. It shouldn't happen here. He didn't plan it like this. He didn't dream it into being. It's too abrupt and unexpected.

He feels for the keys in his pocket. Jutting one at the right angle into her spleen should be enough.

He grinds his teeth as she moves closer.

Chapter 57

Holly

Tyler was right about social media being a weapon. While he so fervently believes that Instagram hurt Frankie, he has no awareness of how he's using it against himself. Holly sees his painfully styled shepherd's pie picture while lying on the bed in her soon to be gone apartment. Such a rookie – the angles are all wrong. She moves quickly, running a brush through her hair and slipping on a hoodie and a coat against the cold. Wait, one more thing. She rifles through the boxes in her kitchen and picks up her sharpest, favourite knife. She has the power to protect herself this time. There is no way Tyler is going to hurt her twice.

Her heart races as she rushes to make it to the Ivy Café in time. She was going to seek him out in a few weeks, when the dust of her confession would have settled in the media, but she keeps being haunted by images of Frankie and that day in the park. After their candid conversation, she didn't hear from her again. Why didn't she think to call her? Why didn't she make the time to find out if her natural remedies were working or if her fears about her relationship were true? Maybe then, she could have been saved.

In her new, clear frame of mind, Holly understands why. If she had faced Frankie's illness, if she had confronted the toll the cancer was taking on her body, she would have had to take responsibility for her role in it and reveal her lies. Back then, it was easier to just forget about Frankie, including her disturbing relationship with her doctor boyfriend.

She runs into the tube station, and is amazed that under the bright lights nobody notices her. People are still making their way home from work, heads nestled in novels and tablets. Four stops later and she is standing outside Marylebone station. Her breath quickens as she paces down the street, hands in her pockets. She stands outside the Ivy Café, looking in on the opulent world she once occupied so comfortably. Now she is nothing more than a beggar watching as the rich men feast. The knife juts uncomfortably from her inside coat pocket. It doesn't feel right walking through the city with a weapon, but she won't make the same mistake twice. Her intentions are good, but who knows how Tyler will react when he sees her.

As Holly hoped, he is still inside, laughing with a pack of well-dressed men who look like bankers, with the same suits, all styled and scrubbed until every inch of them glows. It makes Holly wonder what stench they're trying to cover, what dirt they are really hiding.

She stands around the corner, aimlessly scrolling on her phone until he leaves, calmly deleting the latest batch of hateful comments. What do they matter when her life is about to turn around soon? The wind picks up, its biting force pushing against her. Only when her body is shivering and her fingers are numb does she spot his broad silhouette loping out the door.

Adrenaline pulses through her veins as all the speeches she has practised in her mind converge. She's sorry. She's angry. She still doesn't understand. Her mouth is dry and her throat feels swollen. All the hours of wondering and waiting to confront him ache in these two syllables, in the moment when she shouts out his real name, 'Tyler.'

Chapter 58
Tyler

She runs faster than Tyler expects. Suddenly she is on him, clutching his arm. Her touch lights up the buzz like an inferno. Her desperation thins the air. He always wanted to leave her with nothing, but it is repulsive to see it up close.

Her chaotic, searching eyes try to hold his own. But he won't look at her; he won't. She is the reason he is walking home alone tonight. She is the source of his guilt, his despair, his rage.

'Please, please don't run,' she says softly, holding up both her hands in surrender. 'I'm not going to do anything to you. I just want to say two simple things. I'm sorry about Frankie. I really am. It goes beyond sorry, I am heartbroken. I was mentally unwell for so long and I didn't understand that I was affecting real people. My desire to be liked became an illness in itself.'

The rush of remorse is too late. What good are words when he still can't get to sleep at night without imagining Frankie holding him? When he still buys bottles of her perfume just to remember how she smelt? How he would rewrite history if he could, including stamping out this pathetic, shivering creature far earlier.

She edges closer still, and he lets her. The sharp edges of his keys bring him a faint comfort.

'I remember Frankie,' she says. 'I even met her once.'

He fights the urge to scream, to tear her apart with his bare hands. This is new; she never told him. Why didn't she tell him? Like a lover who has found out his partner's cheating, he needs to hear every sordid detail.

'It was at an event for cancer sufferers. It was her first one. I was the keynote speaker, so of course she thought I was the real deal. We exchanged email addresses and soon became friends . . .'

'You kept in contact?' he chokes.

'Yes, I sent her recipes and introduced her to Dr Ray over email.' Dr Ray, that slimy charlatan, the final nail in the coffin.

'Tyler, you have to believe me when I say that she never told me how bad it was. If only I had known, I hope I would have done things differently.'

The buzz whines and screams as he imagines every email appearing in Frankie's inbox, every word wrenching her further and further away from him. His eyes flicker to Holly, who continues to speak with a faraway, sublime expression on her face. A scarred but healing face, he notices; one she does not deserve.

'What you did was wrong,' she purrs. 'But I forgive you. I need to forgive you for my own freedom and hope that one day you can do the same for me. I had to find you in person to tell you.'

How dare she? After all he's been through. After all he's lost. Forgiveness won't magic Frankie into being once more. The whining pauses, as if catching its breath.

'You disgust me,' he growls, grabbing her arm.

'Wait,' she says calmly. 'There's something else I want to say, a secret I know, about you and Frankie.'

Tyler freezes. There is something about the tone of her voice that puts him on edge. Then he sees it, her mobile phone held up, brazen and threatening as a gun.

'Wait, are you filming this?'

'Do you have a problem with that? You're the heartbroken fiancée after all. Surely you want the public and your new army of adoring fans to know the truth?'

He shouldn't trust her, he should rip the phone straight out of her hands, but the temptation is too great. Isn't this what he always wanted? To see her confess to her fans and to show them all what a fraud she really is?

Holly holds the mobile between them. Tyler notices her hand is shaking.

'Frankie and I met for lunch one day. She looked awful, so pale and stressed. She told me she was worried about her ex-boyfriend, a doctor. Apparently she was angry that he wouldn't support her decision not to undergo traditional treatment.'

The buzz rings in his ears, but it is not the buzz anymore. It's the darkness that used to take him over.

'That's not the way it was,' he says, his voice sounding weak, pathetic.

'That's not all,' she continues. 'She said that she broke up with you, but afterwards she started getting surprise visits from you, didn't she? You turned up at her parents' house uninvited and pushed her around. You made up a whole fantasy about you two still being together, fighting her cancer together and even getting engaged! In reality she just wanted you to get the fuck away from her, am I right?'

Nobody, especially not Holly, could know the beautiful, fragile love they held between them. The love she shattered. How *dare* she act like the expert on what they shared?

'No, no, no!' he shouts.

'It's quite pathetic when you think about it. Someone acting so principled when underneath it all they are a scumbag who cannot take no for an answer. Is that what the Wells way is all about? Forcing yourself and your opinions on others?'

She thrusts the mobile in his face, still filming his every move, defiant. He'll show Holly, he'll show them all.

'She wanted to be with me! She just didn't understand what was best for her. I had to *show* her!'

'So you stalked her and she still wouldn't listen, right? You went to her house one day and showed her who was boss. Oh, don't even try to argue with me – I have already spoken to Frankie's family.'

The buzz snarls in his breath, pulsing through his veins.

'The bitch asked for it, just like you did.' Tyler laughs, the words flowing out of him, unstoppable. 'You think you're so clever, that you can control your health with your little nutrition plans, but you couldn't stop me getting into your apartment, and getting under your skin.'

'Like when you cut me with a scalpel?'

'What else? Someone needed to teach you a lesson.'

A smile creeps onto Holly's face. In Tyler's arrogance and haste, he has given her a full, recorded confession.

He kneels over her and grabs her throat. In a few seconds, this will all be over. He'll have her mobile and will have silenced her for good. Nothing, not prison, nor being unable to ever practise medicine again, stands in his way. His life was broken the moment Holly came into their lives. His fingers lace around her neck one by one. Under the streetlight, he watches her face redden and swell. The mobile falls to the ground and her hands go limp. Tyler shifts more weight onto her fragile neck. Until, he feels a note of discordance, a strength, a powerful push from beneath him.

Chapter 59

Holly

She walks out of the alley alone, head held high, the wind blasting her new skin. A private knowledge of London takes over as her feet move her along the quiet back streets all the way home. Her coat is buttoned all the way up, Tyler's blood stiffening her clothing underneath it. It smells like lead, with a lingering tang of bergamot and sandalwood.

She thought she was sorry when she rehearsed their exchange in her head. She thought she was remorseful when she walked towards him in the alley. The words she said to him and to her friends on the retreat – so heartfelt – could have easily belonged to her. Yet when his eyes changed and he raised his hand, a sleeping beast woke in her soul, a fury that would no longer be still. She was no longer sorry; she was angry.

Holly may have lied, but Tyler had terrorised Frankie, filling the last months of her life with fear. Holly knows too well what that terror feels like. How many hours did she spend as a child, cowering in the corner while her father raged? Living in fear that he was on his way home, ready to punish her for some unnamed crime she hadn't committed? The constant watching makes you crazy, the fear unravelling your grip on self-control.

Tyler deserved the worst punishment of all, so she'd reached into her coat pocket and pulled out her greatest weapon – her mobile.

In the dimly lit alleyway, she provoked him. She played on his pride. Nobody can resist the pull of an audience, of setting the record straight. He got lost in his sad, imagined past. His face filled the video clip, violent with rage. His whole confession and attempt to kill her caught on camera. Three. Two. One. Action.

All she needs to do now is edit the clip and share it to her Snapchat and Instagram Stories. Then the whole world will see his confession and know that she wasn't going crazy. The torment she went through was real, and she wasn't to blame for any of it. There is only one snag – nobody can know what happened next.

A message flashes on her mobile from Zanna. 'Girl, your confession video is killing it! I was cynical at first, but I think this is the beginning of your big comeback.'

Holly smiles. Of course it is, because everything is just a show. When she was loved, she was a character to idealise. When she went wild, she was the jester. People lived vicariously through her, safely experiencing by proxy every-thing they felt was wrong. Why were they so insulted by her fame, by the power of her platform? They were the ones who built it.

The truth doesn't get views, and reality doesn't earn compassion. The story can always be a little bit worse. Mental illness draws the crowds. It's always the most extreme highs and lows that get the most attention. Be sick. Go wild. Shave your head on camera. Be sexy, but not slutty. Don't get too dark, and don't go too crazy, or you will wear your label for good. Don't ask for help, because everyone is just here for the entertainment.

Nobody likes a wild woman, but there was a wildness in her that needed to be freed, a passionate rage that needed to act itself out against his face, his chest. His chest. He fought back, but her months spent boxing made her stronger. He had his fists, but she had a knife. She pounded her anger out in the unblinking silence of one of London's wealthiest streets.

Now her finger hovers over the video clip. Everything she needs to prove her innocence over the past few months is here. However, it will incriminate her in the future, and it will confirm that she was the last person to see Tyler alive. Nobody has to know what happened outside the frame of her heartfelt YouTube confession. Nobody would understand how *necessary* it was.

Holly is now calm, sated and ready to comply. She could delete the video clip, erase his confession and continue to apologise. You were right, I was wrong. She could bow her head and accept the punishment for the things she has done. How her audience will enjoy it!

The show must go on. She'll become the broken face of the fake digital age. Her fallen empire will be rebuilt, as the curiosity of her followers keeps them hooked to see how she recovers, to talk about what she does next. She'll become a darling once again as everyone discovers, with outrage, the truth about Tyler. She'll start a new, authentic nutrition plan that takes the best of her and Tyler's philosophies and promote honesty on Instagram with her own emotional, scarred, make-up-free videos. Perfection is old; righteousness, boring. Mental health should never be sacrificed for an eating plan. She knows that now.

She walks inside her apartment – how she'll miss this place! Her shirt crackles and sheds brown flecks of dried blood as she hides it in the laundry basket. She removes her favourite knife from her coat pocket. Runs hot water in the basin and cleans it tenderly, her thoughts lost in the clouds of pink water blooming around it. She slides it next to the other cooking utensils in a box that will soon be lost in storage. She stands naked on the shower floor for a moment, the central heating caressing her. She reaches for a loofah and scrapes his legacy off her. The first blast of water washes him away, and any residual guilt with it. It stings her scratches clean. She whispers to herself, 'I am better. I am stronger. I am clean.'

Her attack didn't destroy her life, it reset it. The old, timid, people-pleasing Holly was broken to be remade into a tougher model. One who was now no longer afraid to fight back.

Her phone lights up with a string of comments, likes and shares. A familiar thrill awakes, stretching within her bones. It can all be hers still; everybody can love her once again. She selects the video of Tyler, heart pounding. Delete it and nobody will ever know that he was responsible for her torment, for Frankie's. Upload it and she may be implicated in his death.

She makes her decision.

Acknowledgments

Many wonderful people have played a role in bringing this book to life and made the journey to publication exciting and memorable.

Thank you to Jenny Bent of The Bent Agency for seeing the potential in those initial chapters and providing the faith and direction I needed to make *Shame on You* shine. Thank you Sarah Manning for driving the editing process and championing this novel in the UK. Your passion, drive and positivity are unparalleled.

Katherine Armstrong and Bonnier Zaffre were excited about this story from the start and understood the vision for *Shame on You*. Katherine, thank you for your enthusiasm for the book and for your thoughtful, eagle-eyed edits. My utmost thanks goes to every member of the Bonnier Zaffre team that played a role in publishing and marketing *Shame on You*.

Any book takes a village, a network of loved ones that encourage one to keep going. I am so grateful to my writing group – Blaize and Catherine – for their enduring support and inspiration on my journey to publication. You are my first readers and confidantes. Thank you to my dearest friends – Emma, Liesl, Luana, Cat, Debbie, Anna, Claudia, and Thembi – for sharing the highs and lows of this writer's life and always believing in me. Thank you to

Pamela and Kerryn for being such insightful beta-readers and to Liesl B for your considered insights on how it feels to survive cancer.

Thank you, Mom, for teaching me to love language, and Dad for giving me a love for stories from before I could speak. Both of you never doubted that I was destined to write and encouraged me to keep going. My super soul sister Rosie, it is thanks to our shared love for healthy cooking and holistic living that the seed for *Shame on You* was planted. Thank you for your love and inspiration.

Finally, thank you to my great love – my husband Rhys. This story is infused with your voice as sentences and plotlines sprang to life over dinner and walks around our neighbourhood. You held me when I didn't think I could do it. You held us so I could have the opportunity to chase my dreams. There are no words to express my gratitude.

A Conversation with
Amy Heydenrych

What is the inspiration behind *Shame on You*?

A number of separate moments inspired and contributed to *Shame on You*. I used to work in PR and was in charge of selecting social media celebrities to work with big global brands. The psychology of what makes someone influential, and what happens when that influence is revealed as false, fascinated me. As a keen home cook, I was experimenting a lot with vegan cooking at the time and following famous clean eaters such as Ella Woodward, The Hemsley sisters and, of course, Belle Gibson (whose scandal inspired Holly's character to some extent).

How much do you think social media affects our lives and should we be more cautious in what we share online?

I think social media impacts our mental health in a few ways: 1) we can become despondent viewing the highlight reels of other people's lives; 2) we can waste mental energy framing our own lives for an imagined audience and 3) we waste time on social platforms when we could be doing something amazing, like going for a long walk outside, completing a personal project or connecting with someone close to us. As for being more cautious, I think it depends on your own personal views on privacy and what you wish to protect . . . (more on that a bit later!)

What kind of research did you do for *Shame on You*? Social media is so central to the plot; did you talk to people with large followings about how they deal with being recognised?

I met a few Instagram stars with really large followings to discuss their relationship with their newfound fame. I was fascinated by how many were not living the lavish lives they portrayed online – they lived in tiny flats and houses where they had simply identified one or two places with great lighting. I work extensively in the digital industry in my day job and have ghost written a book on social media for an ad agency CEO, so I think a lot of that research and insight into digital filtered through into the book.

I was paranoid about the cancer narrative hurting someone who had been affected by the disease. For that reason I met with cancer survivors and an oncologist to understand what happens emotionally when one is diagnosed with cancer. As for the cooking and recipes, I have basic training as a raw vegan chef so those scenes were based on my own love of cooking and research into it!

***Shame on You* is your debut novel, how did it feel when people first read it?**

I have always hoped that my writing would touch another person, whether that meant making them think about an issue or entertaining them. It has been so thrilling watching strangers read the book and become quite passionate about the characters!

How have you changed your social media habits after writing *Shame on You*?

Before writing *Shame on You* I was a bit of a Holly in that I posted a lot of pictures of my healthy life, from yoga poses to my new favourite vegan recipes. Now that I've written the book I include the moments in between and don't try so hard to live up to an ideal I created in my own mind. Before posting anything I now ask, who am I doing this for, and why?

Living in South Africa, did you find it hard to set your novel in London?

I lived and worked in London for a few years, so a lot of the setting is borrowed from my own experience of the city. However, I did need a bit of help in creating Tyler's wealthy lifestyle. Luckily one of my best friends, Emma, is English and lives in Chelsea. She gave me a lot of help in deciding which bars and restaurants to send him to, and I'd often get her to video them so I could pick up details for description!

Who are the people who have inspired you the most?

In terms of my writing, I am inspired by Jennifer Egan's ingenuity, Margaret Atwood's fearlessness and Elena Ferrante's ability to capture every light and shade of the female soul. When it comes to thriller writing, I look up to Tana French and Emma Donoghue.

What are you currently reading?

I'm finishing up *Anatomy of a Scandal* by Sarah Vaughan – it's a cracker!

If you were stuck on a desert island, which three books would you take with you?

I'd take *A Visit from the Goon Squad* by Jennifer Egan (I reread it once a year), *Le Petit Prince* (my favourite story, and a book that is tied to many of my most favourite life memories) and *The Collected Short Stories of Amy Hempel* (because her writing is perfection and I never tire of her stories).

Can you give us any clues about your next book?

While *Shame on You* centred on the story of a celebrity, the chilling act in my next book could happen to any of us. The main character is just like you or I, but makes a careless decision that changes her life in an instant . . .

If you enjoyed *Shame on You*, read on for
an exclusive extract from Amy Heydenrych's
new book THE PACT.

Coming November 2019
Available to pre-order now.

She never meant for her to die. Truth be told, she didn't know exactly what she wanted. She hated herself while she did it and regretted it the second it was done. But later, beneath her begging and protestations, one fact remained: while she never meant for her to die, she did want to hurt her, just a little.

Chapter 1

What actually happened on the night Nicole died was as vague as a rumour, caught through snippets behind closed doors. By the time the neighbours had guessed what was really going on, it was too late.

Nobody was to blame, because it didn't sound like death at first. A door creaked open. Her musical laugh suggested it was simply a friend stopping by. There were vague sounds – footsteps, clinking cutlery, the low hum of music through her record player. Nothing to cause alarm.

The flats were packed like sardines in the building, so the neighbours did what they always do. They turned the television up, they spoke a little louder, they put on music of their own. It was the usual competing cacophony that never got too loud or lasted after midnight.

But that night was different. Nicole's music got louder – the children in the building couldn't sleep. This was out of character for her and inappropriate for a weeknight. The neighbours below her debated whether it was time to go upstairs and say something.

Every sentence of the conversation was shouted, the laughter raucous. The neighbours tried not to focus on it, to let each word aggravate them further, but it was all they could think about. They should call someone, report it; it was far too loud for a weeknight.

Suddenly, the laughter turned hysterical. It was out-of-control, hooting, belly-aching laughter, the kind that robs you of your breath.

'I can't breathe! I can't breathe,' they heard her choke through the laughter. Something had shifted, it sounded strange, but not strange enough to investigate. The noise came to an abrupt end and all was silent. Soon, the neighbours forgot their irritation and the odd end to the evening, and drifted off to sleep, while Nicole's killer walked past their doorways, while she bled into the carpet and gasped her last breath.

Chapter 2

Now

'Politeness is at the heart of so many suburban murders,' mutters Isla as she parks her old Ford outside the apartment building.

She leafs through her notebook, looking for a blank page to take down a few quotes from the bystanders. In these cases, they always say the same thing.

'Murders just don't happen in this part of town.'

'We're a very peaceful neighourhood.'

'None of us saw this coming. The murderer was an upstanding member of the community!'

Sure.

If pressed for long enough, each neighbour can recall *something*. The night the abusive husband took it too far and the argument ended with smashing glass. The tall, burly men who kept lurking outside the door of the smartly dressed businessman in 12A, who was rumoured to have a gambling habit. Or maybe just a bad feeling about the new family that moved in during the middle of the night.

We are all so polite, so insistent on not overstepping the mark that we neglect the community around us. In our reluctance to offend, we don't give others the opportunity to ask for help. Of course, Isla believes it runs deeper. If we were to pay attention to the signs and notice when something was wrong, we would have to admit that perhaps our quiet suburban lives weren't so safe after all.

Today's case ticks all these boxes. A woman in her early thirties has been brutally murdered, potentially by someone she knew. The police alert issued this morning noted no signs of forced entry and the neighbours have insisted they didn't hear anything other than loud music, animated conversation and raucous laughing. It brings back a memory of her own, a gin-stumbling, stale-cigarette kissed scene that she quickly pushes to the back of her mind. She's safe now, right here, on the other side of the police tape. As a reporter, she has the power to shape the story and take back control.

Isla flashes a media access card and steps into the flat. Technically, she shouldn't be allowed near the crime scene until all evidence has been collected, but in her ten years on this beat she has earned the trust of this division, especially Simon, the lead inspector on the case. The body is in the bathroom – this is evident from the uniforms and the forensic team clustered outside – but there is also a *feeling* a place gets when something terrible happens. No matter how many crime scenes Isla visits, it still chills her to the bone.

She steers clear of the bathroom. To see the body first is too dehumanising for the woman inside. As a journalist, she is more interested in the story behind the story, in who the person was before.

The apartment is small but decorated in a sleek, minimalist Scandinavian style. Every object appears purposeful and of high quality. Isla takes note of the recycling bins in the kitchen and the thriving potted herb garden on the windowsill. This was clearly a woman who had her shit together.

Smaller details in the living room spark Isla's interest. There is a half-eaten bowl of roasted vegetable pasta on the coffee table, a romantic comedy on pause and a magazine on the couch, still in its plastic wrapping. A woman after my own heart, she thinks, a woman who was planning an evening alone.

She grits her teeth as she makes her way to the scene of the murder.

Simon steps in front of her.

'Sorry Isla, this is off limits for you today. We're dealing with a murder of – uh – unexpected horror here.'

Fear grows in the pit of her stomach. She's seen this look in his eyes before – cases like these are hard on the police, as well as reporters like her. They're the kind that push you up close to the face of evil, and give you no option to look away.

'Are you OK Simon?'

He is pale-faced and distracted, his eyes flit to whatever lies behind the bathroom door. His big, rough hand slaps over his mouth. The gesture is clumsy and makes Isla want to lean forward and embrace him.

'No, not really. I think I'm going to be sick.'

'You want a boiled sweet for the nausea?' Isla reaches into her messenger bag. She rummages amidst the plasters, headache pills, hand sanitiser and pens. Whatever crisis arises, there is always a solution somewhere in the chaos of her bag.

'No thanks, unless you have a half bottle of Vodka in there. Listen, I'm going to need you to get out of here, right now. I'll send you the summary of the case when we're done.'

'But . . .'

'*Now*, Isla!'

It's a long walk to the door, and Isla can't help but feel a little disgraced, as if every official person buzzing about the scene knows that she is not meant to be there. She has stood on the frontlines alongside Simon reporting gang violence, bank robberies and more. What about this case has made him wall it off so abruptly?

She clutches the cold railing with shaking hands as she makes her way down the stairs. Best to just to go back to the newsroom, where she can forget this morning and the dread it has stirred within her. As she wrestles her car into gear, she remembers she forgot to interview any of the bystanders. Dammit! What a waste of a few hours.

There is no story without a beginning, no murder without a moment that incites it. Yet no woman asks for this, not ever. Something deeply unjust happened that night, the only question is, what?

Want to read
NEW BOOKS
before anyone else?

Like getting
FREE BOOKS?

Enjoy sharing your
OPINIONS?

Discover

READERS FIRST
Read. Love. Share.

Sign up today to win your first free book:
readersfirst.co.uk